"The baby's kicking. Come closer…"

Ty drew near, close enough to smell Sabrina's light floral scent. "What now?"

"Put your hand over my coat. She's strong, so you should feel her through the added layers."

Feeling a little foolish about placing his hand on Sabrina's belly, he did so anyway. The movement rattled him. "That's her?"

Sabrina nodded. "She must have your leg strength."

Wonder and awe flooded him. *Their daughter*. He glanced at Sabrina's face, bemusement at his reaction written all over her expressive features. "I hope she has your nose," he said.

She tapped hers and grimaced. "It's a button nose. Yours has more character."

"Mine's been broken three times," he countered. "I don't want her following in those footsteps."

He lost himself in the sensation of their daughter pressing and punching. They'd created this person together. He repeated those words to himself again and again. But why did being part of their daughter's life without Sabrina feel like that wasn't enough?

Dear Reader,

Welcome back to Violet Ridge, Colorado! Several years ago, my four-year-old twins and I were caught in an unexpected Georgia snowstorm and spent twelve hours in a minivan as we navigated our way home during a drive that's normally twenty minutes. I was so happy and relieved when my husband met us in a parking lot near our subdivision, and we used a makeshift sled to reach home. With the plot for this book, it was far less stressful and much more fun to strand Sabrina and Ty in a luxurious mountain cabin. And during the holiday season, no less!

Speaking of the holidays, as soon as the Thanksgiving parades conclude, I crank up the Christmas carols. Want in on a little secret? I don't know all the words to "The Twelve Days of Christmas." However, that song became the inspiration for Ty to win back Sabrina's trust. Magnetic and charming on the outside with a gentle and caring core, Ty stole my heart. I hope he'll steal yours, too.

I love connecting with readers. Please visit my website at tanyaagler.com or follow my author Facebook page (authortanyaagler).

Happy reading!

Tanya Agler

HEARTWARMING

*Snowbound with
the Rodeo Star*

—

Tanya Agler

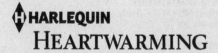

HARLEQUIN
HEARTWARMING

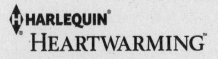

HARLEQUIN®
HEARTWARMING™

ISBN-13: 978-1-335-47552-7

Snowbound with the Rodeo Star

Recycling programs for this product may not exist in your area.

For questions and comments about the quality of this book, please contact us at CustomerService@Harlequin.com.

Harlequin Enterprises ULC
22 Adelaide St. West, 41st Floor
Toronto, Ontario M5H 4E3, Canada
www.Harlequin.com

Printed in U.S.A.

Tanya Agler remembers the first set of Harlequin books her grandmother gifted her, and she's been in love with romance novels ever since. An award-winning author, Tanya makes her home in Georgia with her wonderful husband, their four children and a lovable basset, who really rules the roost. When she's not writing, Tanya loves classic movies and a good cup of tea. Visit her at tanyaagler.com or email her at tanyaagler@gmail.com.

Books by Tanya Agler

Harlequin Heartwarming

A Ranger for the Twins
The Sheriff's Second Chance
The Solider's Unexpected Family
The Single Dad's Holiday Match

Smoky Mountain First Responders

The Paramedic's Forever Family
The Firefighter's Christmas Promise

Rodeo Stars of Violet Ridge

Caught by the Cowgirl

Visit the Author Profile page
at Harlequin.com for more titles.

To my mother, Toni. She passed away too young, but I remember her reading one of my earliest stories that I wrote as a teenager and expressing her belief in me as a writer. Thank you, Mom, for being my first writing supporter and cheerleader.

CHAPTER ONE

"ONCE YOU EXPERIENCE this jacket, you'll never want to take it off."

As soon as the last word left his mouth, Ty Darling closed the black binder with a groan. Who talked like that about outerwear? Or anything, for that matter. His agent had promoted this opportunity, hawking a new line of denim coats as a way to catapult him from the rodeo arena to the silver screen. That promise was a stretch beyond Ty's comprehension, but he was game for anything. Once.

Then again, this chance would be for naught unless he put some effort into it, and why try anything without injecting an element of fun? With a grin Ty hoped would coax his fans and future customers into buying this fleece-lined jacket, he practiced his line, emphasizing each word in turn. He stopped when a blond man with a genial countenance walked toward him.

"Merry Christmas! I'm Carter Webb, the

director." A couple of years younger than Ty, he carried two binders in one hand and a cup of coffee in the other. "Thanks for taking over on short notice. The previous actor backed out at the last minute."

Ty returned Carter's holiday greeting and then fingered the silver buttons on the jacket, suddenly self-conscious. He'd never acted or been on a film set before. "Thanks for taking a chance on a novice. I only arrived in Violet Ridge late last night. Have I missed anything?"

"Not much. There's a production meeting this morning, followed by a fitting for the different coats and outfits you'll wear at each location." Carter juggled the binders and then sipped his coffee. "You'll catch on fast enough. Anyone who can win the National Rodeo Championship two years running has to take direction well. My mom's your biggest fan. She said your last ride at the finals was poetry in motion."

"Glad she enjoyed it. I brought along some extra headshots if she'd like an autographed picture for Christmas." A small gesture, but each fan held a place in Ty's heart.

"That will make me her favorite person for the day." Carter grinned, his affability coming through. "Although my family knows my ten-month-old son really holds that position. He's the first grandchild on both sides."

Ty nodded though he really wanted to shake his head. Having children wasn't anything on his radar. Not that he didn't like kids. He loved his two half sisters, who'd come along when he was a teenager. But after his father died of an unexpected heart attack at age thirty-five, a mere year older than Ty was now, Ty's secure world had collapsed in an instant. Right then, he promised himself no one would cry like that over him. Grief over his sudden demise, practically a given considering his family history, wasn't the legacy he wanted to leave behind.

He realized Carter was waiting for him to say something. "His first Christmas, huh? That oughta be fun. Is he here with you?"

Carter looked wistful. "No, he's in Denver with my wife. I'll make sure this production stays on schedule so we can celebrate the holidays with our families. Shooting in this part of Colorado in December is rather risky, but the designer wants to feature the local scenery since he's from here. His company is sparing no expense for launching this new line of jackets, and the Double I Ranch is the perfect backdrop."

Ty had to agree, plus his agent had negotiated a free ski pass at a nearby resort. The promise of a carefree day of slaloming down the slopes ensured this new venture was worth the time. Besides, he was always more than willing to go along for the ride. "I'll hold you to that. My mother and stepfather are celebrating their twenty-third anniversary on Christmas Eve at their Wyoming ranch, and I'm giving the toast."

Ty could almost taste his mother's special ginger cookies and Hal's eggnog.

"Then we best get started." Carter handed him one of the binders. "This has the updated information, and more. The call sheet, the order of filming and the newest script. The line you're rehearsing went away three drafts ago."

Ty flipped through the pages. So much for memorizing the old script on yesterday's flight from Las Vegas to Grand Junction. The learning curve was steep enough without the extra pressure of fresh lines. "I'll memorize this right away."

"No worries. Most of the time, actors wait around while we adjust the lighting or handle some production detail." Carter glanced at his watch. "Today, we're setting up the camera equipment here at the Double I Ranch. Next week, we're filming at the ski resort, followed by a day at a picturesque cabin. Then we wrap up production at the Irwin Arena on the outskirts of Violet Ridge."

"Speaking of the town, I'm scheduled for an autograph session tomorrow morning at the Over and Dunne Feed and Seed." Ty scanned the script. "Will that be a problem?"

"Your agent, Belinda, told me about that, and I compensated for it." Carter tapped his watch. "I have to adjust the boom, but I'll show you the catering table first. The Irwin family insisted on supplementing the company's normal fare, so there's plenty. I recommend the breakfast burrito."

Carter accompanied Ty to a table overflowing with food. From what Ty had seen the night before, the Irwin family, who was one of his sponsors, did nothing in half measures. The patriarch, Gordon Irwin, had insisted Ty stay at his guesthouse. Arriving after midnight, Ty had marveled at the spacious floor plan, twice the size of his stepfather Hal's Wyoming ranch where Ty hung his hat between rodeos.

His stomach rumbled, and his mouth watered at the variety of breakfast offerings. "This is some spread."

"Everything's delicious." Carter sipped his coffee, then gave a curt nod. "I'll catch up with you at the meeting. It's at the other end—"

A dog's bark interrupted Carter, and then the director's face blanched. Ty turned and found a massive lab mix ambling along the path with an older man hobbling beside him. A huge brace covered the man's left knee and leg. Whether Carter's apprehension was because of the dog or the man's injury, Ty wasn't sure. When the pair neared the table, the man used a hand signal. The dog sat beside him, his tongue lolling, his forceful presence underlying a gentle sweetness.

Carter stepped forward and extended his hand. "Are you the dog trainer, Mr. Lundgren?"

"Yes, but it's Robert." He shook Carter's hand and then tilted his head. "And this is Phineas."

At the sound of his name, the dog wagged his tail and let out a single bark.

"I was concerned about your lack of acting experience and made some adjustments." Carter faced Ty with a guilty expression on his face. "We were fortunate to retain Phineas's services."

Hence, the script changes as there was no dog in the original commercial. Too bad no one had informed Ty.

"Phineas is quite the entertainer. You might have seen him on his hit television series, or one of his other projects." Robert recited a lengthy list.

"I don't watch much television," Ty confessed and picked a plate off the top of the stack.

Between training and traveling to rodeos, Ty's life was pretty full. Or, at least, it had been until he committed his biggest mistake on his last birthday by breaking up with the only woman he'd ever loved.

He'd been meaning to find Sabrina Mac-Grath and ask for a second chance, except his life had been a roller-coaster ride over the past few months. First, he'd hired an assistant who'd gone too far in his duties, believing he was sheltering Ty by limiting his exposure to the outside world. The subsequent mayhem from that debacle had taken a high toll, and he'd fallen out of position for a spot in the championship finals. No one had been more shocked than Ty when he'd clawed his way back into the standings and defended his title.

"Phineas is in high demand." Pride laced Robert's voice. "He's a bullmasador, combining the best qualities of Labrador retrievers with the work ethic of the bullmastiff."

Ty was well acquainted with bulls, and Phineas was only slightly smaller than a newborn calf.

"Good to know." Ty selected a breakfast burrito and some sausage links. Then he faced Robert, that knee brace looking pretty imposing. "Can I fix a plate for you? I can carry both on my tray." Ty kept a careful eye on Phineas, amazed the dog hadn't tried to jump on the table. Then again, he'd been around more sets than Ty and was used to the atmosphere.

The older gentleman caught sight of the selection and nodded. "I'd appreciate that."

Ty grabbed an extra plate and added it to his tray. Then he eyed Phineas. "Does your dog need anything?"

"He eats his own special mix of food designed to keep his coat bright and full. At the production meeting, I'll review Phineas's training regimen and rules with the crew. I limit his interaction on set to actors so he won't be confused about cues." Robert sniffed the air and squinted at Ty. "The most important rule to remember is never to feed him except for his special treats, which are diced carrots and celery."

Ty's face grew hot as he'd almost slipped sausage into his pocket to sneak to the dog and win him over. "I'll keep that in mind."

Robert scanned the place cards of the different breakfast offerings. "Could you grab one of the chorizo and black bean burritos along with some guacamole?" After a heaping spoonful, Ty looked at him, and Robert nodded his approval. "Thanks."

"What happened to your knee?" Carter asked. Some color returned to his cheeks.

Robert bent and tapped on the brace. "I wrenched it at a rest stop yesterday when I didn't gauge the distance from our bus to the ground correctly. I shouldn't be walking, but the show must go on."

"Is there another trainer on the way?" Worry lines popped out on the director's youthful forehead. "Or should we delay the shoot?"

"Phineas is a pro. He's been acting for the past three years." Robert brushed away Carter's concern. "I'm as much of a guide as a trainer at this point."

"Do you need a crew member to help you?" Carter asked. Ty could see the wheels turning in the director's head as if calculating extra time into the schedule.

"Phineas is trained and well-behaved, except for loud noises. That's his one weakness." Robert pointed to the sour cream and then nodded when Ty scooped enough.

"This should be a quiet and efficient set," Carter reassured Robert. "I'll let the two of you get acquainted. Give Ty any tips for working with Phineas. I'll bring the crew over to you for the production meeting in ten minutes."

Ty carried the tray over to the seating area.

"Thanks. I know from previous experience the less weight I put on my leg, the faster I'll be back to normal," Robert said, accepting the tray with a smile.

Ty situated the chairs so Robert could prop up his knee. In return, the dog handler regaled Ty with stories of Phineas's successes. Ty hadn't laughed this much in months. Not since breaking up with Sabrina, the most honest and refreshing person he'd ever met. Why had he ever let her go?

Pushing away her image, Ty looked at Phineas, still patient, despite sitting in the same position for ten minutes. In his shoes, or paws in this case, Ty would be antsy. Didn't the dog ever have a little fun?

With no warning, a huge quake reverberated through the valley. The ground shook. Shouts from a nearby meadow coincided with crew members sprinting in that direction. Something must have crashed to the ground. Ty's attention turned to Phineas, who was shaking. Then Phineas took off running.

The dog could get hurt on a working ranch. Ty grabbed the sausage off his plate and dashed after him. "I'll bring him back!" Ty said.

Out of the corner of his eye, he caught Robert struggling to rise. The trainer called Phineas's name, but the dog didn't stop for breath. For such a big dog, he sure was fast. Ty followed on his heels, not wanting anything to happen to the sweet fellow.

The stable loomed ahead, and Phineas made a beeline for the entrance. Ty hesitated. The last thing he wanted was to scare the horses, but Phineas might bring harm upon himself if Ty didn't look out for him.

Ty slowed and approached the open double sliding doors. "Hello? Anyone in here? I'm coming for Phineas."

He didn't hear any response, so he ventured inside. Entering the stable was like coming home, with the aroma of the horses and feed familiar and comforting. Gordon Irwin's reputation for producing quality foals preceded him on the rodeo circuit. Ty ventured inside, the layout here the same as Hal's ranch. A wave of longing to spend time with his family crashed over Ty. Christmas awaited him in Wyoming, but first things first. *Phineas.*

Ty's eyes adjusted to the dim light. Soft whinnies came from the stalls. He searched the area and spotted Phineas in the corner, quivering.

"It's you and me, Phin." He crept deeper into the Double I's stable. A quick glance confirmed they were alone. Any grooms or trainers must have left to check on the cause of the noise.

Ty couldn't leave the poor dog. The lab mix had seemed so big before, but he cowered in the corner, his teeth chattering, his short brown fur quivering. Robert's advice not to give Phineas table scraps flittered across his mind, but this was an emergency.

He reached into his pocket and pulled out a sausage link. "I know this isn't good for you, but I'm sure it's okay, just this once. That noise scared me, too."

Phineas's huge brown eyes met Ty's. The dog must have decided anyone offering him sausage was decent enough. He let Ty approach and gobbled down the treat. Ty reached into his pocket for the other sausage, and the dog downed it in one gulp. Kneeling beside him, he soothed the big guy. "This will be our secret. I won't tell Robert." Keeping secrets wasn't Ty's favorite trait, actually it was his least favorite, but Phineas's lips were sealed. "Ready to go back and face everyone?"

Phineas licked his lips. A line of drool formed and coated Ty's hands.

"Excuse me? Are you part of the commercial shoot? The stable is off-limits." A woman's voice issued forth from behind. "And what's with that noise? I've spent ten minutes calming the horses in the paddock."

Ty's head shot up. He'd recognize that voice anywhere. *Sabrina MacGrath*. His biggest regret.

Covered with a fine layer of dog drool, he realized, wasn't the way he wanted to reacquaint himself with the woman he'd let get away. However, these next two weeks had just become that much more interesting.

He shifted his footing and faced her. Even in the dim light, she was striking. She pushed up her cream-colored cowboy hat, two chestnut braids falling on either side of her swan-like neck. Her cheeks were fuller than he remembered. And how had he never noticed that glow around her? She was radiant.

Her brown eyes registered confusion and then hurt. "Ty Darling. What are you doing here?"

The temperature outside hovered around freezing, but it was warmer than the frigid interior. Phineas settled by his side. Ty was most grateful for the small show of support. *Sausage for the win.*

Her face ashen pale, Sabrina folded her arms over her long, puffy turquoise coat.

"Turquoise is your favorite color, isn't it?" he asked. "That color suits you."

"Yes, but flattery doesn't answer my question. Why are you inside Elizabeth Irwin's stable?" From her edgy tone, it would take a lot more than sausage to convince her to give him another chance.

"I'm here for the commercial shoot. They're actually paying me to sell a product." He plucked at the jacket and chuckled, hoping she'd follow suit. Instead, her frown remained intact. "What are you doing here?" he asked.

She stood resolute in her dusty brown boots. "I'm the barn manager for the Double I Ranch now." She jutted her chin toward Phineas. "Since when do you own a dog?"

"He's not mine." Her face fell as if owning Phineas would have given him a mantle of responsibility. "I'm playing his owner in the commercial."

He laughed again, but she remained unmoved. In all fairness, considering how he ruined their last meeting, he couldn't blame her.

Robert appeared at the archway, his hand over his heart. "Thank goodness I found you. Is Phineas okay?" Ty nodded. "Phineas, come."

The dog rose from his haunches and went over to Sabrina. He sat as if guarding her, and Robert repeated his instruction. This time, the dog obeyed his handler and left. Ty already missed Phineas's presence, as if the only one in his corner was gone.

He was alone with Sabrina, and he had so much to say. Where should he start? How he missed their long walks? How he freaked out upon turning thirty-four, one year younger than the age when his father, grandfather and great-grandfather all passed away? How his life wasn't the same without her?

Ty opened his mouth, but she spoke first. "Please tell the director to be more careful. The noise spooked the horses."

She also looked spooked, as if she had something to fear from him. He knew he messed up by ending their relationship without any warning, but this was something else. Her earlier words about her employment situation penetrated his senses. "Why are you working at the Double I Ranch?" Her natural rapport with horses endeared her to rodeo competitors and fans alike. "You love being a rodeo clown."

"Like I said, I'm the new barn manager. The safety of the horses is my responsibility, and I report about each of them at the end of the day to Elizabeth Irwin, the daughter of the ranch owner. This type of commotion isn't good for them." He stepped toward her. She shook her head, her arms remaining folded over her chest. "You broke up with me and didn't answer my calls or emails, so my occupational status is none of your concern. Goodbye, Ty."

Several of the horses whinnied, and their well-being mattered. "Merry Christmas, Sabrina."

With a backward glance, he left the stable. Before the commercial shoot was over, he intended on making amends with Sabrina. Then he could go home to Juniper Creek and celebrate Christmas with his family with a clear conscience.

"YES, LITTLE ONE, that was your father."

Her unborn daughter kicked her ribs, and Sabrina MacGrath leaned against the stable post. She placed a protective hand over the baby bump hidden by her bulky coat. Ty's parting words had sounded more like a farewell than a hello. Another sign she'd been right to accept the barn management position. Even with irregular hours, it didn't present danger at every turn, like her previous career as a rodeo clown. Better yet, her best friend, Will Sullivan, and his new wife lived on the adjoining ranch. Will and Kelsea promised they'd help with the baby. Moving to Violet Ridge was the logical step, the safe choice. Just what her daughter deserved.

And her job allowed her to remain around horses. That was the best part. Sabrina murmured soothing words to the nearest horse, Elizabeth's sweet Appaloosa. "Yes, that pole crash was earth-shattering, but the production crew will be gone soon."

And good riddance. After repeated emails with no reply, she never expected to see Ty again. Emotions warred within her, anger giving way to sadness at him forgoing a relationship with their child.

Sabrina checked on the next horse, cooing her encouragement and concern. Come to think of it, though, Ty acted clueless, almost as if he didn't know about the baby. That couldn't be possible. After the urgent care visit when she found out about the pregnancy, she sent him an email. And another, and then another. The low point had come when she was admitted to the hospital for dehydration. Against her better judgment, she'd done the unthinkable and called him. He didn't pick up, so she left a voice mail. For days she'd waited for a reply or a call or, even better, him showing up and admitting he'd been wrong to break up with her. That he loved her and their baby. That they'd be a family.

Then the days stretched out into weeks, and then months. She'd accepted the fact he'd meant what he said during those romantic walks about never wanting to father a child. At the time, that had been fine with her, considering her mother's desertion and rocky childhood.

She quit the rodeo and interviewed with Elizabeth for the barn manager position, being upfront about her impending motherhood. Elizabeth, her immediate boss, hired her on the spot. Sabrina had kept riding horses until the baby bump touched the pommel of the saddle. Then, she'd temporarily hung up her reins. Fortunately, the grooms and other ranch employees exercised the horses.

There was something about Ty's demeanor, though, that made her doubt he was aware of their daughter's impending arrival in a mere six weeks.

If he didn't know, she had to tell him.

Except…

She didn't need yet another permanent goodbye in her life, and he didn't want children, two excellent reasons for moving on without him. By Christmas, the camera crew would be gone, as would Ty Darling.

It was for the best this way.

Sabrina saved her mare, Cinnamon, for last. Part of her salary included stable privileges for her Morgan horse and room and board in a tiny converted bunkhouse. Elizabeth performed double riding duty, taking Cinnamon out after exercising her own Appaloosa. Cinnamon pawed the ground with her front left hoof, and Sabrina calmed her by rubbing her muzzle.

"Did that noise scare you?"

Of course it did. Horses despised sudden, loud noises, and whatever happened on the set was as unexpected as Ty's reappearance in her life.

"Everything's fine. In a few days, they'll be gone, and life will return to normal."

Whether she said that for her benefit or the horse's, she wasn't sure. Ty's presence left her rattled. *Whew, it's getting hot in here.* She started unzipping her coat.

"*Normal?* That's so overrated." Ty's voice startled her. She hurried and zipped up her coat once more before facing him. Those mesmerizing blue eyes paired with that thick black hair caused backflips in her stomach that had nothing to do with the baby. There was no reason her body should still perk up when he was around. Yet her attraction to him flamed to life once more, and she willed it to go away.

"What are you doing back here?" Too aware of her baby bump, she folded her arms over her abdomen and grimaced.

Maybe this was why he returned. To talk about the baby. A bead of sweat started around her neck and trickled down her chest. The coat was sweltering, but that wasn't the cause of her discomfort. This man had always sent her emotions soaring, but he'd sent them plummeting when he broke up with her.

"I gave up too easily a few minutes ago." He smiled, his features dazzling and perfect. She upped her guard against the sheer devastation that was Ty. "Same as I gave up too easily on us."

That should provide some comfort, and the baby kicked as if telling Sabrina to hear him out. "Hmm, maybe you should have returned my emails and voice mail before now. Seven months is a long time."

"*Seven months?* It can't be that long." He frowned as if doing the calculations in his head. "Oh, yeah, it has been. I've been busy. Rodeo commitments, personnel issues, winning a second championship buckle."

"Not one call or text, Ty." If so many things occupied his time, he might not have time for their daughter. She couldn't and wouldn't let that happen.

"Seems like we've both been too busy for each other. While I'm here, we can be busy together." There was that devastating grin again. "And maybe I can convince you to come back to the rodeo. You wouldn't believe how many fans have asked me where the pretty rodeo clown is. The other competitors have, too. They feel safe when you're in the barrel."

This was news to her. As much as she appreciated the sentiment, though, protecting and raising her daughter in a home full of love without fear of abandonment were Sabrina's new priorities. "That's quite the compliment, but I'm happy here."

Tell him. Tell him about the baby. She ignored the voice in her head, same as she was ignoring the quivers from being this close to him again.

"Before I leave, do you want to hit the slopes? I seem to remember how much you wanted to learn to ski. We could make a day of it." Ty looked too eager for her response.

"Some of us can't take the day off whenever we feel like it." She finished stroking Cinnamon and headed for the tack room.

He followed, and she gave him credit for this newfound persistence. "What about tonight? I owe you a drink and an apology about the way I ended our relationship. I'd like to renew our friendship."

His voice softened, and she relented. While she might not want to be friends with Ty anymore, their baby deserved a relationship with both of her parents. "I'll consider it."

She selected the liniment she needed for the swollen foreleg of Copper, one of the ranch mares. Ty continued to follow her as she entered the horse's stall. He stayed on the other side.

"Um, about the breakup." She stopped and wiped her brow, the air thicker than it was in Texas, where she'd grown up with her grandparents. She rubbed her stomach and groaned. "There's something I need to tell you."

Someone cleared their throat from the direction of the entrance. "Ty? Are you still in here?" Sabrina noticed a man in his late twenties, tall and blond, standing at the archway. "I've been looking all over for you. The production meeting is about to start."

"I'll be there in a minute." Ty reached over and patted Sabrina's arm. "My mother has acid reflux. If that's what's wrong with you, it's treatable. See you soon."

After she tended to Copper's foreleg, Sabrina hustled back to the tack room. She then paused while locking the medicine cabinet. Ty's mother had acid reflux. She didn't know that or anything else about Ty's family's health history. The baby kicked once more, and Sabrina rubbed her belly. "I know. I have to tell him about you, but I'm not sure he'll like this."

"Like what?" Elizabeth's voice came from behind, and Sabrina startled.

"I didn't hear you." She willed her heart to slow down. Too much excitement wasn't good for the baby, and this day had been full of surprises.

"Sounds like you were having a pretty intense discussion with yourself." Elizabeth entered the tack room and removed a bridle from the wall. Her green eyes gave Sabrina an appraising look. "You're rather pale. Do you need to take the rest of the day off?"

She reached for Sabrina's forehead.

"I'm fine." Sabrina set aside the concern with a shaky smile. She updated Elizabeth on Copper's swollen leg. "Why didn't you tell me Ty Darling was here for the commercial?"

Elizabeth set the bridle atop a saddle and shrugged. "I didn't think it was important. Besides, the company said the cast and crew would keep to themselves. I already spoke to the director about that noise. That type of disruption is unacceptable around the animals."

A bundle of energy, Elizabeth kept up a steady stream of conversation while Sabrina helped her saddle Andromeda until something her boss said struck a chord. "Repeat that last part."

"The Double I is one of Ty's sponsors. My father insisted Ty stay in the guesthouse until Christmas." Elizabeth tightened the cinch and then straightened. "That's the second time you've asked about him."

"He's a popular figure on the rodeo circuit." Sabrina bristled at the defensive edge in her tone.

So much for her idea to wait until the end of the shoot to tell him. With Ty staying at the guesthouse located right next to her bunkhouse, it was inevitable he'd learn about the baby sooner rather than later.

"The Violet Ridge Roundup Rodeo was this past May, and then you transferred to the women's circuit for a month before you applied for this job." Elizabeth's gaze went to Sabrina's baby bump.

"You remember my résumé well." Sabrina handed Elizabeth the reins. "Look at the hour. It's time to muck out the stalls."

"No one has ever been that happy about that chore." Elizabeth sent a pointed look Sabrina's way. "Does Ty know he's going to be a father?"

Sabrina's shoulders slumped. So much for keeping Ty's role a secret.

"I don't think so." Giving Ty the benefit of the doubt wasn't something she'd have done before this morning, but, to be fair to him, he'd shown no evidence of knowing. "But I have to tell him, and soon."

Sabrina was one of the first female rodeo clowns on the modern circuit. Performing her act in makeup and a big rubber red nose was as natural as breathing. In fact, she loved every minute of her former career, missing it every day since she left. She'd rescued many a contestant from the pounding hooves of a massive bull.

Yet informing Ty Darling of his impending fatherhood scared her more than any stunt she'd ever performed.

CHAPTER TWO

Ty's SECOND MORNING in Violet Ridge promised to be even more exciting than the first, considering how many people were waiting for his autograph. The line, mainly women, snaked around the front porch of the Over and Dunne Feed and Seed and extended to the parking lot. This was one of his favorite parts of his job. When his fans carved time out of their schedules to meet him, he listened to every person and offered a kind word in return. That bond was why he always tried to arrive at these signings early. Today, however, he couldn't help his tardiness.

It wasn't his fault. Not really. Robert's knee was worse than expected, and Ty was the only person involved with the commercial shoot the trainer trusted. He hadn't had the heart to tell Robert that he and Phineas were bonding over sausage rather than positive reinforcement. Phineas's walk took longer than expected. He'd have brought the huge, lovable dog to the feed and seed, except there was nothing to keep him occupied while Ty signed autographs.

Ty clutched his disposable cup of coffee and hurried to the rear. He caught sight of an older woman with two plaits of reddish-brown hair pacing at the doorway. She noticed him and tapped her watch. "You're late."

"Sorry about that. I had to park a couple of blocks away." Ty flashed a grin he hoped would smooth over his transgression. "You must be Regina Dunne. Somehow, I don't think we've ever met on my previous visits to Violet Ridge."

"No, and the name's Regina Dunne-Sullivan. I recently married the uncle of one of your former rodeo competitors. This signing was my niece's idea to raise awareness of our recent addition of a consignment store, and she hasn't steered me wrong in her other business decisions yet." She gestured with her hand, and he followed her through the storage room.

He had a strong feeling Regina would prefer for him not to be here. So far, he was batting a thousand with his presence. He hadn't been Carter's first choice, and the director had added a dog to make Ty look good. In the stable, Sabrina hadn't been happy to see him, making it clear she'd have preferred it if they'd never crossed paths again. And now Regina dismissed him out of hand for being ten minutes late.

There had to be something he could do to get on everyone's good side.

Upbeat instrumental holiday music greeted him in the main selling area. Festive garland with red balls hung on the end of every aisle. A life-size ceramic cow wore a necklace of colorful twinkling lights and sported an ugly Christmas sweater. "Nice decorations. They really liven up the place," he said.

"Christmas is my husband's favorite holiday." Regina's features softened, and she led him past the women standing in line. "He says he wants our first Christmas together to be big, really, really big."

She laughed, and he felt like he'd missed the gist of an inside joke. At the start of the line, a small table with a red tablecloth and a gingerbread house shared space with a Christmas tree decorated with horseshoes and vintage cowboy boot ornaments, each with a price tag. Someone muttered his name, and several oohs and high-pitched squeals filled the air.

"Merry Christmas!" Ty tipped his hat at the crowd. "Thank you for coming and making my trip to Violet Ridge much more special. The holidays wouldn't have been the same without meeting all of you."

A murmur of delight buzzed through the crowd. He grinned, no longer feeling like anyone's second choice. Regina helped him get settled in his seat, and Ty posed for selfies and signed autographs for a good hour. If this crowd was any indication, his future decision about whether to leave the rodeo and segue into acting just became that much harder. His agent, Belinda, was trying to convince Ty that there was no time like the present to change his career.

Earlier this year, she'd been ready to fire him as a client after he hadn't returned her emails or phone messages about a cameo on the hottest Western streaming series. It was only then that he'd discovered his assistant was filtering emails and messages, keeping Ty away from anything that might prevent him from training for the rodeo.

After Ty fired him and changed all his passwords, he discovered a monthlong gap in emails and other correspondence, even phone messages. While it was more time-consuming to handle his business dealings without an assistant, there was comfort in knowing any mistakes from here on out were his and his alone.

Another selfie, another smile, another satisfied fan.

"Merry Christmas!" Ty waved at the departing woman.

A pair of older women, one wearing a bright purple jumpsuit and the other sporting a neon red holiday sweater with a three-dimensional image of Rudolph, approached the table. The resemblance ended at the identical features on their tanned, weather-lined faces. The one in purple styled her green hair in a pixie cut while her twin's hair was long and silver, capped with a bright multicolored beanie.

"I'm Zelda," the one with green hair said, "and this is my twin sister, Nelda. I'm the former mayor…"

"And we run the Violet Ridge Grandmas for Ty Fan Club." Nelda finished her sister's sentence.

"We're your biggest fans," they said in unison.

Ty grinned. They'd fit right in with Hal's mother, Eugenie, a candidate for the world's best grandmother. She had always treated him with the same love and tender care as she did her biological granddaughters.

"It's mighty fine to meet you." He reached for a photograph. "Do you want me to make one out to each of you?"

Nelda shook her head. "Can you make mine out to Jaxon?" She spelled the name for him. "He's my seven-year-old grandson. We watched your appearance at the finals on television together and used your scores to make addition fun. Your endurance was such an inspiration."

"Perfect." Ty's grin grew even broader, and he looked around the pair. "Why didn't you bring the little fellow with you?"

"He's in school," Zelda answered before her sister. "He's in first grade with Sofia, my granddaughter."

"I'll be in Violet Ridge for two weeks. I hope I meet both of them before I leave." Ty stood and walked in front of the table. "How about a selfie?"

Ty removed his cowboy hat and reached for Nelda's phone. With his arm extended, he flipped the screen and snapped a picture. Before he handed it back, he searched the screen. Could it be?

Yes, that was Sabrina at the front of the store.

"This is better than the blue ribbon for my quilts." Nelda thanked him and showed her phone to Zelda, who squealed.

"This picture's going on my fireplace mantel with my Christmas gnome collection."

Ty heard the praise and nodded absent-mindedly, his focus honing in on the pretty brunette. Somehow, he had to set things right with Sabrina. Yesterday left a nasty taste in his mouth. What's worse, her brown eyes didn't sparkle like they had when they dated. Even if it was for these few weeks until he left for Wyoming, he'd provide a happy distraction. After all, it was Christmas time, the season of good tidings and partridges in a pear tree. *Ho, ho, ho!* While he probably wasn't on her nice list, he hoped he'd get off her naughty list and part on better terms this time.

Besides, in this instance, a goodbye didn't have to be permanent. He'd be back in Violet Ridge next May for the rodeo roundup. They could either reconnect then, or she'd have come to her senses and rejoined the circuit. He'd seen the way she captivated the crowd with her humor and athletic ability.

There wasn't anyone else like her in the sport. Anywhere else either.

For the first time since he broke up with her, hope she might become a fixture in his life again flowed through him.

He excused himself, promising the next fan he'd be back in two shakes. A couple of groans greeted him as he made his way to the spot where he'd seen Sabrina, but she wasn't there.

He kept searching until he found her in a different section of the feed and seed where the smell of fertilizer and other supplies was more pronounced. She stopped her flatbed cart in front of a display.

Before he could offer to help, a woman with auburn hair, Gordon Irwin's daughter, if he wasn't mistaken, rushed to Sabrina's side. "You weren't about to lift that heavy bag of horse feed in your condition, were you?"

Condition?

"Leave it to you to find me and remind me about that. As if it was ever far from my mind. Life as I knew it had to end sometime." Sabrina's nervous laugh reached him, and the building swayed around him. Did she just say her life was ending? "I'm not ready yet, but then again, from what I've heard, no one ever is."

Sabrina was dying. He should have known her condition had to be something major for her to quit the rodeo, but he didn't expect anything this catastrophic. His heart thudded as if falling down a hundred-floor shaft. Everything on either side of him faded, and the aisle narrowed as if elongated. He reached out for something to steady his wobbly legs, and some bags of feed fell to the concrete floor, causing a thud. Sabrina and the other woman faced him, and Sabrina's eyes widened like a doe caught in the headlights.

"Ty."

"Sabrina." Her name came out in a croak of anguish. He still couldn't believe this devastating news. He rushed over and held her hands, two blocks of ice. "Why didn't you tell me?"

Whatever was wrong with her, he wanted to endure it with her. Their time together had been the best days of his life. She wouldn't go through this alone.

"I emailed you, but you never answered me." Color started coming back to her cheeks. "I thought you didn't care."

"Shh. That's all in the past." He brought her to him, stroking her silky hair, the mere presence of her filling him with a calm he never knew he possessed. Her bulky coat gave rise to layers of padded clothing, obviously necessary in case the winter cold bit right through her delicate frame. His throat clenched; the thought of a world without Sabrina was like a world without horses and open vistas. "I'm here for you. How much longer until…"

He couldn't finish his sentence, and she hurried away from him.

"You should know. About six weeks, give or take. Probably sooner." Sabrina hiccupped and glared at him. "But I can't believe you're so accepting of this."

"Accepting?" He blinked. She thought that little of him she couldn't see the sharp ache inside him. "Hardly, but that's not important. What's important is making you as comfortable as possible."

"There's a little ankle pain, but nothing I can't handle. A month from now might be a different story. Some of the online videos and podcasts?" She shuddered. "I thought I wanted to go through it naturally, but I reserve the right to change my mind."

She was so brave, standing there with her arms around her middle. To think he dismissed it as acid reflux.

"Six weeks?" *That little time left.* Dizziness

engulfed him. "Maybe the doctors are wrong. Have you had a second opinion?"

"The doctors are pretty convinced they've seen this before. The circle of life, you know." Sabrina narrowed her eyes and gazed at him with suspicion.

Elizabeth Irwin stepped forward and cleared her throat. "It's nice to see you again, Ty, but I think there's a communication problem here." She faced Sabrina. "I think he thinks you're dying."

Sabrina unzipped her coat and revealed a baby bump.

"You're pregnant."

He did the math in his head. There was only one answer. He was the father.

Suddenly feeling woozy, he reached for anything solid and grabbed a shelf nearby. The wood gave way under him, and he fell to the floor. His bottom banged against the cold concrete, rattling him. His head jostled against the metal of the shelves. Something bonked the back of his skull, and bags of feed landed around him. One bag's seam must have split open. Pellets landed in his hair and down his shirt. He groaned, and alfalfa landed in his mouth. He spit it out and sat there, stunned.

Within seconds, a crowd gathered around him. *Perfect*. One of the lowest moments of his life, and his fans had to witness him, reduced to falling on his backside. Regina hurried over.

"What in tarnation is going on?" Regina asked, her eyes round with consternation.

Just when Ty didn't think the situation could get much worse, people snapped pictures with their phones. No doubt they'd go viral within the hour.

"Nothing to see here." Elizabeth stepped between Ty and everyone else.

Apparently, she was good at taking charge. The crowd dispersed, except for Regina, Elizabeth and Sabrina. Every bone in Ty's body screamed out in pain, but his brain was numb. He sat there, speechless, too numb to move.

Regina huffed out a breath. "My husband, Barry, told me this was going to be big. He just didn't know it was going to be a big disaster. Look at this mess."

A young blonde appeared with an employee, a couple of sweeper brooms and big black trash bags. She patted Regina's arm. "Nothing is ever as bad as it looks. All publicity is good publicity."

As carefully as he could, Ty rose from the

mess. A stretch confirmed his ego was more bruised than anything else.

Ty reached for a broom and a trash bag. A little hard work might be exactly what he needed. Where to begin? Shreds of paper and mounds of ruined feed loomed large. Clean up first, then he'd offer to help fix the shelves. A little reinforcement couldn't hurt. "I'm responsible. I'll see it through."

"Our baby is an *it* to you?" Sabrina's words held a note of fury in them.

Our baby. He loosened his grip, and the broom clattered to the floor. *Our* baby. Her meaning penetrated his brain, still foggy from having a bag of feed fall on it.

A long time ago, he'd promised himself he'd never leave a child behind, someone who'd have that same gaping hole in his or her life as Ty did that fateful day when he was eight.

He'd never been good at keeping promises.

Shock and disbelief fought for space in his mind. How could this have happened? Well, the how was obvious. What was going to happen next was the genuine mystery. He stumbled backward but caught himself before he collided with any more shelves. "I'm the father."

The blonde hugged Sabrina. "See, I knew he'd step up."

"Hmm, we'll see, Kelsea." Sabrina's voice held a note of disbelief.

How many people knew of his impending fatherhood? It appeared he was the last to find out. He didn't know what was worse: his broken promise to himself or his being this late to the party.

Elizabeth and Kelsea surrounded Sabrina as though they'd appointed themselves her guardians. He appreciated that bond of friendship and support now more than ever, considering not one person in the rodeo had contacted him about the impending event.

He stared at the baby bump. It wasn't often he didn't have a glib word or response. He'd learned fast after his father died that a funny quip drove away the look of pity in people's eyes. That had served him well on the circuit, with him gaining a reputation of being witty and charming. He didn't feel that way right now. He rubbed the back of his head, a goose egg his reward for this morning.

Worse yet, he'd let down his fans, many of whom were leaving without a signed picture. They'd come to support him, and here he was, covered in animal feed. Hardly his best look, although he'd looked a lot worse after some of his falls.

He winced and stopped rubbing his head. He'd maneuvered his way into this mess, and he would fix it yet. Mom and Hal had raised him a sight better than he was acting at the moment. "Mrs. Dunne-Sullivan." He craned his head until he met the gaze of the owner of the feed and seed. "I'm most sorry about the damage I've done to your shop and by not fulfilling my obligation to my fans. I'll be in town until a couple of days before Christmas. I'd like to reschedule and make it up to them."

"Seems like you have to make something up to someone else, too, but I'll make the announcement." Regina propped the broom against the end of the display case and headed toward the signing table.

Ty turned and found Sabrina. If anything, her friends moved closer to her, flanking her with their protection. "Thank you for your support—" Sabrina touched Elizabeth's arm, then Kelsea's "—but I think Ty and I need a minute."

She'd had seven months to process all of this. He needed more than sixty short seconds. How could he have missed the signs yesterday? People always talked about an expectant mother's glow, and she radiated like a beacon.

Elizabeth and Kelsea gave her a backward glance from the end of the aisle. Shock continued descending into his consciousness. Sabrina pulled something from her purse and handed him a small, black rectangular piece of paper. "This is our daughter."

A daughter? A healthy daughter to love and teach how to ride a horse, snowshoe and sleep under the stars, the world at her fingertips. All the things Hal had taught him and his sisters to do. He reeled even more. He'd missed so much in the past months. His heart melted at the sonogram picture with the head up close and in plain view. At least he thought that was the head. He'd never paid this much attention to one of these before.

The margin of the photo caught his eye. "Baby Girl MacGrath." With some reluctance, he returned it to Sabrina. "Now that I know about her, she'll be little baby Darling."

Sabrina accepted the photo and placed it carefully in her wallet. "I don't think so."

"What do you mean? She's my daughter. I'd like her to have my name." Frustration dulled the shock. "What's the deal, Sabrina? You waited until now, in public, to tell me I'm going to be a father. Why didn't you tell me yesterday in the stable or come and find me at the Double I after your shift?"

"When I found out I was pregnant, I emailed and called you. It wasn't until after you left the stable yesterday that I realized you might not know." Sabrina found the broom and swept the floor.

While her decision to halt her career as a rodeo clown made much more sense, he was still wary, especially considering she'd waited so long to tell him. He reached out and stilled her. "Regina and her crew will clean up."

"I'm responsible. I'll stay and help." This stubborn streak was the first sign he'd seen of the old Sabrina, the woman he'd fallen for.

The woman who kept their baby a secret from him.

"I had no idea about the baby." He reached for the other broom and pushed the feed into one large pile.

"How was I supposed to know that? All you've ever told me was how much you didn't want children, and then you never responded to any of my emails or my voice mail." Her nostrils flared, and she used part of a broken bag as a dustpan. "I thought you didn't want us."

He swept the feed onto the brown paper, and she deposited the remnants into the black bag. Their work ethic and style always had meshed. They would have made a great team.

Except...

Trust, once broken, was next to impossible to repair. She didn't trust him because he broke up with her. And as far as he was concerned?

She kept the single, most important event of his life a secret.

So much for trust and second chances. There was no way to go back and rekindle that spark that had roared to life last spring. It was extinguished for good.

"My itinerary has never been a secret." The shock was now giving way to rational thought. And anger at something this big being kept from him. "You could have shown up at any of the rodeos and told me."

And that was the least of it. There were a number of possibilities for getting in touch with him. He'd talked often of growing up in Wyoming with his mom, Hal and two sisters. Any of them would have connected Sabrina to him.

What would his mom and Hal think of the mess he'd made?

Here he was, about to become a father, and

judging from Sabrina's stance, she wanted nothing to do with him. She set aside the broom and pulled out her wallet. "Here. I think you should have this."

His fingers brushed hers as he accepted the sonogram image.

"Ty Darling?" A woman with big silver circle earrings and bright red layered hair squealed from the end of the aisle and rushed toward them, waving a black T-shirt in one hand and a silver Sharpie in the other. "They said you were already gone, but it's my lucky day. You're still here."

With reluctance, Ty tucked away the image in his wallet and then transferred his attention to the newcomer. He flashed a wide grin. "Just waitin' for you, darlin'."

The woman giggled and shot a look at Sabrina. "Are you finished with her?"

"Yes, he is. I'm leaving." Sabrina set aside the broom and waved the woman forward.

The woman thrust the marker in his face. His gaze followed Sabrina as she left the building. They weren't done talking. Not by a long shot.

LATER THAT AFTERNOON, in the stable's tack room, Sabrina frowned at the drawers that someone hadn't pushed back into the set shelving unit. A couple of the cowboy hats weren't on their proper pegs, scattered about on the floor. Someone had rifled through the room, and Sabrina wasn't happy one bit. Since the grooms and other ranch hands would never leave the room in this condition, it didn't take much of a leap to guess the cause of the mess. *The commercial crew.* Mr. Irwin had assured her she wouldn't notice their presence, but that was all she could concentrate on since their arrival. Or at least the one specific member of the shoot who had once more lodged himself under her skin.

Ty was back. And he hadn't known about the pregnancy. She reached down and rubbed the bump. Her reward was a swift kick. Whether she should be relieved or nervous that he knew, she wasn't sure. Relief that she didn't have to hide anything anymore reared up, along with anxiety over his next move. The navy flecks in his eyes told her too much. So had his words. He didn't enjoy finding out about the baby in public. She couldn't say she blamed him much on that point.

She thought she'd been diligent in trying to track him down. Emails. A phone call. A voice mail. All ways to communicate without looking someone in the eye. And he'd been right. She'd stayed away from any place where she'd confront him in person. Had that been the easy way out so she could raise their daughter alone?

When her mother had dropped her off at her grandparents' house vowing she'd come back for her once she hit it big on the music scene, six-year-old Sabrina watched her mother's car disappear into the sunset, never to return. With her mother prioritizing fame and success, Sabrina learned from an early age people didn't fulfill their promises. After Ty broke up with her, his promise of forever fading like the sunset, she watched his trailer pull away in a haze of dust.

If he'd said he loved her and still ended their relationship, would he disappoint their daughter in the same way? Sabrina would do everything she could to protect this little one. She might never keep all the bad out of her life, but she'd try her best to shelter her from as many tribulations as possible.

Was Ty a storm or sunshine?

Sabrina sighed and righted the room. Jamming her cowboy hat on her head, she left the stable and headed for the set. Once and for all the crew had to get it through their heads, they needed to keep their distance from the stable, both for their safety and the animals' well-being.

The chill in the air did her mind a world of good, helping to calm her ruffled feathers. She drew strength from this land she'd adopted as her own. The craggy mountains rose to meet the bluest sky she'd ever seen. Those mountains had been around a long time, and they'd still be here after the camera crew left. So would she.

Five minutes later, she arrived at the meadow where the crew had set up their massive lights and other equipment. *Two weeks.* She could make it through that time, but the crew had to respect that the stable was off-limits.

People milled about a table loaded with food. That seemed as good a place as any to find the director. Someone noticed her, and it was as if the conversation ground to a complete halt. Five sets of eyes bore down on her, and there wasn't a familiar face in the group.

"Excuse me?" A youngish man with a baseball cap and a heavy black coat frowned. "Can I help you? This is a closed set."

"I'm the barn manager, and I need to speak with the director about the stable. They're closed to anyone who doesn't have proper authorization." Sabrina didn't want friction between the two camps, but she'd defend those horses to Pikes Peak, the famous Colorado landmark, and back.

The light lines on the man's forehead creased. "I'm Carter Webb, the director. I communicated the info about the stable to the crew, and they respect the boundary. That was the deal I made with Mr. Irwin."

Sabrina stretched to her full height of five-seven, thankful for the couple of extra inches her cowboy boots afforded. "And I assure you, Mr. Webb, I'll be speaking to Mr. Irwin about how someone in your crew disregarded those orders."

She turned on her heel and started for the ranch house, when a familiar voice sounded behind her. "Sabrina? Is something wrong?"

Ty's voice held genuine concern, enough for her to retrace her steps. His tone was a bit of a surprise given how badly this morning had gone. She'd expected…

What did she expect from him? Better yet, what did he want from her? This baby now bound them together, whether she liked it or not.

She faced him and saw him approach with a woman holding a tape measure trailing behind him. Her ire grew into full flame. If she didn't have proof it was the camera crew before, she did now. Ty was wearing Mr. Irwin's special cowboy hat, taken from the tack room. "Carter said he informed everyone on the set the stable is off-limits. The rules apply to you, too, Ty."

He removed the cowboy hat, rubbed the back of his neck and winced. "Give me a break about yesterday, Sabrina. Phineas ran in there, and I was worried he might hurt himself or another animal. It won't happen again."

"You entered the tack room today." Frustration bubbled inside her, and she pointed to the evidence resting in his right hand. "That's Gordon Irwin's lucky cowboy hat. The one he wore when he won the steeplechase championship a couple of years ago. It's his favorite."

The older woman next to Ty placed her hand over her mouth and gasped. "Oh my stars!"

Ty faced the woman, her large black glasses overwhelming her face. "Maureen, are you okay?"

"I'd used the measurements of the cowboy we originally hired, and his hat didn't fit you. I saw someone riding a horse and asked him where I could find one. He told me to go into the stable and borrow the one with the green brim." Terrified, her gaze went from Carter to Ty and then back to Carter. "Am I in trouble? Did I get the wrong hat?"

Maureen didn't know it, but she'd received permission from Mr. Irwin himself. "I'm sorry for jumping to conclusions," Sabrina said. "It's all good."

With a nod at Carter and Ty, she headed to the stable.

"Wait!" Gravel crunched behind her, and she knew it was useless to outrun Ty.

While she agreed with him they needed to talk, this wasn't the right time. Not with her basically accusing him of trespassing and theft just now. And that was on top of him feeling betrayed she didn't tell him about the baby. Once again, she found herself turning and facing him.

His open expression floored her. It was like he expected to clear the air between them. Still, she'd like some niceties for this long overdue conversation. A warm room, a cup of tea and a practiced script, not necessarily in that order.

"I don't want to keep you from your work," she said. The wind swirled around them, picking up in intensity. From what she'd heard, December in Colorado could get unbearably cold. She pulled her woolen cap over her ears. "The horses are depending on me."

"I just finished the costume fitting when you showed up. I'm done for today, and that was quite a bombshell you dropped on me this morning." Shock laced his words. "I never expected to hear those words from anyone."

Nothing close to happiness or joy came through in his voice or his closed stance. A little excitement would have been nice. Then again, they'd talked so often about a future without children that he'd made his position on the matter quite clear. Suddenly, the idea of him rejecting their daughter as easily as he'd rejected her left her dizzy.

The same way she'd felt the first time Ty kissed her in a meadow of wildflowers, the sun streaming down on their faces.

The same way she'd felt the night of her seventh birthday when it sank in that her mother wasn't coming to her party.

"Later. I have a tack room to clean and horses who need me."

"Sabrina, I grew up on a ranch. I know the horses come first, but I'm asking for fifteen minutes, thirty tops." His jaw stiff, this determined man was a far cry from the reckless guy she'd fallen in love with almost a year ago.

And as hard as it was to admit, he deserved more of an explanation than the bare minimum she'd given at the feed and seed this morning. "I'll meet you in front of the stable in a few minutes."

They went their separate ways, and she tried to gather her wits when she remembered she hadn't checked on the mare's foreleg yet. Copper, one of their most reliable ranch horses, was still experiencing some swelling, and she needed to change the wrap. She was in the middle of her examination when she heard Ty's voice asking to come inside the stable.

She gave him credit for that. "Back here." She ran her hand up the horse's foreleg, checking on the swelling present for the past couple of days. It had decreased, and she looked forward to giving Elizabeth a positive report. In no time, she bandaged the foreleg.

She looked up and saw Ty watching her. "You always had a way with horses," he said. Appreciation of her efforts shone on his earnest face.

"Thank you." It wasn't by chance that she

agreed to talking here at the stable. Familiar and comforting, this was her second home. Besides, she spent most of her waking hours here, getting to know the personalities of the different horses, assisting the vet and farrier and modernizing the office setup. Taking over from someone older and much admired by the staff had been daunting before she'd placed her stamp on the position. So far, the technological strides she'd adopted made her job that much easier.

She rose and gathered her supplies. Exiting the stall, she wondered how to proceed. No longer were they Ty and Sabrina, letting down their masks and falling in love. They were strangers about to become parents, and the dance of avoidance was over.

"How long—"

"When are—"

Their voices overlapped, and the tension grew thick. She shifted the bag with the supplies from one hand to the other. "What do you want to know, Ty?"

"Are you returning to the rodeo after the baby's born?"

At least he started with a straightforward question. "No." Sometimes she'd fall asleep so exhausted from the day's work on the ranch, she didn't have time to miss her old job as a rodeo clown. "I'm the permanent barn manager for the Double I Ranch."

She led him inside the tack room and started putting away the supplies.

"I'm surprised you didn't move back to Texas. Isn't that where your grandparents live?"

He remembered. That warmed her, and a tug of attraction kicked up once more. "They're older, and not in the best of health." She had considered returning there, but she hadn't wanted to leave her friends behind, who she also considered family. "When I asked Will for a job reference, he told me about the open position here at the Double I."

"Will Sullivan?" He leaned against the door frame, the denim jacket showing off his broad shoulders. "The same guy who used to compete on the rodeo circuit?"

Will, along with Lucky Harper, were more than rodeo competitors to her. Bonding on the tour long ago, they'd gone through thick and thin for the past ten years together. There'd been that time when she and Will had sung "Happy Birthday" and Lucky revealed this was the first time anyone had ever bought him a cake. A month later, Lucky had given both her and Will handcrafted chess sets he'd carved himself. She and Lucky had spent many an evening playing chess while Will read a book nearby.

Then there was the time she'd sprained her wrist while she was working at a different rodeo from Will and Lucky. They'd driven all night to make sure she was on the way to recovery.

After the death of Will's parents, she and Lucky had made their first, but not last, visit to Will's ranch.

They were more than her friends; they were family.

"Yes. Walk with me to my office?" More like a broom closet, but it was hers. Another sign she belonged at the Double I.

He nodded, and she flipped off the switch. They entered her office where he dominated the small space with his commanding presence.

"So, Will Sullivan recommended you for this job?" She thought she detected a note of jealousy, but that was just wishful thinking.

"Will owns the Silver Horseshoe, the next ranch over. The bunkhouse there is full, so he told me about the opening here." When she'd come to Violet Ridge to tell Will about the baby, she wasn't surprised he was engaged to Kelsea Carruthers after a whirlwind few months. Kelsea had arrived in town without ever having stepped foot on a ranch before. Getting a crash course in ranch life, Kelsea had found herself stranded when the tires on Will's lone UTV deflated. That had forced Will to come to terms with the accident that had claimed his parents' lives and confront his feelings for Kelsea. "He and his wife have been so supportive. They've agreed to be the baby's godparents."

"That's a big decision." His brow furrowed, and he leaned forward on the small wooden chair, his elbows propped on his knees, close enough for her to inhale his woodsy scent.

"You weren't around, Ty." *Breathe, Sabrina, breathe.* "I've done everything on my own for the past seven months. I'll do everything I can to make sure she has a secure home, surrounded with love."

"From here on, I'd like to be consulted on decisions of that magnitude."

"From where? The magazines were full of articles of you closing down the bars having a good time. Or what if I need you while you're wrestling with a bull ten times your weight?"

That was another reason Sabrina couldn't go back to the profession she loved so much.

What if she were injured while working? She'd had a few close calls while distracting the bull enough for the rider to get away. Cuts and scrapes were the least of her previous injuries, which included a broken clavicle and a couple of concussions. No matter what, she'd always downplayed the close calls to her grandparents, unwilling to cause them any extra stress, but the underlying danger was still there. That same danger would accompany Ty through his remaining days in the rodeo. As the Double I Ranch's barn manager, there'd be less chance of significant injury.

"There are plenty of rodeo contestants who are fathers." Ty stood and removed his jacket, a fine sheen of sweat dotting his forehead. "I just never imagined I'd be one of them."

Her heart sank at his stony face, resolute and unmoving. When the nurse told her about the baby, she'd gone through a gamut of emotions in sixty seconds. Shock and disbelief had quickly given way to love and acceptance. While she didn't expect him to overcome his feelings that fast, she hoped for some glint of happiness about the baby.

But he stood there, perspiring as if a two-ton bull was about to stampede him. "I'm not asking for you to change anything about your life. You deserve to know you have a daughter, but that's all. Your responsibility ends here."

Ty frowned. "I'm not following."

"I'd like to raise our daughter by myself."

CHAPTER THREE

BY MYSELF. Every time Ty threw the tennis ball to Phineas while the crew worked on the lights, Sabrina's earnest entreaty from the day before asking him to give up any claim to his daughter haunted him. Did she expect him to walk away so easily? Then again, he'd done it once before. He couldn't blame her for thinking he'd do so again.

Phineas brought the ball back and laid it at Ty's feet. He rewarded the dog by throwing it even farther this time. At least he was good at this. He'd tried to help the crew and ended up accidentally tripping someone carrying an important camera part. They'd relegated him to keeping Phineas busy, and Robert encouraged him to bond with the dog. That he could do. Making inroads with the crew, though? So far he'd struck out with them, same as he had with Sabrina.

So much for rekindling the past. Two days ago, when they reconnected in the stable, she sparked something inside him. During their relationship, she'd brought a new depth to fun. Like it had a purpose.

It seemed like just yesterday when they searched out rodeos where they could work together. Whenever they landed at the same arena, they blocked off any free time for each other. Not that there was much of that with his sponsorship commitments and her intense preparation for what some called the toughest gig at the rodeo. Still, they always found a day to themselves.

Every time, he hunted for the most offbeat places in whatever town they were visiting. One week, they toured a house converted from an oil storage tank. The next week they strolled through the Cathedral of Junk in Austin, an unusual structure cobbled together out of people's garbage. No matter where they visited, Sabrina had made him appreciate each attraction, bringing a unique perspective that spurred him to think hard. Just by being her spunky self.

And those places had paled next to her husky laugh. He remembered the afternoon they were hiking in the countryside when the thunderstorm left them soaked in an abandoned barn. Her laughter when he shook the moisture out of his hair was the moment he knew. He loved Sabrina MacGrath and wanted to make her happy always. It had been the best day of his life.

Had he thrown love away out of fear she might be left alone without him, or out of fear she might leave him if they stopped having fun?

Phineas retrieved the ball once more, now a gooey, drooly mess. *Oh, well.* The dog loved it. Ty faked throwing it in one direction before sending it in an arc over the field, a thin layer of snow not slowing down Phineas in the least.

Phineas returned without the ball, wagging his tail in an obvious ploy for attention. Ty obliged. "Why did I throw it all away, Phin?"

Over a promise he made to himself when he was eight? There was no way three premature deaths in his direct family line could be a coincidence. There had to be some hidden defect. His heart skidded. Would his daughter have the same issue?

"Ty?" Carter repeated his name. "If you and Phineas are done having fun now?"

"Sorry about that." Ty blinked and glanced at the crew carrying out their responsibilities. If he kept his head in the clouds, he'd be letting down all these people from the best boy to the gaffer.

He might enjoy having fun, but he prided himself on working every bit as hard.

"Are the lights fixed?" Ty asked, still petting Phineas.

"Take five," Carter called out to the crew and then motioned for Ty to follow him. "Thanks for entertaining the dog, but you have to stay on top of what's happening on the set."

Ty stood straight. He could see the reasoning behind Sabrina's criticism, but this? "I thought I was staying out of the way. Remember yesterday?"

"I see your point." Carter scrutinized him with a keen eye. "I was against using you in the commercial, but your screen test made a believer out of me. Today though? You seem like a different person than the lighthearted guy who was here the first day."

Robert came over and murmured his thanks before leading Phineas away. Ty already missed his companionable sidekick. He faced Carter, who stood waiting for an answer. "The crew's like a family. I'm the new guy."

"That's one way of looking at it, but it's more like you're distracted about something." Carter's lips pursed in a straight line, and Ty waited for the boom to fall, figuratively not literally like the other day. "What happens in the rodeo when you're distracted?"

Ty didn't have to think twice. "Bulls will leave you in the dust or eat you for lunch."

Carter nodded. "The camera is equally unforgiving, although differently. When your mind is somewhere else, the camera picks up on that."

And his mind was on Sabrina and the baby.

"Got it." Ty had always separated fun from work in the arena. Somehow, he'd have to do the same here.

"Aha!" Carter snapped his fingers. "I get it now, and it's more common than you think."

That a man found out he was going to be a father and the mother didn't want him involved in her life? Ty raised his eyebrows at Carter's statement. "I don't think so."

Carter dismissed Ty's statement with a wave. "Nerves. It happens to the best of them. You're the new kid on the block, and you're intimidated by my crew, who's worked together for years."

"That's one explanation." Not the right one, but Ty didn't correct Carter's false impression.

"You seem like the guy who knows the

best places to kick back and unwind." Carter waited while Ty considered his statement.

Was that the quality everyone noticed about him? That he was fun-loving Ty?

Still, it rankled a bit that he knew just the place. "The Bighorn Blaze has a great craft brew selection, one of the largest in the state." And in Colorado, that was saying something. "They also make an epic bison burger."

Carter pulled out his phone. "An evening bonding with the crew is in order. I'm sending out a group text now. Everyone on the set will get to know you. You'll get to know them. By tomorrow, we'll be one big happy family."

If only Ty could say that about him and Sabrina. There wasn't anything he could do about that tonight, so he might as well salvage this chance. "Sounds good. I'll be there."

"We'll have a last rehearsal and then film tomorrow once you're more comfortable around everyone."

Carter walked away, and Ty responded "going" to the group text. He went to replace his phone in his pocket when he received a text from Sabrina.

I was out of line earlier. Talk this afternoon?

His heartbeat accelerated. They'd both lost faith in each other, bad choices leading to consequences that seemed impossible to overcome. She believed the worst about him to such a degree she asked him to stay away from their daughter.

Forever was such a long time, and yet it seemed like yesterday that he'd cried for the father who never came home. As hard as it was to leave someone behind, it was harder to break their heart by not being part of their life. He couldn't do that to his daughter.

Still, the hard truth of the breakup was his to face, and he had to confront the past now before it cost him this job, or worse yet, a chance at a future relationship with the baby. He'd broken Sabrina's heart, and now she didn't want him to do the same to their daughter.

How could he persuade her that seeing that little black-and-white image had changed him?

That wasn't the only thing biting at him. He'd seen the pain on her face. He thought he'd spare her any grief by breaking up with her, and instead he'd caused her pain.

Her incoming text stopped him before he could reply. Sick gelding. How about dinner tonight?

He was about to answer yes when he remembered the crew get-together.

How about tomorrow? Have work appointment tonight.

They settled on a time, and Ty returned to the set, whistling his favorite Christmas carol. No sooner had Carter wrapped up production for the day than Ty changed his clothes and borrowed one of the ranch trucks. He didn't even need to use his GPS to find the Bighorn Blaze. The plain brick building with its gravel lot hadn't aged a day since the last time he'd visited Violet Ridge. The outline of the establishment was decorated with bright, colorful Christmas lights, the kind Hal loved.

Upon entering, country met Christmas in the tunes coming from the speakers. The yeasty smell of the craft beers hit him, along with the greasy aroma of the grilled burgers. His stomach rumbled, and he waved at the crew, who'd already pushed a couple of tables together.

Noise and camaraderie might help him put his troubles with Sabrina on the back burner for one night. A little fun never hurt anyone.

Ty had barely stepped inside the door before a couple of old-timers patted him on the back. "Way to go, Ty! Knew you'd come back. You deserved that win."

That type of mindset would have been mighty handy in the summer months when, more than once, he'd laid flat on his back, trying to ignore the stars swimming around his eyes as much as avoid the two-thousand-pound bull aiming for a piece of his jeans.

"You're why I do what I do. It's your support." He pasted on his widest grin. "That's what pulled me through."

Every word was the truth. He obliged them with selfies and autographs, laughing and joshing with them. Others came over and congratulated him, and he spent time with each of them, smiling and posing for pictures.

For years, he believed this type of casual contact was all he needed. Sabrina had proven him wrong. Sad inside but beaming on the outside, he waved to the crowd and made his way to the crew table, sitting in the only open spot, next to Carter.

As he hung his coat on a hook on the pole, laughter greeted him. Normally, he wasn't this late to any party. Too often, he *was* the life of the party. Yet his arrival in Violet

Ridge turned his world inside out. He wasn't sure of much about anything anymore.

The server delivered the crew's dinner and recited Ty's order back to him, promising to return with his bison burger and fries as soon as they were ready. By the time his food arrived, everyone else was raring to go to the billiard room. He waved them away, holding up his lemon water, as he didn't have a designated driver. "As soon as I'm done with this, I'll join you."

The crew departed to let off some steam. Carter gave him a pointed glance, but Ty raised a fry. Carter shrugged and left while Ty concentrated on his food. The mound of fries should have already been halfway gone, yet he wasn't hungry. He swirled one in ketchup.

He ate a couple bites of his burger and gave up the ghost. His appetite had vanished when Sabrina announced her request for him to stand aside. How could she think he didn't want to be involved?

Their walks and talks resurfaced in his mind. *Children aren't in my future. I never want to leave a child behind. Fatherhood is for other men, not me.* With lines like that, he could see why she believed she was offering him an easy out. Problem was, this might be his only chance to experience fatherhood, even if only for a short time. His father had eight years with him, and it wasn't like his father left by choice.

He wanted to be there for his daughter for as long as he had left.

All he needed was a chance to prove himself to Sabrina. But to what end? A relationship with their daughter or another attempt with Sabrina herself? While both would be nice, he wouldn't deceive himself. Sabrina didn't love him anymore.

He raised another fry before throwing it back on the plate and pushing it away.

Cheers came from the direction of the billiard room, but he was too tired to join them. Suddenly, the price of fun came crashing down. The true cost of valuing fun over substance might be a relationship with his daughter if he didn't think of a solution, and fast.

Was it already too late to salvage even a friendship with Sabrina?

Losing her friendship would be the worst part of all of this. He shivered and headed toward the bar. Why did he venture this way? He wanted nothing clouding his already stormy mind. The bartender came over, his

red-and-green-plaid bow tie a matched set
with his vest.

"What can I get you?" The bartender placed
a bowl of peanuts in front of Ty.

"I'm good."

Someone called out for the bartender, who
threw the dish towel over his shoulder and
scurried away. Ty steeled himself for the billiard room and a chance to bond with the
crew. This wasn't personal; this was work.
Besides, a game of pool might be a great way
to unwind.

"Howdy, cowboy. Buy me a drink?"

Ty turned and found a woman in her late
twenties sitting on a stool. She smoothed her
bright blond layered hair, abundant and wavy,
and licked her lips. Her green glitter tank was
paired with a brighter jacket. She crossed her
legs, her red thigh-high boots coming up almost to her knees.

Before he could answer, he looked over the
woman's shoulder. The crowd parted, and he
spotted Sabrina near the servers' stand, her
mouth open. Disappointment glistened in her
eyes. She said something to the two people
next to her.

"Sabrina!" Ty jumped off his stool and
tried to make his way through the crowd, a

large party of holiday goers who'd come in together blocking his path.

"Aren't you Ty Darling?" A middle-aged woman tugged at a man's sleeve. "Look, honey, it's Ty."

Before Ty could get to the front, the man grabbed Ty's hand and pumped it. "Congratulations on that brilliant run in the championships."

Ty smiled, not wanting to let down his fans. He posed for a selfie with the couple and waited for the wife to find a pen in her purse. After he autographed a napkin, he nodded and searched for Sabrina.

She'd already left.

HER BEST FRIENDS, Will and Kelsea, were sweet enough to take Sabrina straight home after the disaster she'd just witnessed. Earlier, when they'd offered to buy her dinner, Sabrina jumped at the chance. The baby definitely agreed a grilled burger from the Bighorn Blaze sounded like a great idea. With Ty unavailable, a night with friends was what she needed. *Some evening.* Looking out the rear passenger window, Sabrina wiped the tear off her cheek. She and Ty weren't committed to each other. He had every right to flirt with a beautiful woman. The sooner the camera crew wrapped up their production, the better. Then she wouldn't see Ty again.

Numbness spread through her. Ty had progressed from breaking up with her to making up excuses to avoid her. That was some leap for the handsome rodeo star.

To think she once believed they'd spend a lifetime together.

Will and Kelsea accompanied her to her front porch. Sabrina didn't miss the look of pity Kelsea sent to Will.

"How about I stay with you? It'll just be the two of us. Will can come back later and drive me home. In the meantime, we'll bake Christmas cookies." Kelsea rubbed her hands together with glee. "And even better, eat them warm out of the oven."

"Kelsea keeps telling me about her grandmother's recipe." Will sent a look of pure adoration to his new wife. "I'll gladly offer myself as the taste tester."

What would it be like to work through your differences and fight for love like Will and Kelsea had done? Sabrina wouldn't know, as the people in her life cut their losses and moved on, leaving her behind. First her mother, and now Ty.

"Thanks, but go home and bake them together." Sabrina entreated her friends. "I need some time alone."

After some well-meaning protests, Will and Kelsea took their leave. Sabrina stared at the walls of her living room, a former bunkhouse Elizabeth had offered her as one benefit of the job. The holiday decorations looked too festive, too bright. She needed the earthy aroma of the stable. Better yet, she'd be around animals that didn't claim to have work appointments when they didn't. She might as well get a head start on tomorrow's work list.

Besides, the unconditional love from the horses sure beat sitting around, feeling sorry for herself. In no time, she changed, donned her boots and headed to the stable, where she swapped out her puffy turquoise coat for a jacket with deep pockets.

She greeted and checked on each of the ten horses. The groom had handled the evening feeding, but a glance at Mr. Irwin's mustang, Margarita, gave Sabrina pause. Margarita was all anyone could want in a lead ranch horse, intelligent with a stamina of steel. The mare responded to Mr. Irwin's commands before he even had to ask. Tonight, though, the normally composed horse was agitated about something.

Sabrina entered the stall and found the problem on the wooden post. "That nail must have popped out. I'll remove it and then check your leg."

She reached for her multiuse tool in her pocket and used the pliers. In no time, she extricated the offending nail. Then she ran her hand over Margarita's hind leg. She felt a couple of superficial scratches, but nothing that required further attention. "You're doing fine, sweetheart."

"Calling a mustang a sweetheart?" Ty's voice came from the aisle outside the stall, and Sabrina clutched her hands over her chest. "That's a new one."

"Give me some warning next time, before you turn up."

"There's going to be a next time? The way you left the restaurant, I imagined the worst." Ty grinned and leaned against a post, those dimples standing out in the soft glow of the lights. Tingles shivered up and down her spine.

Sabrina returned her focus to Margarita's leg, the mare still far from being her usual composed self. Was something else bothering Margarita? She'd check on her first thing in the morning. If she still acted this antsy, Sabrina would call the vet. With a pat and murmured words of reassurance, Sabrina left the stall.

"*Next time* was a slip of the tongue, that's all."

"How about clearing the air?" Ty's grin slowly expanded, and she ignored the funny feeling in her chest.

"About what? Tonight? You could have texted me the truth. That you were going to the bar for a fun night, and more." Extra proof her original plan of raising their daughter alone was for the best. "My offer still stands for you to sign your parental rights over to me. You'll probably be happy once this is behind you. Then you can continue to surround yourself with attractive women and your adoring fans with no distractions."

The baby kicked as if interceding on her father's behalf. Sabrina ignored the movement and faced Ty, popping her hands on her hips. That grin turned into a frown, a rare occurrence. That concerned her. He wasn't thinking of countering her offer, was he? He could assert his paternal rights, but that wasn't the Ty she knew.

Ty's head craned in one direction and then the other. "Who's in the stable with you?" Not the response she expected, but she'd go along for a minute.

"You." She exchanged her stable coat for her turquoise one.

He stared into her eyes, his usual mischievous gleam absent. "It's late at night, and you were in a stall with a mustang. What if the horse had kicked you?"

Was that a flicker of fear in the back of his eyes? Surely not.

"Margarita is a professional, as am I."

"Accidents happen, Sabrina. And you're six weeks away from giving birth." He straightened, as alert as if he was in the rodeo chute before the bell clanged. "What if you'd gone into labor?"

She transferred her multiuse tool and phone to the pocket of her turquoise coat. "I'd call Elizabeth or one of the grooms." She zipped her coat. "You don't have any cause to worry about me."

He placed his hand on her arm, concern for her written all over his face. "You think that little of me?"

"You lied to me tonight."

"What?" He shook his head. "I did no such thing."

"That woman didn't look like a work commitment." Sabrina reeled at her jealous tone. Why should she care what he did in his off hours?

Ty's nostrils flared, and he tapped the ground with his boot. "What you didn't see was the camera crew in the billiard room. I've been in a state of shock about the baby all day. Carter's worried I'm suffering from nerves, which I am, but it's over your pregnancy, not the shoot. He thought bonding with the crew would put me more at ease. Yes, a woman approached me, but I wasn't interested. I'd have been here sooner, but I couldn't find you at the restaurant and then I got sidetracked with the crew. I came straight here. I didn't even run by your house first. Somehow, I knew you'd be in the stable."

"Um." He knew her well, and she'd ran away instead of approaching him for an explanation. "Maybe I should have stayed and talked to you. We need to get to the heart of the matter."

In more ways than one.

"Talking was never our problem before. Why is it so hard now?" Ty looked straight at her.

Maybe it was because they no longer were wearing rose-colored glasses about the other.

Now they both saw the good and the bad in each other. Doubt had taken a strong hold upon her heart. At the restaurant, she'd jumped to the wrong conclusion too fast, something she wouldn't have done this time last year. The instant trust from the first time she navigated a bull away from him in the arena was now gone.

Cutting ties now, before the baby's arrival, would spare the three of them pain down the road. "Because there's someone who matters now."

"You matter, Sabrina." He jammed his hands in his pockets. "To me. You always did."

She wanted to believe him, but the ease at which he walked away from her seven months ago said otherwise. "The horses are settled for the night. We can go somewhere where we can sit down." She began walking toward the stable doors.

He stayed where he was. "What will you do once the baby's born? Will someone else check on the horses at night?"

New alarms clanged in her head. These weren't casual, off-the-cuff questions. These were serious ones that almost sounded, dare she think it, *fatherly*. Hope he might want to be a part of his daughter's life sprung inside of her. *Hope?* Where had that come from? She wanted him out of her life. Didn't she?

"Kelsea and Will live nearby and have offered to help with the baby. Then there's the staff. As the barn manager, I have several grooms and ranch hands who report to me. They'll help at night. If there's an emergency, I'm friends with several employees who work in the main house and live nearby. A few have offered to watch the baby."

He frowned. "So, you're not hiring a full-time nanny?"

"I'll provide for her just fine without a nanny." Fear struck at her about where this conversation was going. "Come on."

She enlisted his help in pulling the stable doors shut for the night. Together, they pushed until the clank of steel meeting in the middle echoed through the valley. Night had fallen, and a myriad of stars shone overhead without light pollution diminishing their glow. Little puffs of water vapor greeted her. The crisp Colorado air stung her cheeks, but she relished her favorite season, winter's quiet stillness calming her unsteady emotions.

"I admire how much you inspire a fierce loyalty in your friends," he said.

Sabrina didn't expect him to say that. He

always found a way to surprise her and keep her on her toes. She'd missed that about him, and more. His friendship. His magnetism. Those kisses. She blinked that away.

"And you're always the life of the party, Ty. People crowd around you, wanting a piece of you. I'm offering you a chance at more fun nights with no recrimination. You can still be free to live your life as your own."

He shoved his hands in his coat pockets. "Why does everyone assume I only want to have fun? You know me better than that."

She thought she had before he walked away. "It's late, and I'm heading home."

"I'll walk with you. Make sure you get in okay." Ty strolled alongside her, the path to her bunkhouse clear with only a trace of snow shoveled to the side. "After all, I'm living next door for the next twelve days."

It's just temporary. Don't get your hopes up. "If you need that time for your decision, that's fine with me. I've spent seven months thinking I'd be raising her alone. Twelve days won't matter much." She rubbed her baby bump and kept looking straight ahead, too scared of admitting any feelings, which was exactly what she'd do if she glanced his way. "I've built a secure world for her."

"Maybe I want to be a part of that world."

Absolutely not. Her mind rebelled at the very idea, flashing back to the drawn-out agony while waiting for her mother, who promised she'd sing for Sabrina. Her mother never came. She didn't want their daughter waiting for a father who promised to come for a holiday or her birthday and didn't follow-through.

"What if you get caught up in chasing the finals and forget to call?" Her voice grew more squeaky with every syllable. She breathed in and out, practicing her technique for next month. Oxygen flooded her system and, once again, she regained her levelheadedness. "Or say it's her birthday, and she's waiting for you to open her presents. She might even fall asleep—"

"Sabrina—" he laid his hand on hers "—I'm not your mother."

Until now, she'd forgotten she shared that memory with him. She'd never even told Will Sullivan or Lucky Harper about that fateful day. The three of them had shared most of the details of their lives over countless evenings of heartfelt confidences and fun times. Lucky spent his childhood in a series of foster homes while she'd lived with her grandparents—

another thing that had bonded them. "Well, it could happen."

"How about a deal?" Ty grinned, that same dare in his voice as the first time he'd asked her out.

She should say no. "I don't…" The baby kicked as if asking for Sabrina to hear him out. Whether or not that was wishful thinking on her part, she wasn't sure. However, the least she could do was listen. She owed him that, if for no other reason than for not telling him about the baby in person. "What kind of deal?"

That grin grew even wider, and those tingles along her spine spread to her arms. She was just cold, that was all. "You've heard of the twelve days of Christmas?"

She rolled her eyes. "And every parody of the song."

"Well, how about the twelve days of Ty?" He scrunched his nose. "That doesn't sound good. The twelve days of Darling?"

"More like twelve days of charisma," Sabrina muttered under her breath, and his eyes lit up.

"See, that's why we make a good team. You polish my roughness and make me shine. For twelve days, I'll show you my charismatic, lovable self so you can see I'm trustworthy."

She climbed the steps to her front porch. "What if you fail?"

"Hardly," he scoffed. "I'll charm your socks off."

She looked down, her boots not visible with the baby bump protruding. "What if I'm not convinced at the end of those twelve days?" She produced a key from her pocket and unlocked the door.

"Of charisma." He entered behind her and shut the door. "You can't leave off the most important part."

She placed her coat on the coatrack. "And you're not answering my question."

His chest heaved. "If you don't think I'll make the best father, I'll sign the papers."

That easily? She was disappointed in herself for thinking he might stick around this time.

"You have an especially steep mountain to climb. Since anyone who's willing to give up with such reckless abandon surely isn't in it for the long haul."

He didn't seem deterred as he reached for the doorknob. "That's where you're wrong. I'm trustworthy because I'm listening to you and going along with what you think is best for the baby."

He extended his hand, and she weighed

his words. Slowly, she nodded and shook his hand. The warmth from him spread through her, gnawing at the numbness that had settled over her when they broke up. She found herself drawn to him once more. "You have yourself a deal," she said.

"Be prepared to be Ty-dazzled."

With that, he detached himself and raised two fingers to his forehead in a mock salute. When he left, a whiff of his woodsy cologne lingered in her living room. Something about the confidence he had in himself made her question whether she was right in asking him to sign away his rights. Anyone who was that sure of himself could teach a child how to have a healthy dose of self-esteem and resilience. He could end up being a good father.

But anyone that sure of himself might also be immune to the sound of someone else's heart breaking. Either her heart would shatter again or their daughter would suffer if he disappointed her in the future. Neither prospect was appealing.

Suddenly, being Ty-dazzled was scarier than the prospect of labor.

CHAPTER FOUR

HEADING TOWARD THE town square located a block away from the pastel storefronts of Main Street, Ty admired the large red bows on the black antique lampposts. Today's shoot had gone smoothly, and Carter claimed last night's dinner broke the ice. Ty hadn't confided that Sabrina's warming up to him was the real reason he was more relaxed and happy.

After watching the daily rushes, Carter had offered to call Ty's agent with an opportunity for another acting role. Ty had declined. While acting was a pleasant change from the rodeo, he wasn't giving up his lariat forever. If anything, this week proved he belonged in the arena for at least another year, if not longer. Dare he hope the Darling genes might spare him from the same untimely demise that claimed his father, grandfather and great-grandfather at the tender age of thirty-five?

But if they didn't, he'd leave his daughter behind. Maybe he should take Sabrina up on her suggestion and allow her to raise the baby alone. After all, his daughter couldn't miss what wasn't in her life. Could she?

He reached into his pocket and pulled out his wallet. Tucked into the lining was the sonogram picture Sabrina had given him. Examining it, he fingered the white glossy edge, careful not to smudge the image of their daughter. Maybe this wasn't about the baby missing him, but what he could give her in the meantime. A swell of love overtook him for someone he'd never met.

Well, except he'd felt this same emotion, although differently in a romantic way, during those months with Sabrina when he'd wake up each morning with her next to him, wanting to make her life a little better. Thinking of ways to coax that smile that lit up her entire face was fun. He hadn't considered how hard it would be to never see her again when he ended their relationship.

That made the next twelve days all the more crucial, a test of whether they could be friends again. He shivered with anticipation. Beginnings were always a herald of fun and adventure around the bend. Excitement welled in him at the challenge set before him. He was going to do whatever it would take to impress Sabrina until she admitted there was room for both of them in their daughter's life. When Sabrina had custody, she'd show their daughter how not to be afraid of anything. When their daughter lived with him, Ty would make her laugh and find joy in the everyday existence.

Suddenly, the thought of a home without Sabrina didn't seem like fun.

With careful deliberation, he tucked the photo back in his wallet. He only had an hour to prepare everything before Sabrina would meet him in front of the giant Christmas tree in the town square. His stomach flipped at the prospect of fulfilling one of her life goals that she'd confided in him while they dated.

Fifty-nine minutes later, in the growing twilight, he stuck a couple of bills in the red pot next to a worker ringing a bell. With his arms full of packages and boxes, Ty felt free and ready to take on the world, Sabrina included. He hurried toward the gigantic pine tree with twinkling, colorful lights and a delicate dusting of snow. Then he spotted Sabrina, and his heart skipped a beat. She'd pulled her shiny brown hair back with a green-and-red headband with little holly sprigs dotted all over it, her gaze serious and reflective.

He neared her and performed a mock bow. "My lady."

Her face instantly paled, and he muttered an apology. That was the way he'd always greeted her on their dates.

"That's okay." She exhaled a deep breath and reassured him. "We're both adjusting to this new normal. You know this isn't a date, right?"

"Of course it isn't, but it seems like an audition of sorts." Which was crazy. An audition for his commercial? Most understandable. Tryouts for fatherhood? Was it even possible to rehearse for such a situation?

"Maybe it is a bad idea." She stepped away, a frown marring her pretty face.

"I didn't say that." He was on the cusp of losing her again. Where did that thought come from? They weren't a couple now, and they never would be again.

These next days were only about proving to her that he'd be a good father, and nothing more. For eight years, his father had been the best. After his mother remarried, his stepfather, Hal, had done more than just make his mother happy again. Hal had met a frightened boy trying to adjust to his new life on a ranch and diligently worked at the relationship until he won Ty over. Hal was more than his step-father; he was his second dad.

That kind of example was a hard act to follow, but if Ty could hold on to a rope attached to a bucking bronc for eight seconds, he was made of sturdy stuff.

"Why did you choose this place? Did you hide something in the tree?" Sabrina looked over his shoulder, and he turned his head in that direction.

"No, it was just a convenient meeting spot. Why do you ask?"

"The first day of Christmas. A partridge in a pear tree? I assumed you'd connect the experiences to the actual song." Her eyes sparkled with some of that patented Sabrina spunk.

He laughed and reached into the first package for the teddy bear he'd purchased. He stuck it on a branch and shrugged. "A teddy in a piñon tree?" He shook his head. "Doesn't have the same ring to it, but it'll have to do."

Come to think of it, he'd have to up his game and think of a different corresponding event for each day.

"Thank you. I'll put it in the baby's nursery when I get home." She reached for the bag, and he frowned.

When he touched her hand, sparks of static

electricity prickled his skin. "Maybe it's for you."

She looked at him like he'd just been thrown from a bull. "For me?"

"Everyone should have something warm and cuddly to hug." He kept his tone light and brought out another box. "And something sweet and delectable."

He winked. This was going to be fun, after all.

She opened the box with a dozen chocolate éclairs and gasped. "You remembered!" She selected one and bit into it. "Yum. So good. I've been craving these."

A light pink blush spread across her face, the same color as the sunset surrounding them. "After you finish, I have a surprise for you."

"A teddy in a piñon tree and my favorite éclairs. This is already too much."

It didn't seem like enough, but it was a start. "You mentioned this activity often on our walks. You're going to love it."

"With an intro like that, it sounds wonderful." A look of bliss crossed her features. "But I'd have been happy with just this."

That was so Sabrina. Down-to-earth. Genuine. Always herself. He longed to keep up.

"We have a couple of minutes until it's

ready." He pointed to the bags. "Can we put these in your car?"

"Did you buy out Violet Ridge?" Her eyes grew wide.

"I just bought a few outfits." And a pair of baby cowboy boots, tiny and adorable. He hadn't been able to resist purchasing what would be her first pair. "The salesperson showed me the softest blanket. You'll love it."

"Sounds perfect. My car's this a way." As they walked, they fell into the happy rhythm of telling each other about their days. She regaled him with stories about the different horses. Too soon, he loaded everything in the trunk of her Subaru. She closed her liftgate and faced him. "Is this surprise within walking distance, or do you need a ride?"

"We can walk." He could barely contain his excitement as he guided her back to the tree. "Remember the story you told me about your first jewelry box?"

She wrinkled her nose. "How I pretended I was an ice-skater instead of a ballerina like the one that popped up and danced to the music? Rather difficult in West Texas."

He stopped at the ice-skating rink within sight of the tree. "I rented this for the next two hours." He performed a mock bow. "Hal taught me how to skate, and I'm rather good, if I say so myself."

"Is this a joke?" she blurted, and halted at the gate. "It's not funny, Ty."

"What's wrong? You always said this was one of your dream experiences."

Her throat bobbed. "No sushi, no hot tub, no alcohol, no ice-skating. And Elizabeth is riding Cinnamon for me." She tapped her five left fingers with her right hand. "An internet search. Two minutes, and you'd have found out it's dangerous this late in my pregnancy."

Soft fluttery snowflakes began falling, and they dotted her nose and cheeks. The beauty of the night was within their grasp, and he'd blown it. "I didn't think."

He reached out to brush the flakes off her face, and she stilled him. "I can do it myself." She wiped her nose. "Thank you for the éclairs. I'm going home."

Too often since he arrived in Violet Ridge, she walked away from him. He watched as she did it again.

LEAVING THE TOWN SQUARE, Sabrina slowed her pace. One teardrop, then two, and she stopped in the nearest archway so she could collect herself. The last thing she wanted to do was trip on an icy sidewalk and go into premature labor.

Why had she agreed to the twelve days of charisma? It would be so easy to get wrapped up in Ty's exciting world and lose sight of herself. Not that she'd done that while they had dated. If anything, Ty had encouraged her in her career and in life in general. Without him, she'd never have sought out quirky side attractions on her own like a pine tree rooted in granite or the hot springs.

"Sabrina?" A woman called out her name. "Are you crying? Is everything okay?"

Sabrina found Emma Graham locking up her shop, Rocky Road Chocolatiers. "Hi, Emma. I'm fine." Sabrina wiped away her tears and faked a smile. "Thanks for asking."

"I don't think that's the complete story." Emma twisted the key and then pulled it from the lock. "Was there something wrong with the éclairs?"

"How do you know about them?"

"Ty Darling came into my shop early this morning and bought out my supply of molten lava chocolate mini Bundt cakes for the camera crew. He asked if I made éclairs. I know the Blue Skies Coffeehouse is legendary for theirs, but for the price he quoted, I brushed off my culinary school recipe." Emma laughed and pocketed her key. "Macy's been wanting a pink Lego set for Christmas, and now I can get it for her."

Macy was Emma's adorable four-year-old daughter. So, Ty had remembered Sabrina's favorite dessert and arranged a special order, just for her. "I tried one already," Sabrina admitted. "They're delicious."

Even better than Blue Skies, but she didn't want to jeopardize her standing with them.

"Thanks. Ty was so excited when he picked them up a few minutes ago." Emma looked around Sabrina. "Where is he?"

Back at the skating rink where Sabrina had chewed him out in no uncertain terms. He'd gone through hoops for her, and she'd reacted rather harshly. "I left him at the town square."

"Well, tell him I could use a new coat, so if he wants another special order for the crew..." Emma chuckled.

"I will." Sabrina's smile wasn't fake this time.

Emma gave Sabrina's arm a quick squeeze before hurrying in the opposite direction. The light snowfall tapered off, the trace of powdery flakes barely registering on the pastel storefront facades. Each window was decorated for the holiday season with eye-catching displays. Any other time she'd have loved lingering and looking at the little details that captivated tourists and residents alike, but she had to find out if Ty was still at the rink. She owed him an apology. She'd start there and then head to the guesthouse if he wasn't.

She turned the corner and stopped. The rink's lights were on, and she made out Ty's laughter above the Christmas carols playing on the speakers. Ty took center stage, twirling and performing figure eights among a small group. He said he'd rented it out for her, and yet people were skating and having a great time.

It was nice to see that; nonetheless, she was confused.

"Sabrina!" A familiar voice kept her from leaving.

An older woman named Zelda Baker, whom Sabrina recognized as the town's retired mayor, removed her green-and-red-striped elflike woolen cap with a white pompom and rushed over, her green hair ruffling in the evening wind.

"Hello, Zelda. Merry Christmas. Sorry I can't stay and chat. I was just heading for my car."

"Not without my hat, you're not." Her red sweater blinking with holiday lights, Zelda thrust her cap toward her. "I won't have you catching cold with that baby due so soon."

Zelda might have retired from her position as the Violet Ridge mayor, but she, along with her identical twin, still looked out for every resident. The sisters were the first to welcome Sabrina when she moved here. "I'm going straight to my car. I'll be fine."

Zelda looked unconvinced, rolling her eyes. "Nelda has a spare. She always does." She glanced over her shoulder and called out to her sister standing at the rail.

Nelda turned, replacing her frown with a smile. She came over and clucked over Sabrina. "You're not wearing a cap. Zelda, why didn't you offer her yours? You know I always carry an extra one because Jaxon can't keep from losing his."

"She did, but I refused." Sabrina rushed to Zelda's defense. "I'm on my way home."

Zelda reached over and stuck her cap on Sabrina's head. "There. Now we..."

"Both feel better." Nelda completed the thought.

"Thank you." Sabrina adjusted the hat. "I'll return it the next time I see you."

"Before you go—" Nelda linked her arm through Sabrina's, her bright orange snow-suit almost fluorescent in the twilight "—you have to watch my grandson Jaxon take a lap around the rink. You won't believe what just happened."

"Ty Darling is letting us use the rink, free of charge," Zelda blurted out and beat her sister to the scoop.

"It just made us love him even more. This is definitely going in the Grandmas for Ty Fan Club newsletter." Nelda pointed to the rink. "This is Jaxon's first time on the ice, and Ty is teaching him how to skate."

"Sofia's been skating for three years." Zelda gave an emphatic nod. "She was so disappointed when she saw the sign the rink was closed. Then Ty came over and said it was a misunderstanding. He helped them lace their skates…"

"And turned it into a fun math lesson for Jaxon." Nelda finished Zelda's sentence as she often did. "He's the greatest."

Sabrina glanced at the ice. Ty marched and then turned back to Jaxon, who mimicked Ty's actions. The boy slipped on the ice and fell on his bottom. His lip quivered until Ty held out his arm and whispered something in his ear. With a determined look, the boy rose, brushed himself off and started again.

Her heart melted a little, and she followed Zelda and Nelda to the rail. Who was the real Ty Darling? The man who left her without a backward glance or the man she saw before her, taking time with each child?

He looked her way and waved. A wide grin broke out on his handsome face. Would their daughter have that grin? The one that made her insides melt? He whispered something to Sofia and Jaxon. The girl helped Jaxon to the rail. Then Ty executed a figure eight, followed by a double jump. The cousins clapped and cheered, and he took a bow.

The proverbial life of the party was in his element, with an audience and adoring fans. He always could make the best of any situation. As much as she didn't want to admit it, he deserved these twelve days. Once trust was reestablished on both ends, they'd decide what was best for the baby from there.

That was why he was doing this, though. For the baby's benefit, not hers.

AFTER SAYING GOODBYE to his new friends, Ty followed Sabrina's older-model Subaru back to the ranch. He should have known pregnant women shouldn't skate. What he didn't know about pregnancy could fill a rodeo program. Come to think of it, it had been some time since he'd been around babies. How was it possible that so much time had elapsed since his half sister Devon was crawling toward him with admiration in her gaze? Now she was about to celebrate her nineteenth birthday. But it was like roping a steer, right? It would all come back to him.

He parked the ranch truck in Mr. Irwin's pristine garage and headed to the guesthouse. Without a second thought, he veered toward Sabrina's bunkhouse.

Knocking, he stood back, the puffs of air evaporating in a cloud of vapor. Sabrina answered in no time, still wearing her coat. "Did you forget something?"

Yes, to give her a good-night kiss.

Huh? Where had that thought come from? He couldn't kiss Sabrina any more. Not after breaking up with her. "I need to talk to you. Devon's eighteen, going on nineteen."

"Is Devon your older sister or your younger one?" Sabrina shivered and then opened the door more than a crack. "Come on in."

"Peyton's older." Ty entered and basked in

the warmth of her home. "Thanks for inviting me in."

He stopped and admired her holiday decorations. A large Christmas tree occupied center stage, the smell of fresh pine filling the air. On her mantel, green garland interwoven with small white lights drew attention to two stockings, one with her name and one with Baby scrolled across the top. What names did Sabrina have in mind? Would he be a part of that decision?

"Did you want an éclair?" She picked up the tote bag and led him to the kitchen. "I was about to put them in the refrigerator when you knocked. Any particular reason for the late-night visit?"

She brought out two plates and then handed him one éclair, her brown eyes sparkling. Would their daughter have her eye color, perhaps with his darker shade of hair? Would she gravitate toward people and crowds like he did? Or would she weigh the gravity of the situation and then ride to the rescue like spunky Sabrina?

"I remember Devon loved her baby swing. Does the baby have one?"

"Come look at the baby's room." She washed

her hands and then gestured for him to follow her.

The hallway was narrow, small enough for him to inhale the light floral scent she always wore. She flipped on a switch, and he was impressed. The walls were rosy pink, as was the coatrack in the shape of a cacti in the corner with tiny garments attached to the hooks as well as a weighted bottom so it wouldn't fall over. The cream-colored crib was in front of a wall with pieces of lumber nailed in the shape of a barn. Hanging in the middle was a sign reading MacGrath.

"Sabrina…" Now was as good a time as any to settle the baby's last name. Maybe a compromise? MacGrath-Darling was rather long, but their baby could make it work.

Her phone rang, and she checked the screen. "I need to take this."

She hurried into the hall, and he stood in front of the crib. His daughter's room looked like something out of a baby magazine, and he hadn't been a part of picking the theme or decorations. He hadn't been there when Sabrina selected the glider in the corner or the fluffy white rug underfoot. If he hadn't shown up now, he'd have missed everything.

Her raised voice from the hallway caused

alarm bells. Rushing toward the door, he collided with something soft. Sabrina wobbled, and he reached out. Her form was curvy and familiar, but oh so off-limits. He waited until they were both steady on their feet, and then let go. "What's wrong?"

"Nothing." The earlier smile had faded, and worry was now etched on her forehead.

"Is everything okay? Is it your grandparents?" He was hesitant to overstep his bounds.

"They're fine. This call had nothing to do with them." She blew out a deep breath, a stray strand of her long brown curly hair escaping and falling over her forehead. She tucked it behind her ear, and he missed the touch of the silky hair between his fingers. "It was Luis Rodriguez from the rodeo circuit."

"Why was he calling so late?"

Sabrina went over and settled in the glider, hugging the brown pillow in the shape of a cowboy boot to her chest. "You might have to help me get off of this gracefully."

He sat on the ottoman, unaware it also glided. He went flying and landed on the floor. She hid her laugh the best she could before she couldn't hold out any longer. Her rich laughter filled the room, followed by a distinctive snort. She whipped her hands over her mouth, but he realized he'd missed that signature snort of hers at the end. And so much more.

He rubbed his bottom, wincing as there'd be a bruise there tomorrow. "I don't recommend my method for the dismount."

She wiped away something from the edge of her eye. "Sorry, but you have to admit, it's funny."

He grimaced. "Just don't tell anyone on the rodeo circuit your ottoman bucked me off in a second flat."

"Your secret's safe with me." The word *secret* hung in the air, and she shifted on the glider. "Luis offered me a raise to come back as a rodeo clown."

"On the same circuit as me?" This was perfect. He'd see her and the baby more often than originally expected. "Six weeks will give us plenty of time to arrange everything."

The future opened up before him. Life would be a sight better returning to his traveling RV with Sabrina and the baby.

Sabrina and the baby? They weren't a package deal. Well, in one way, they were, but not for him. Living arrangements would need to be sorted, along with a search for a traveling nanny, one who'd work with whatever arrangement they hammered out.

"I turned him down. My rodeo days are over, Ty." Her firm voice cut into his daydream. "I've hung up my clown gear for good."

Ty's gaze swept over all the little Sabrina details that made this room perfect. From the cream-colored changing table to the tiny pink clothes in the closet, everything here screamed permanence.

"You're the best rodeo clown on the circuit." He should know. She'd saved his caboose from being bull fodder more than once. "And we work great together. What's holding you back?"

"It's a dangerous job. I've suffered three broken bones and multiple concussions." She rubbed her head and winced. "My daughter needs a mother who's there for her."

"Being around any horse has an inherent risk of danger. How is being a barn manager that much different?" Her raised eyebrow hinted he was treading water in the deep end. Okay, he was reaching and he knew it. There was a huge difference between managing an efficient operation like the Double I and distracting a two-thousand-pound bull from a fallen rider.

"I'm staying in Violet Ridge, Ty." Emotion deepened her voice, and her chest heaved. "You've met Nelda and Zelda, who gave me the hat off her head. I could go on and on about the different residents. I love this town."

So much for the dream of them traveling together. He couldn't imagine life without the rodeo. For so long, he believed his life would be cut short, the same as his father, grandfather and great-grandfather. It was one thing to be a traveling vagabond when he lived like there was no tomorrow out of fear there wouldn't be. But now? One more year on the tour seemed about right. A goodbye of sorts. What came after that? Asking Hal for a job on the ranch? Acting? With a new reason to think about tomorrow, he needed to do just that.

So, what did he want to do after the rodeo ended?

Be a good father, for one thing.

He picked up a monitor on the table and turned to Sabrina, who yawned. She needed her sleep, and he made some excuses.

With a nod, he left and started walking to the guesthouse. In the freezing cold of the December night, puffs of his breath came out fast and hard, disappearing in an instant. He looked back. Sabrina created a bubble of security around her with friends, a steady job and a home. Where did that leave him?

persona. Maybe you need a costume —
either that, or your friends are worse
role-models. When did that happen?

CHAPTER FIVE

THE NEXT EVENING, dusk descended on Ty and Sabrina while they waited for the bus shuttle that would carry them to the Mile of Lights holiday display. This second day of charisma had to go better than the previous night's disaster. Then again, that wasn't a high bar. Ty sneaked a peek at Sabrina bundled in her bright turquoise coat and a matching knit cap. Her face, framed by her lustrous brown hair, glowed, taking his breath away.

To his surprise, they had their choice of available seats on the shuttle. He'd expected larger crowds, but it was early in the evening yet. They walked right onto the rear of the bus, and he sat next to her. "This wasn't my original plan. I tried to snag two golden tickets for tonight's Evalynne concert, the one at Irwin Arena, but it's been sold out for weeks." He laced his tone with a note of apology. Whether it was about the concert or more, he wasn't quite sure. He continued,

"We never talked about music much, but she's one of those singers everyone seems to like."

"She's my grandparents' favorite musician." Sabrina paused as if she wanted to add something but didn't. Instead, she gazed out the window, the stillness of dusk settling upon the mountains. "I've heard her lullabies, but not for quite a long time."

"The Mile of Lights is supposed to be spectacular." Ty wanted to reach for Sabrina's hand, but last night proved how much distance now separated them.

If everything went as planned, and it normally did, these days would rebuild the trust that once existed between them. And yet that wide gap seemed insurmountable, if that faraway gaze of hers was any indication.

But if the rodeo had taught him anything, it was the importance of hanging on tight when odds seemed against you.

"Trust me, I'd rather be here than at an Evalynne concert." She turned away from the glass window toward him, her smile crooked yet real. "Besides, I've wanted to see these lights. I wouldn't have come without you."

Finally, that gap didn't seem as far apart. They had always spurred each other to seeing new vistas with gusto. "Carter recommended it. He and his wife came here last year when she was preg—"

The bus screeched to a stop. He and Sabrina jolted forward. Without hesitation, he threw his arm in front of her, coming in contact with her soft, puffy coat. Gasps echoed through the bus. Then the driver swung the hinged door open and announced that they had arrived. Sabrina's face scrunched into a grimace, and his chest constricted.

"Is something wrong with the baby?" He held his breath, his hand inching toward his phone.

"We're fine." She laughed it off. "That was unexpected, that's all."

They walked to the entrance, the glow of the lights a bright halo around them. His mouth dropped open. The display was well worth the trip and then some. The owner of an apple orchard had taken the mile-long road to his house and transformed it into a winter wonderland. An archway was illuminated with metal snowflakes outlined with blue and white lights. Beyond that, decorated trees extended as far as the eye could see. Instrumental Christmas music played on the speakers, and the lights were in sync with the songs. He was wrong. This was the golden ticket after all.

And he was sharing it with Sabrina. That made the evening more special.

The attendant handed her a brochure, and she opened it. "The Violet Ridge Mile of Lights is an interactive display with a singing Christmas tree and an ice sculpture spectacular that will stay with you through the holiday season and beyond. Be sure to visit our concession stand and gift shop."

They found themselves under strings of icicle lights, hanging from suspended ropes like crystals and looping from dark blue to white before starting the dance over once more. "It's like walking through a fairy garden," he said.

Sabrina chuckled. "Not a sentiment I thought I'd hear from a rodeo champion."

"Two younger sisters." He shrugged. "They'd bribe me to attend their tea parties with food, knowing that would get me to do their bidding. Petit fours, cookies, you name it, and I was there."

"Tell me more about these parties." Sabrina placed the brochure in her purse. "How old were you?"

"I was sixteen when Peyton was four." He rubbed his bottom. "Those tiny chairs left a permanent imprint on my rear."

"Ah, that must have been so cute." Her brown

eyes twinkled with the lights reflecting in those sepia flecks.

And he'd do the same all over again with their daughter. "Anything for one of my mom's huckleberry tarts."

"You light up when you talk about your sisters. Spill the dirt."

He shrugged. "Devon looks just like my mom, while Peyton looks like my stepfather, Hal." Not for the first time, he wondered whether their daughter would have his dimples or Sabrina's cheekbones. No matter, the baby already had him tied around her little finger, although he hoped she resembled her beautiful mother.

A couple pushing a stroller passed by, laughing while their hands interlaced around the handle. Ty looked with longing at them. That could have been him and Sabrina next year, a family taking their daughter for her first Christmas outing. Too bad it could never be them. Not with her staying here in Violet Ridge, and him only now waking up to the possibility of a future, the rodeo calling him with its different venues and packed stadiums. Any chance at a romantic entanglement was gone for good.

"How much younger are your sisters?" Sabrina asked.

"Let's see. Peyton's almost twenty-two, and Devon's eighteen." Each of his sisters had trailed after him from the time they came home from the hospital. His teen self hadn't been impressed, but now? He loved being their older brother. "I taught them to ride the same as Hal taught me. They're naturals. Princess tomboys. I wonder if our daughter will be, too."

"She'll be her own person." She waved her arms at the wonders around them. "What do you want to see first? The ice sculptures or the singing Christmas tree?"

"You had to ask? I want to find out what a singing Christmas tree is." He grabbed her gloved hand and pulled her along. He'd forgotten how well their hands fit together. Walking alongside her, there was a peace about him he hadn't felt for a long while. Seven months, to be exact.

In no time, they reached a three-story lofty structure that rotated human singers on different levels designed to look like the layers of a tree. They crooned Christmas carols to the passersby.

"And we ended up at a concert after all."

Sabrina sang along, her voice off-key. Then she turned bright red and clasped her gloved hand over her mouth. "I can't carry a tune. Only one in my family who can't sing."

"Ah, that'll be my job then. To sing our daughter to sleep." He chuckled and then his cheeks relaxed, the stubble a protective layer against the dropping temperatures. "And don't worry. Hal can't sing either, but he and my sisters are like this."

He crossed his right index and middle fingers together to indicate the closeness.

"Hal's had a big impact on you, hasn't he?"

"Of course." And the thought of another man having that same impact on his daughter? He wasn't sure if that made him happy or sad. "He works hard on the ranch, but he also knows when to sit back and appreciate the small things. He has a great sense of humor."

They listened to the next carol and then clapped along with the crowd. Sabrina faced him, her cheeks rosy with the cold. She tried to hide a small shiver but didn't succeed. He removed his scarf and wrapped it around her neck. She fingered the wool, her lips turning upward. That smile did him in every time. "Thanks. How old were you when Hal married your mom?"

"Twelve." He remembered the long nights after his father died. His mother tried to put up a good front, but after he went to bed, he'd hear her crying, the walls only muffling the sound. "After my father died, my mother tried the best she could. Now that I'm older, I appreciate her effort to make everything safe and familiar, but that also put pressure on me. I wanted to make her smile again and kept telling her how much dad would want her to have fun again."

Whether it was time or Hal that brought that lovely feature back, he wasn't sure, but he was grateful Hal came into their lives when he did.

"What did they say about…" Sabrina looked down at her coat, which hid the baby bump. "Well, you know."

He wasn't sure whether he should deliver the news about their first grandchild over the phone or in person. Maybe Sabrina would have some insight. "I'm still deciding whether to tell them now on a video call or wait until Christmas and tell them in person." A light bulb went off. "Why don't you come with me to Wyoming? It's their anniversary on Christmas Eve. They're having a big party to celebrate. You'd be more than welcome."

She hesitated, a shadow falling over her face. "I don't think so. That would give them the wrong impression about us." She edged her fingers up and down the end of his scarf. "Besides, traveling that late in the pregnancy isn't a good idea. I can't fly, and that long of a car trip away from my doctor is out."

Another reminder of how much he had to learn. "I guess I should call them." Get it out in the open before he arrived home for Christmas.

A reminder he wouldn't be spending his favorite holiday with Sabrina.

"Then again, you had a valid point when you said I should have told you about the baby in person. Communicating with people face-to-face seems the way you roll, and it has its benefits."

The carolers launched into the next song, and he reached for her hand, her gloves a barrier to her soft skin. "Thank you, and I should have contacted you sooner. After all, I never texted or reached out either."

She squeezed his fingers. The crowd started singing along, and he chuckled at her warbling. Sabrina wasn't kidding when she said she couldn't carry a tune. Still, she threw her whole heart behind her effort. He'd never enjoyed this carol more.

After the song ended, she turned to him. "What next? Food or the ice sculptures."

"From the way you said that, I think there's only one right answer," he said.

"The baby's hungry."

"Then, you had me at food."

They started for the concession stand when she stopped. "Wait a minute."

His eyes widened. Despite the cold, sweat popped up on his brow. "Are you going into labor?"

"That's the second time you've asked that tonight. You can't think that way every time I make a sudden move, or you'll worry too much and not have any fun." She rolled her eyes. "The baby's kicking. Come closer."

He neared her, close enough to smell her light floral scent. "What now?"

"Put your hand on my coat. She's strong, so you should feel her through the added layers."

Feeling a little foolish about placing his hand on her belly, he did so anyway. Movement rattled him. "That's her?"

Sabrina nodded. "She must have your leg strength."

Wonder and awe flooded him. There was

a person inside Sabrina. Not just any person. *Their daughter.* He glanced at her face, bemusement at his reaction written over her expressive features. "I hope she has your nose," he said.

She tapped hers and grimaced. "It's a button nose. Yours has more character."

"Mine's been broken three times. Them's the breaks."

She groaned. "Okay, we'll just have to wait and see what she looks like. The main thing is that she's healthy."

He lost himself while feeling their daughter's kicks and stretches. They'd created this person together. Pretty amazing when he thought of it that way.

Then he noticed the faint laugh lines around Sabrina's eyes. She looked happy again, and he liked being here, seeing the holiday lights, with her. Was she the reason it didn't feel like enough—to be a part of their daughter's life without Sabrina too?

SABRINA DRANK THE last sip of her delicious hot apple cider and then threw away the cup, her gaze never leaving Ty. She gave him credit. He was turning this unexpected, life-changing news into an experience of a lifetime. She'd been meaning to come see the Mile of Lights with Elizabeth or Kelsea, but something always interfered with the plans. Ty was the one who made it happen.

It was more than that, though. His sheer magnetism was wreaking havoc with her heart. He'd always had that ability.

They started walking, and she caught sight of the ice sculptures. Her mouth dropped at the magnificence in the details. The story of *The Nutcracker* played out before them with life-size replicas of Clara, mice and gingerbread soldiers. Lowlights projected color onto the distinct characters, and they looked like they were about to spring to life. "I've never seen anything like these," she said.

"Me neither."

"Have you ever seen the ballet?" Her favorite, she'd introduced her best friends, Will and Lucky, to the production. She had yet to see a version that matched the first one she'd attended.

"Never had the time. Before we moved to the ranch when I was twelve, Mom worked two jobs. Then she married Hal, and the ranch is quite a distance from town. We always celebrated the holiday at home with Hal's family."

"You'd like it. I can't wait to take our

daughter to see it. *The Nutcracker's* all about friends helping friends and gifts spreading joy when they benefit both the giver and the receiver." The lights changed from red to blue to green, and the enormity of what he was doing for their daughter gripped her. "I think I get it now. These twelve days are your Christmas gift to the baby."

She stood on her tiptoes and kissed his cheek, the heavy stubble tickling her lips. What had she done? She moved away quickly. The baby brought them together, but that was all. Security beckoned in Violet Ridge, and Ty made her feel anything except secure with her heart beating this frantically. She'd stay behind while he pursued the excitement of the rodeo, where action and danger reigned side by side. Who knew where he'd be three months from now while she was juggling middle-of-the-night feedings?

He moved closer and reached for her hand. Soft holiday music surrounded them, and the air was electric with energy. Somehow, she knew that energy had nothing to do with the crowds and everything to do with them. Maybe they couldn't recapture the past, but they had to find some way forward for the sake of the baby.

"Sabrina."

Movement in the distance caught her eye, and she stood on her tiptoes and squealed. "I can't believe it."

"It's the time of year to believe again." Ty's husky words deflected off her as she glanced over his shoulder.

"I must be dreaming." She pulled him along until they reached a group of three heading toward them.

She blinked, but her eyes didn't deceive her. Lucky Harper was here at the Mile of Lights. Will had offered Lucky a place to stay until the rodeo circuit started back up again next year, but Lucky was a wanderer at heart. In the ten years since they'd met each other, she'd never known him to stay in the same place longer than a month. Until this moment, she hadn't realized how much she missed his happy, laidback self.

In less than a second, she released Ty and embraced the man she loved like a brother. "You didn't tell me you were coming to Violet Ridge. How did you find me?"

She separated from Lucky, his dirty blond hair longer than usual, peeking out from under his cowboy hat. He tipped it toward Ty, with Will and Kelsea standing nearby. "I know how much you love anything to do with *The Nutcracker.*"

Seeing that show was one of the last outings with her mother before she took off in pursuit of success, which she found in droves. That day had been so much fun, the two of them happy in their seats, watching the ballerinas. Sabrina's young heart had been full. Only to have it wrenched from her just a few weeks later.

But where were her manners? She reached for Ty, his jaw uncharacteristically resolute. "Ty, you know Lucky Harper, right?"

Ty nodded and reached out his hand. "You're a great adversary, Lucky. Always a pleasure."

"Wish I could say the same." Lucky folded his arms and glared at Ty. "Will and I look out for Sabrina. Anyone who hurts her isn't high on my list."

"Sabrina's a good rodeo clown. She can look out for herself, don't you think?" Ty challenged Lucky, continuing to keep his hand extended.

"And I'm right here." Sabrina inserted herself between the two. "Lucky, Ty didn't know about the baby. We're using this time to think about what's best for her."

Lucky seemed to relent and shook Ty's hand.

"Sorry if I came on a little rough. I think the world of Sabrina."

"I can only imagine what you thought of me." Ty winced but kept shaking Lucky's hand. "My reputation seems to precede me."

Sabrina turned back to Lucky, excitement curling her toes. "Are you here until New Year's?" Her voice held out hope that he'd stay until the baby was born.

Lucky's face fell. "Just passing through. If Violet Ridge had a training facility, there's nowhere else I'd rather be."

Sabrina's spirits deflated. Lucky never stayed in one place for any prolonged period of time. "How long are you staying?"

Lucky winced and slipped an arm around her shoulders, his solidity familiar but only a comfort, providing no jolt unlike Ty's electric touch. "I'm leaving for Texas tonight. A friend needs my help."

Then again, he never turned away a person in distress, either. She loved that about him. Flustered, she moved back and examined his face. "You aren't kidding."

"I wanted to check on you." That carefree gleam didn't fool her. He cared deeply for everyone he met.

"You'll come back when you're done and meet her, right?"

"Wouldn't miss it for the world. I'm still hoping I can convince you to return to the circuit after she's born. I'd feel a sight better if you had my back." Lucky prodded and nudged her side.

"My clown nose is retired for good." She rubbed her baby bump. "This one needs a stable home."

"Home is where you hang your hat," Will interjected, looping his arm around his bride.

"And where your friends and family wait for you." Kelsea smiled and leaned into him.

Once again, the story of how Will and Kelsea found each other in a turbulent time struck Sabrina in the gut, and she glanced at Ty. Too bad they hadn't had that type of perseverance. She waited for the familiar anger at their breakup to resurface, but it didn't. She let go of the negativity, preferring to bask in the glow of being surrounded by friends.

Ty cleared his throat. "This is my cue to let you get on with your evening." He turned toward Will. "I trust you'll give Sabrina a ride home."

With some reluctance, Sabrina separated from her friends and latched on to Ty's arm.

"I love you all, but Ty promised me twelve days of charisma. I'm not letting him off the hook."

After hugging Lucky goodbye, she found herself on the path alongside Ty.

"I'm surprised you chose me." Ty stopped and examined one of the mouse sculptures.

"There should be some mystery surrounding a person, don't you think?" A fine one to be talking, as Ty was much more mysterious than he appeared on the surface.

"Does that mean you're going along for the ride?" That tone of his held a hint of a challenge.

She rose to the occasion. "Maybe it's time for me to sit in the audience and enjoy the show. You always deliver a fine performance while making it seem effortless."

"Hopefully not too much so, considering there's a two-ton busting bronc involved." He chuckled that rich deep laugh that made her heart skip a beat. The lights glinted off his black hair, only making him look that much more debonair. Goose bumps dotted her arm under her layers of clothing. "Then again, I could choose the simple route. There's always a first time for everything."

A bit of that Ty charm resurfaced, but the

Ty from their walks, not Ty the rodeo star. This was the man she fell for, the one who had a whisper of vulnerability about him.

"Except I've seen you at too many rodeos, and you never take the easy way out. You have to be pretty stubborn to win the national finals two years in a row." A bit of a daredevil, a bit of a rogue and the heart of a champion. His fans recognized this and loved him for it. "You have the scars to prove it."

She reached over and traced the fine white line hidden by stubble where his chin met his jawline.

"This old thing?" he asked.

Among others she'd seen and one she even helped treat after the rodeo doc stitched him up. "Isn't it from your first rodeo? That was quite a wild, practically unbelievable story about the bull that almost ended your career before it began."

He glanced around before crooking his finger. She approached, and the lovely aroma of coffee brought a sudden urge to kiss him.

She was having serious coffee withdrawals.

"I'll let you in on a secret, but you can't tell anyone."

They both knew she could keep a secret. "What?"

"That's not the real story."

Her chuckle confirmed she'd known otherwise. "Somehow, I didn't think the bull gave up that easily."

"Peyton was upset Mom and Hal brought a baby home from the hospital, rather than a playmate her age. Anyway, I used Hal's rolling chair as a bucking bronc, and I fell off." His eyes crinkled at the sides. "Peyton laughed really hard, almost as hard as the hug when she realized how much her big brother loved her, but Mom was rather upset at me."

They reached the last of the sculptures, a giant nutcracker with red floodlights. "You're right. The actual story, while my favorite, might not go along with that daring image of yours you've cultivated so well." And here they were at the end of the exhibit. "Ty, tonight was a lot of fun…"

He waggled his finger. "This is only the second day. Your gift to me is the full twelve days."

She would never go against a promise. "But are we dancing around the hard truth rather than meeting it head-on?"

"Fun and trust go hand in hand sometimes, and this is one of those times. Sabrina Mac-Grath, you have two doors before you." He bowed with a flourish. "Which one do you choose?"

She eyed him with suspicion. "Is this like that old game show where I have to choose a door without knowing what's behind it?"

He shook his head. "I'm going to tell you everything. No secrets. No surprises."

"But you thrive on surprises." Until now, she hadn't realized how much she missed his spontaneity.

A devilish gleam sparkled in those blue eyes. "Ah, I intend on keeping you on your toes."

She laughed, and it felt good. "You're making my ribs hurt from laughing so much."

"Laughing was never our problem, but we've come to a fork in the road."

They had built their previous relationship on a flimsy foundation of fun, rather than anything substantial. "Then what's behind door number one?"

"Sabrina MacGrath, today is your lucky day." His deep announcer voice brought forth more giggles from her. "Behind door number one is a lifetime supply of diapers and a fully funded bank account that will allow Baby MacGrath to choose her own path when she graduates high school."

The use of the baby keeping Sabrina's last name didn't escape her. "Let me guess. This is my easy way out. A path of security."

He brushed her hair behind her ear, and she leaned into his touch. Then she righted her head, not wanting to give an inch. "If this is what's important to you, I won't stand in your way." His low voice sent shivers down her spine, his blue eyes almost black with fear she would go this route.

Her heart shattered. "You're giving up this easy, Darling?"

His thumb glided over the soft spot at her temple. "You haven't heard what's behind door number two yet, MacGrath."

"I don't have to." Her breath caught as she inhaled the woodsy scent of his cologne. She wasn't about to cut off this ride before it played out to the end. "I already know which door I'm selecting."

CHAPTER SIX

DURING A BREAK on the set, Ty waited for Phineas to go about his business. There wasn't a prettier place around for it. The mountains rose high in the surrounding countryside, their snow-capped peaks majestic and proud. Gray clouds on the horizon promised a heavier dusting of snow in the near future. So far, the accumulation had been rather light for Colorado in December, although that could change at any second.

"Carter said he'll be ready for us in half an hour, Phin." He extricated his phone from his coat pocket. "So, you have ten minutes before I have to report to Maureen for my fitting and makeup." The dog wagged his tail vigorously as if replying.

Ty shuddered, as the pancake makeup was his least favorite part of acting. Along with the waiting. And the lack of action.

His phone started vibrating, and his agent's name flashed on the screen. Belinda Wasilewski preferred emails, so this must be important. He pressed the green button. "Merry Christmas, Belinda. I didn't expect to hear from you until after the new year."

"Carter called me last night," Belinda said straightaway. "By the way, Merry Christmas to you, too."

Ty stopped tapping his foot. Was he getting fired by proxy? So much for Carter's request to Ty to walk Phineas as a favor to Robert, whose knee was still out of commission. "The first day was rough, but he assured me yesterday's rushes were much better."

This shoot was his ticket to stay in Violet Ridge. More so, he wanted to stick this out. It was more than proving to Carter that he could improve. He had to prove to himself that he could finish what he started.

"Relax, Ty. I have good news. Carter's advertising agency was awarded a contract with a saddle company. He wants to know if you're available next year. I negotiated a nice fee for you with residuals this time around." He heard the sound of shuffling papers in the background. "And the promise we could show the rough cut of both ads to other producers who've reached out to me."

While he wanted to finish this commercial, he didn't love acting enough to make a career change. "I'm already committed to several rodeos next year." Including the Violet Ridge Roundup Rodeo.

"That's great for the short-term, Ty, but you're on the upper end of rodeo longevity."

And if he followed in his father's footsteps, and his grandfather's and great-grandfather's… He shuddered. He had to get past that negativity. Still, if he didn't fall victim to the same early demise, what did he want to do with the rest of his life? Act in commercials and work his way up to bigger roles? Continue to be the latest rag doll for a series of bucking broncs? Or was there something else in his future? Something in Violet Ridge with Sabrina and their daughter. Last night, Lucky Harper had mentioned how there wasn't a training facility in the area. What if there was one? Perhaps he could start it. Sabrina could demonstrate how to become a rodeo clown while he worked with competitors.

The silence on the phone dragged out a second too long, and Belinda cleared her throat for his answer.

"Carter's satisfied with my performance, then?" That was the important part of this conversation.

He'd disappointed too many people recently. Somehow, though, Sabrina was the one he didn't want to let down again.

"He needs an answer by the end of the shoot. Rodeo competitors are a dime a dozen, but you have as solid a stepping path to an acting career as I've ever seen before. There are other offers coming in. Some producers have expressed interest in featuring you in a cameo for a couple of programs, and a few magazines want you for their covers. We'll schedule a follow-up appointment." Belinda ended the call.

Phineas spotted something and took off into a full run. Ty didn't let go of the leash, instead pumping his legs for a full workout. "Good dog, Phin."

He commended the dog on his excellent taste. Not a foot away from him, Sabrina looked beautiful with her rosy cheeks and pregnancy glow. "Nice recovery, Ty." She reached down and began rubbing the back of her calves. "I think we overdid it last night with all of that walking. I woke up with leg cramps."

She grimaced, and alarms rang out louder than Christmas bells. "Is that normal? Should you be working? Did you call the doctor? Is the baby okay? Is that a sign of early labor?"

The questions poured out of him, and his chest tightened. What if something happened to the baby? What if something happened to Sabrina? His breathing came erratic and heavy, and sweat poured off his forehead.

Her hand reached out and massaged the upper part of his arm. "I've had them throughout the whole pregnancy, so to answer your questions, yes, yes, no, yes, and no."

"Are you sure?" He breathed a little easier, his heart no longer racing like a barrel horse.

"Positive." She looked down and released his arm like it was a hot brick. "As positive as I am about my answer last night."

"It was the second surprise of the evening." The first had been choosing to spend time with him over Lucky and her friends. The second had been her snap decision. Normally, he was the impetuous one. Last night, she'd opted to continue with the twelve days of charisma. He'd been surprised but pleased she hadn't taken him up on the offer that promised security and no involvement on his part.

"I think I surprised myself and Baby Darling, too."

A wave of shock came over him. "You've changed your mind. She'll carry my last name?"

"Yes."

Suddenly, he wanted to shout out from the rooftops: he, Tyrone Darling V, was going to be a father. His mother would adore being a grandmother, and Hal? He'd be thrilled, too, about becoming a grandfather. "So, I'll be a part of her life?"

"She'll carry your last name. Let's hold off on any major decisions until the twelve days are over. Ouch!" Sabrina reached down and continued rubbing her calves, her face scrunched in pain. "These leg cramps are fierce."

Phineas sat in front of her as though he elected himself her personal guard dog. Far be it for him to do anything to upset the Lab-bullmastiff mix.

"It's been like this the whole time?" Concern for Sabrina coiled inside of him, and he wanted to do something, anything to make this easier on her.

She straightened and flexed her ankle before her face showed a modicum of relief. "It comes and goes," she said. Her face finally reflected the end of the cramp, and he breathed out his worry. "Something troubled me last night. In your mind, will our daughter be on equal footing with the rodeo?"

"I'm still getting it through my head I'm going to be a father, but she'll never be on an equal footing." Sabrina's gasp made him realize how that sounded. He reached out and stroked her chin. "She'll always be more important."

"Oh." Sabrina's chin quivered with the true intent of his words lightening her face. "Not all parents feel the same as you. Sometimes it's easier to act as though someone doesn't exist, and that can be as damaging as anything else." She pointed toward the stable. "I need to get back to work."

And yet he wanted more time to talk to her. He reached for some reason to extend the conversation a little longer. "We're still on for tonight, right? The third day of charisma?"

"I need a rain check. It's going to be an early night for me."

The thought of spending an evening in his guesthouse all by himself wasn't appealing, no matter how spacious and luxurious his quarters were. "What if I join you? I'll bring dinner."

She looked conflicted. "I don't want you to go to any trouble."

Her tone was clear. She didn't want him there. After everything, they really did only have the baby connecting them.

That seemed wrong.

"No trouble." He smiled at the bump, knowing the baby would be a surefire way to get Sabrina to accept his offer. Perhaps that was underhanded of him, but he was desperate. From here on, he'd couch everything in terms of the baby, building on her need for security. "What does the baby want?"

"Enchiladas."

"Then that's what the baby will get."

LATER THAT NIGHT, Sabrina laid her head against her turquoise couch's cushioned armrest. She twisted to her side, unable to get comfortable. Her leg cramped, and she flexed her foot until the charley horse was gone. Thirty-four weeks pregnant would do that to a person. The baby kicked as if to say she'd be here soon enough.

"And your father is accepting the idea of you."

She gave Ty credit. When he suggested the twelve days, she believed he'd tire of this experiment before it ended, the same as he tired of her. Now, though, it might be backfiring on her. He was getting involved all right, but tonight he'd be staying for dinner.

And she'd have to resist that legendary Darling charm.

The doorbell rang, and she was relieved

at the break from her thoughts. Her stomach rumbled, and she hoped Ty brought enough food.

Opening the door, she blinked at the sight of a man in a tuxedo standing on her front step with a large laminated paper in hand.

"Ms. Sabrina MacGrath?"

She nodded, and he pointed to a catering van parked behind her Subaru. "I'm Feliciano. My siblings and I own Tres Hermanos, the food truck voted the best of the best at over fifty different rodeos." Then he offered her the menu. "It's our pleasure to serve you and Mr. Darling tonight. Can you show me your dining room so my crew can set up everything for your dinner?"

"Crew?" She'd envisioned takeout with some containers. Something simple. "I think there's been some misunderstanding."

"No mistake. Mr. Darling hired us, and we do it all from setup to clean up." He turned and gestured with his hands. Two others emerged from the van. "What type of enchiladas would you like? Enmoladas covered in mole sauce? Enchiladas Suiza with swiss cheese? Salsa verde enchiladas?"

They all sounded delicious. "What do you recommend?"

"Our specialty is enchiladas de Camaron with our homemade tortillas." He recited the ingredients, and her mouth watered. "We take our fried tortilla and fill it with shrimp, corn, onion and chiles. We garnish them with Crema Mexicana, avocado slices and grated cheese."

The baby kicked and expressed her approval. "Exactly what I've been craving today. That sounds perfect."

In no time, her tiny dining room looked like something out of a magazine with a colorful table runner and matching place mats livening up her secondhand oak table. Tiny cacti plants next to huge pink and yellow tissue flowers doubled as a centerpiece. Sabrina marveled at the transformation while her stomach rumbled at the delicious aromas of cilantro and peppers coming from her kitchen.

"Ty!" Feliciano greeted him from the other room. "Long time, no see."

Sabrina walked over to the threshold and saw the men exchange a hearty handshake.

"Thanks for traveling all this way. The baby wanted enchiladas, and your brisket enchiladas are the best I've ever tasted," Ty said, patting Feliciano on his back.

The baby. Sabrina sighed at how Ty was bending over backward for his daughter. She couldn't help but wish he was doing some of this for her.

While Feliciano and Ty chatted, Sabrina rested at the dining room table, eager to get off her feet. The farrier had visited today, keeping Sabrina busy while she'd inspected each horse's shoes. Cleaning, trimming and shaping the horse hooves had taken the whole day, and Sabrina was thankful someone else was preparing dinner.

Ty entered the dining room with a basket of tortilla chips while Feliciano carried bowls of green and red salsa. They both thanked Feliciano, who disappeared from sight, and Ty sat across from her.

"The green salsa's hotter than the red." Ty dipped a chip in the green and munched, contentment spreading over his face. "They're both delicious."

"Thanks, Ty." She rolled her neck. "I appreciate this even though you went to way too much trouble. But after the long day, I'm grateful."

"What happened?"

With the salsa alleviating her hunger pangs, she launched into an animated discussion of the different horses and their attitudes toward the farrier. "Andromeda holds her head high and pretends to tolerate everything while the farrier trims her hooves. Cinnamon likes the attention and preens."

Ty listened and gave some excellent suggestions for next time. Then it was her turn to listen while he shared stories from the set. In no time, she stared at an empty plate. Had she really consumed three of those divine enchiladas? Feliciano collected the baskets and bowls.

"Thank you, Feliciano." Sabrina wiped the corner of her mouth. "I have to agree with Ty. Those are the best enchiladas I've ever eaten, and I'm from Texas."

"I'll convey that to my brothers. We'll be out of here shortly." He nodded and took his leave.

The smell of the aromatic food lingered in the dining room after the plates were cleared. Ty excused himself. Feeling relaxed, Sabrina closed her eyes. A tap on her shoulder woke her up, and she found Ty looking at her with concern. She yawned. "I can't believe I fell asleep in here." Then she snapped her fingers. "Tres hermanos in place of three French hens. Very cute."

Ty perched himself on the edge of the table.

His mouth opened when the doorbell trilled. Sabrina stretched for a second before opening the front door. An older woman with short gray hair and an efficient manner stood there, a large bag at her side. "Ms. MacGrath?" The woman made her way inside without waiting for Sabrina to confirm her identity. "I'm Nancy Snyderman. Where would you like me to set up?"

"For what?" Sabrina asked as Ty joined them.

"Thank you, Ms. Snyderman, for coming on short notice." Ty turned to Sabrina and winked. "She's here to give you a prenatal massage. Your legs are cramping, and that can't be good for the baby."

The flicker of hope that he'd arranged this just for her sake was extinguished in the blink of an eye.

"This is too much for one evening." *Dinner and a massage?* She rolled her neck and let the feeling of being pampered sweep over her. To her surprise, she liked it.

"Nothing's too much for the mother of my baby." Ty rubbed her shoulder, but her inner glow deflated.

All of this was for one reason, and one reason only. So she could trust him with their daughter.

Ms. Snyderman set her bag on the cherry hardwood floor and looked at Sabrina with some expectation. "I'm a licensed traveling prenatal massage therapist. Where should I set up my equipment?"

"In the living room? I'll be right there after I talk to Mr. Darling." Ms. Snyderman reached for her case and headed where directed while Sabrina faced Ty. "This is too much."

"It's not enough as far as I'm concerned. Are you Ty-dazzled yet?"

She'd been Ty-dazzled for months. "You still have nine more days to spread out plenty of Christmas cheer."

"I'm just getting started." He folded his arms and leaned against the wall, the sight of him in that tight black Henley shirt sending flutters down her spine.

"You don't have to impress me."

"Don't I?" His gaze held that challenge again, and her glow had nothing to do with the meal.

Ms. Snyderman came back to the foyer. "Mr. Darling mentioned your leg cramps." She waited until Sabrina gave a lingering nod. "This should help with that, as well as aches in your back and neck. Then you'll get a better night's sleep. There are studies to show having this done once a week between now and when your baby is born will reduce your stress and increase your blood flow."

"I should talk to my doctor first." Sabrina was running out of reasons but, for the life of her, she didn't know why she was stalling.

"I can send a summary to your doctor tomorrow."

"Sabrina." Ty tapped her arm. "It'll do you both good."

A half hour later, Sabrina only regretted she hadn't thought of indulging herself with a prenatal massage earlier. Her legs hadn't felt this good in months. She thanked Nancy, who promised to return next week.

Sabrina found Ty in the dining room with a plate of churros with caramel sauce on the side. "Want one?"

"You're spoiling me."

He held up his hand. "Considering how hard you work, you're not spoiled in the least. You put in long hours with those horses. I know you love being around them."

He held out a churro, and she accepted one. Their hands touched, and her gaze was drawn to the cinnamon sugar lingering on the side of his mouth. She used her free hand and patted the side of her lips. He neared, and she inhaled the woodsy scent of him mixed with the spicy scent from the Mexican food. "Sabrina."

This was the Ty she had missed, the one that swept her off her feet, the man who made her laugh. She moved toward him, intent on finding out if his kisses were as magnetic as she remembered. He must have had the same idea, and she tilted her head, ready for the kiss.

The doorbell rang, breaking the spell. She stared at him. "Three French hens. You didn't hire someone to bring me birds, did you?"

He grinned. "I might have one more surprise up my sleeve."

A catered dinner, a prenatal massage, and now something else? Everything kept escalating, and he made a simple night in into anything but casual. Still, she couldn't remember the last time anyone went to this much trouble for her.

"I'm afraid to ask."

"After dinner and a massage, the baby needs a lullaby."

There it was, *the baby*. His determination was touching, but she couldn't help but wish he'd done it in an attempt to win her back. She faked a yawn. "If these are singing lessons, I'm too tired." The massage did leave her rather languid, a wonderful feeling after a full day of physical labor.

"Nope, and really, I saved the best for last. Her concert was sold out last night, but my agent tracked down her phone number for me. I was shocked, but Evalynne agreed to come here tonight. And she's right on time."

Stunned, Sabrina stood rooted to the spot. "Evalynne?"

Ty opened the door. There, on her front doorstep, stood the person Sabrina had waited by the window for so long the day of her seventh birthday. The woman was older now, but her hair fell in soft red waves over her shoulders, and her brown eyes were as familiar as Sabrina's own. Her figure was still slim, the turquoise leather jacket with fringe one Sabrina could see herself wanting to borrow from her, if her mother hadn't chosen fame over family, over her. "Evalynne."

CHAPTER SEVEN

"SABRINA, DARLING. I didn't know…" Evalynne's words faded into the night.

Ty stepped forward, too aware of the tension crackling around the women. He set out to put everyone at ease. "My mother and stepfather would love to be here right now." He smiled at Evalynne, who was actually here, in Sabrina's home. "Thank you for agreeing to sing tonight."

"What are you doing here?" Sabrina's jaw clenched, an edge to her voice he'd never heard before.

"It's not every day a rodeo champion calls you and asks if you'd consider giving a private concert for his closest friend."

"Surprise. She's here to sing to the baby." He couldn't understand Sabrina's reaction to a world-famous singer arriving for a private concert. He turned to Evalynne, becoming flustered at her presence. "We have some enchiladas left if you haven't eaten dinner yet. If you have time."

"I'm sure she's busy with work commitments. After all, she's very successful." Sabrina folded her arms, and he wondered what was happening. This wasn't the reaction he'd expected.

"Violet Ridge was the last stop on my tour. I'd love an enchilada if you have any to spare." Evalynne's soft voice carried inside, a small quiver at the end.

A stiff wind carried into the bunkhouse, almost as chilly as the reception Sabrina was giving Evalynne. This was most unlike the pretty woman who greeted horses and people with a warm welcome. "Feliciano left enough for tomorrow's dinner and extra freezer meals for after the baby's birth."

Evalynne's face paled, and her gaze went to Sabrina's stomach. "You're pregnant? I had no idea."

"Grandma didn't mention it?" Sabrina's eyebrow inched upward, and she stood resolutely, her arms folded, her stance closed.

"Not a word."

"Could someone tell me what's going on?" Perplexed, Ty rubbed his arms. His black Henley provided little protection against the cold.

Anguish was written all over Sabrina's face. "I promised myself I wouldn't keep any more secrets from you, but…"

"What she's trying to say is that I asked her and her grandparents to keep her identity a secret from the world, one I've regretted ever since." Evalynne rubbed her arms. "Can I come in, Sabrina? Please."

A swift nod of the head was enough for Evalynne to hurry inside, and Ty rushed and closed the door behind the singer. "Can someone explain in clear terms what's going on?"

Evalynne started unzipping her jacket, then stopped. "Will I be staying long enough?"

Emotions played all over Sabrina's face before she gave a slower nod. "Ty must have paid a substantial fee for your appearance tonight."

"Nothing." He blurted out the word, and they both stared at him with the same luminous brown eyes. "I mean, she agreed to do this out of the blue."

Evalynne looked around and walked over to the mantel, fingering a frame with a picture of a young Sabrina in a cap and gown flanked by two older adults, no doubt her grandparents. "I have this picture at my home. Mom sent me a copy after your high school graduation."

"You could have been there." Sabrina sat on the couch, her jaw firm with displeasure.

Ty went over and settled next to her, reaching for her hand and holding it tight. What was supposed to be a relaxing night was turning into a disaster.

"How do you two know each other?" Ty turned to Evalynne, then to Sabrina, unsure of which woman would answer first.

"Sabrina's my daughter."

He almost fell off the couch. A knock at the door caused everyone to turn in that direction, the tension thick. Sabrina balled her hands into fists next to her sides. "Who else did you invite here tonight?" she asked him through clenched teeth.

"No one. Just dinner, a massage and a lullaby." Instead of three French hens, he'd substituted three calm moments of Zen. Some pampering that might help relieve stress and lead to a new start between them. How wrong he was.

Sabrina released him and returned a minute later with Gordon and his daughter, Elizabeth. "Look who dropped by." She introduced her bosses to her mother.

"We've seen cars coming and going all evening and decided to check on you." Elizabeth frowned and felt Sabrina's forehead with the back of her hand. "You're rather pale. Are you feeling okay?"

"Thank you for your concern, and I'm fine. It's just that Ty arranged a rather eventful evening."

That was one way to put it. Not that this last part was going as planned, but then again, nothing about his relationship with Sabrina was ordinary. Time with her was never boring.

"Lullabies are overrated." Ty tried to put a light spin on it.

"Lullabies." Gordon stepped forward, his gaze focused on the singer. "Evalynne? You're singing here? Tonight? You probably don't remember me, but we met the other day. I had the privilege of seeing you in concert. It was unbelievable, the best I've ever attended. I'm a huge fan. If there's room for two more…"

"Gordon Irwin as in the Irwin Arena?" Evalynne squinted and her cheeks became bright pink. "It's hard to forget the man whose arena you performed in last night."

"Then it's settled." Gordon gave a perfunctory nod. "My daughter Elizabeth and I would love to join your party."

Evalynne sent an apologetic glance his way. "I left my guitar in my hotel room."

"I have one." Sabrina gasped, almost as if the words escaped before she could stop them.

She hurried away, and Ty followed. Someone needed to carry the guitar case for her. At least, that would be his cover story if she asked, and he'd stick to it.

SABRINA ENTERED THE nursery and leaned against the closet door. For the first time tonight, she was alone. She let the rush of emotion take hold, and the nerves of tension knotted her neck worse than before the prenatal massage.

So much had happened tonight. It would take from now until the baby was born to process everything, but she had her boss, her mother and her ex-boyfriend, the father of her child, waiting for her guitar.

"Hey, there." She jumped at the sound of Ty's voice coming from the hallway.

She turned around, and it wasn't fair. All night, she'd worn these stretchy black maternity pants and a T-shirt that she'd never gotten around to cutting up for rags, and he looked amazing with the hall light hitting the ebony strands of his hair and that Henley stretched across his shoulders. His presence filled the room. He entered, and it took all her willpower not to reach out for a hug. While she craved the moral support, he wasn't her boyfriend. She wasn't even sure they were friends.

"I can make excuses for you." He ran a hand over his stubbled chin. That even looked good. "Not that they would count as excuses under the circumstances."

She smiled at him wanting to help her, and tapped her forehead with her index finger. "But that would be taking the easy way out."

They grinned at each other, and she let the joke flood her with inner peace.

"It would take a lot of guts to return to that living room, MacGrath." A slight dare entered his voice, and his eyes gave the encouragement she needed.

"It took a lot of guts to call your agent so you could contact a world-famous singer you've never met before, Darling." She didn't want him leaving without some acknowledgment from her about the lengths he'd gone to in order to make this evening happen.

Because, for better or worse, it had happened.

"I could pluck out the strings of the guitar for you." He sent a wicked grin in her direction.

"Yeah, but you won't." She reached into the baby's closet and pulled out a long black guitar case.

He hurried over and reached for it. "Then the least I can do is carry it for you."

"Ah, but that you could carry something else for me for ten minutes." She grinned so he would know she was joking.

Well, mostly joking.

His hand covered hers, and shivers of awareness rocketed through her. "I'd do it in a heartbeat."

He neared, and she brushed away the cinnamon sugar dotting the side of his warm lips. This time, there was nothing to keep her from kissing him.

Nothing except the fact this easy camaraderie had always come naturally with him. It took more than dynamite kisses to sustain a lasting relationship. She thought she'd known the true Ty when they'd been involved, but she hadn't known the ease with which he could say goodbye, the same ease Evalynne had shown when she abandoned Sabrina with her grandparents and pursued a music career that catapulted her to the top of the charts.

There was something about Sabrina that brought out the best in others, but only after they left her.

She couldn't go through that again.

Especially not with a little one who'd be depending on her.

His gaze held expectation, but she couldn't give in to her feelings without something substantial and real to bind herself and Ty together. Not without a tangible rope, so the baby would have an anchor, a shelter in the storm. Sabrina had been lulled into a false sense of security in her relationship with Ty once. Those days were gone forever. It was best to build a solid home so the baby would never look out a window, believing someone would return when the bright lights of a career beckoned with even more intensity than those from a welcoming home.

"Ty..."

"My father sent me to find out if you really own a guitar." Elizabeth's voice came from the hallway, and Sabrina jumped away from Ty. "But I seem to be interrupting something."

"Not at all." Sabrina pointed at the case. "I'm not in Evalynne's league, but playing the guitar is a hobby of mine. It made learning the ukulele for my rodeo days quite easy."

Why had that slipped out of her? She was the one who chose to put that time in her life behind her, although she missed the sport with a fierce sharpness.

She brushed past her friend and settled in the living room. Ty handed Evalynne the guitar case, and she gasped. "So, this is where it went." She opened the case and pulled out the Gibson special, running her long fingers over the polished wood with tenderness. "I sang at every bar in a hundred-mile radius of our house to earn enough money for this beauty."

"I missed something." Gordon ignored the hush coming from his daughter. "Why would Sabrina have your guitar?"

Evalynne stopped tuning the instrument and sent Sabrina a wistful smile. "She's my daughter." She brushed her eye with the back of her hand and then strummed the strings. "And I dedicate this version of 'Misty Morning' to her. After all, she's the inspiration behind the song."

Elizabeth sent Sabrina a pointed look, and Sabrina returned the favor. Before long, Evalynne's lilting clear soprano entranced the small audience, even her. The notes reminded her of years gone by when her mother would tuck her into bed and reach for that same guitar. Her songs were her bedtime stories, lyrical melodies of love and hope. Every night, Sabrina would close her eyes and try to stay awake for the closing chords. Every night, she'd fall asleep with a smile, dreaming of mountains and misty mornings turning into days spent near river streams with love waiting around the bend.

Someone tapped her shoulder, and Sabrina woke with a start. She blinked and found herself in her living room instead of her childhood bedroom with candy pink walls and a white canopy bed. Just like in the past, Evalynne's soothing songs had once again lulled her to sleep.

She found Ty hovering over her, his look of concern touching. "You've been asleep for over an hour. Elizabeth said she'll arrange for the other grooms to perform the early morning duties and not to arrive at the stable until afternoon."

That wouldn't do. If the staff could function without her, that could cost her the job she loved so much, especially if Elizabeth and Gordon thought she could afford otherwise. Just because Evalynne had found success didn't mean Sabrina was wealthy.

But one look around the living room only brought Ty and Evalynne into focus with Evalynne near the hearth, placing the guitar back into the case, her eyes teary. Sabrina knew what she had to do: return the guitar to its rightful owner. "That's yours. Please take it with you."

Evalynne shook her head. "I left it behind. I left too much behind." Sabrina couldn't argue with that, so she didn't even try. "I'm spending Christmas in town, and am staying at the Violet Ridge Inn for the next few weeks. Perhaps we could have lunch at that cute little Italian bistro."

"I work here at the Double I as the barn manager. That keeps me pretty busy." Iron entered her voice. She wasn't that little girl by the window anymore.

"Dinner then?" Evalynne hesitated, but kept her distance. "You're also invited, Ty. I want to include you, seeing as how you're a part of Sabrina's life. The two of you are so in love. How long have the two of you been together?"

"We're not together." Sabrina's words came out with more force than intended.

Evalynne glanced at Ty, then Sabrina. "Hmm. Okay. If you say so."

"I have an early call." Ty reached for his coat on the coatrack. "Good night."

He headed for the door, and Sabrina didn't want him to leave like this. "Wait a minute." She held up a finger to Evalynne, indicating she'd be right back, and hurried after Ty, whose hand was on the doorknob. Ty halted in the foyer. Sabrina continued, "It's fine with me if the fourth day of charisma isn't quite this eventful."

Those blue eyes sparkled with his normal exuberance once more. "I get the feeling it's not me who's causing the excitement."

"How do you top this, anyway?"

He winked. "Never underestimate a Darling."

He slipped out the door before she could come up with a retort. How did he do it? Make her feel like her life wasn't quite the same without him in it while knowing he'd leave her, and she'd have to confront the loss all over again.

Although she'd like to mull that over, her mother was waiting in the living room. Everyone expected her to forgive and move on. If only life was that easy.

Or could it be as simple as finding a way to forgive while not forgetting?

She detoured into the kitchen before returning to the living room with a plate of enchiladas and refried beans. "You said you hadn't eaten dinner yet."

"This wasn't quite what I had in mind when I asked you to dinner, but thank you." Evalynne accepted the food with a grateful smile. "When's your baby due?"

"Next month. I already know I'm having a daughter."

"How wonderful!" Evalynne wiped the corner of her eye before taking her first bite. "This is delicious. Thank you. When are you due?"

Sabrina gave some basic information without revealing anything too personal while Evalynne ate her enchiladas.

"Didn't Grandma or Grandpa tell you?" Sabrina tried not to be too self-conscious as she sank into the couch.

"They're protective of you. Since their health battles took a turn for the worse, I've reflected on what a mess I've made with them, with you." She pushed around the last of the refried beans on the plate, her gaze not meeting Sabrina's. "I'm not expecting forgiveness from you or an instant mother-daughter bond. I hope we can use this time to forge a friendship."

"A friendship?" Sabrina echoed the last words while the disbelief rushed through her. "I needed a mother."

Evalynne gave a slight nod and placed her empty plate on the hearth. "You're right. Merry Christmas, Sabrina."

Evalynne paused, her glance lingering over the guitar case, before she started buttoning her coat. Sabrina let the regret over what could have been between her and Evalynne subside while weighing what she wanted. She'd asked for a quiet night in, but Ty had turned this evening into a three-ring circus. Regardless of whether he was aware of it, he amplified everything.

Last year, they'd visited offbeat places she never would have found by herself. Tonight he arranged for a prenatal massage when she would never have indulged in one and called a world-famous celebrity to sing her a lullaby.

How could she accept that type of larger-than-life quality while sheltering her baby?

Maybe the first step was accepting what

Evalynne and Ty were offering, olive branches for a new beginning. That didn't mean she had to forget, but holding on to grudges? That seemed wrong with a baby on the way.

It would be wrong even if she wasn't pregnant.

Evalynne picked up her purse and headed for the foyer.

"Hold on." Sabrina followed her and then plucked on her coat sleeve from its resting place on the coatrack as if it was suddenly the most interesting thing in her house. "It's Christmas, and Grandma and Grandpa would like it if I give you one more chance. There are several good lunch places in Violet Ridge."

"Maybe, just maybe, I'll earn that chance. After all, this is a season of hope and peace and resolutions." Evalynne brushed the back of her hand against Sabrina's cheek. "I'll hold you to that date."

Sabrina closed the door behind Evalynne, not liking this sense of uncertainty. She had everything figured out before Ty came to town. Working as the Irwins' barn manager provided a steady income and a chance to be around horses without the danger of the rodeo. And now?

That stable security was sliding out from under her, and she wanted her feet back on solid ground.

CHAPTER EIGHT

CARTER HADN'T BEEN lying when he said an actor spent most of his time waiting for the production crew to prepare for the next shot. Ty stood by the catering table finishing a late lunch, more convinced than ever a career change to acting wasn't in his future. No matter what opportunities his agent touted, Ty preferred forward motion and activity.

While it was fun trying something new, he missed the open trails riding a horse attuned to his every move. He even missed the rhythmic motions of rubbing the orange-scented saddle soap into the leather afterward. With the baby coming, it would be even longer until he enjoyed such a ride again. And he'd have to postpone the beginning of his strenuous training regimen for the upcoming year, as there were no facilities nearby. Yet another reminder of such a need in this town.

He wouldn't call this time in Violet Ridge

a waste, though. These twelve days were crucial in gaining a foothold in Sabrina's life.

The baby's life, that was.

There was too much water under the bridge for him and Sabrina. The chemistry was still there, probably always would be, but that couldn't overcome the problems arising at every turn.

Now, he'd have to be content with becoming a father and fashioning a joint custody agreement somewhere down the line.

Still, he gave Sabrina credit. She kept her mother's identity a secret because of a promise. Keeping her word was more than commendable. Last night required a great deal of courage on her part to leave the nursery and attend Evalynne's impromptu concert. He wouldn't have blamed her if she'd gone to bed, yet she faced the situation head-on with grace and spirit. Or maybe he hadn't seen all her positive attributes the first go-round because he'd been too busy planning fun side trips, wanting to impress her.

He stopped and let the hope wash over him. Was another attempt at a relationship, one with depth and meaning, feasible? Was Christmas providing them with a second chance?

"Ready for you." The production assistant motioned to Ty.

He hurried to the set and waited while Maureen powdered his nose, a concession to the harsh lights. Ty adjusted the denim jacket until Carter nodded his approval. Then Robert brought Phineas over, giving him a treat and ordering him to stay. The older man then limped to Carter's side and reached for a long metal stick with a tennis ball on the end, his training method for Phineas's performance.

"Action." Carter delivered the command.

Robert brought the tennis ball to his cheek. On cue, Phineas barked once and then licked Ty's cheek. Ty smiled for the camera and delivered his line.

"Cut." Carter ended the scene.

Robert hobbled over and gave Phineas a treat, lavishing him with praise. "Good boy."

"That's a wrap for this location," Carter announced to the crew. "Meeting at the catering table in five."

From the previous days, Ty knew the director would take the next few minutes to review the footage. Ty entered the costume trailer and traded the denim jacket, more suited for a Texas spring day than a Colorado winter, for his coat. Although the past day hadn't provided any new powder, gray clouds were gathering on the horizon. If he had a chance to hit the slopes at the ski resort, the next location of the shoot, he'd welcome the opportunity to find inspiration for new ways to impress Sabrina. Maybe a sleigh ride? Everyone liked a night under the stars with jingle bells guiding a sled through a snowy meadow, right?

He thanked Maureen and hurried to the catering table. Carter nodded at everyone. "There's been a change of plans. Without December's expected snowfall, the ski lodge isn't at its most photogenic. Violet Ridge is expecting a few inches this weekend, so we're filming at the cabin first, then the lodge. The catering crew has already delivered the food supplies. Ty and Robert, you can take tomorrow off while we set up the equipment."

With a whole day in his pocket, he'd ask Sabrina to take the day off. The stress of the past week must be rather trying. Relaxation and rest might be more of a necessity than anything else. The ski lodge could be the perfect follow-up to the prenatal massage.

He strengthened his case in his mind. A complete spa treatment, a five-course dinner followed by a sleigh ride with five jingle bells. That was it. The perfect solution for the fifth day of charisma.

Phineas's bark brought him back to the meeting just in time to find everyone staring at him. Ty nodded. "Sounds great."

"That's settled. Ty, you'll drive Phineas and Robert to the cabin," Carter said, clasping his ever present black binder to his chest. "We'll get back on schedule and wrap this up by Christmas Eve."

Robert made his way over to him. "Thanks for driving. From everything Carter said, there's not enough room for our bus up there."

"No problem."

Ty arranged a time for them to meet two mornings from now so he could chauffeur them to the site. He smiled when the dog nudged his leg, seeking his affection. Phineas was a sweetheart, enough so Ty even considered adopting a dog for the first time. His busy rodeo schedule had never lent itself well to walking a dog or keeping up with a cat. But he could see teaching his daughter how to lasso a cow with a dog running beside them.

Where would he do that? *On Hal's ranch?* Hal had always treated him like a son, but Peyton and Devon grew up on the ranch. Peyton even graduated early, finishing her college degree in ranch management in three years instead of four. Ty assumed Hal's daughters would carry on Hal's family's legacy.

On the road? Going from rodeo to rodeo was fine for a bachelor or even a family man who had a home base. What sort of life was it for a child, even in a trailer that rivaled some houses?

In Violet Ridge? The town was growing on him. This morning, Regina had begrudgingly admitted he'd done a fine job after he fulfilled his promise for a longer autograph session. Nelda and Zelda kept him laughing with their quirkiness. Emma's baked goods were up there with the best he'd ever tasted. Opening a rodeo training facility could provide a real service. A perfect opportunity to merge his past and his future.

For too long, those would be problems he'd leave to his future self to solve, knowing all the pieces would fall into place as they always did until the Darling genes caught up to him.

Now, though, he had something, and someone, to think about before himself.

Shouldn't I have thought about Sabrina like that before I broke up with her?

He'd professed his love for her, yet he hadn't

regarded her feelings, hadn't been open and honest about his fears of dying young.

Maybe part of these twelve experiences should include that type of openness. He started for the stable.

SABRINA SHOVELED THE last of the hay into Cinnamon's stall. Putting the shovel aside, she rubbed the sorrel muzzle of her Morgan horse. "Elizabeth doesn't have time to ride you for a couple hours, but she promised me she'd take you on a long run today."

"What about me? Do you trust me?"

Ty's voice came out of nowhere, and Sabrina faced him. "Trust you?" That wobble at the end was rather unlike her, and Cinnamon nudged her with her muzzle as if concerned. Their bond was yet another reason she couldn't wait to ride again after the baby was born.

For a second, she even allowed herself to miss the rodeo.

"To let me ride Cinnamon, of course." He grinned before his face took on a more serious bent. "I came here after the afternoon's filming wrapped. I was hoping I was wrong."

Stroking Cinnamon, Sabrina struggled to put everything together. Maybe last night muddled her mind more than she thought. "Wrong about what?" *Breaking up with her? The twelve days of charisma?* Pins and needles pricked her spine.

"You being here instead of resting at home." He walked toward her, stopping in front of Cinnamon's stall. "I thought you were taking the day off."

"Just this morning." A defensive note entered her voice. She didn't have to justify herself to him, but she appreciated his concern.

"Last night must have packed a wallop."

Least of all Evalynne's admission she'd made a mistake years ago. Where this new friendship would lead, Sabrina wasn't sure, but she couldn't change the past, only the future.

"Evalynne left me with my grandparents. After she hit it big, she never came back for me." Never acknowledged her existence in public either, although from what she'd seen on the internet, that might have benefited Sabrina. Children of celebrities often were thrust into the spotlight. While she loved the attention in the arena, she wore clown makeup and a costume. In that way, she could entertain others and maintain her privacy. "You're the first person to know, outside of my grand-parents."

Not even Will or Lucky knew about her relationship with Evalynne. She supposed she'd better tell them today so they wouldn't hear it secondhand.

"I'm honored. Thank you."

"Evalynne is the one to thank." It felt good that someone else finally knew about Evalynne. "If you'll excuse me, I have a morning of work to catch up on."

"I thought you said there were grooms and a staff to help you." Ty glanced around the stable. "You're alone."

"The afternoon groom is eating lunch…" Her voice faded. Then his concern touched her. "Cinnamon and I go way back. We trust each other. It's sweet of you to make sure I'm okay."

She looked at him in a different light, this level of thoughtfulness new about him. If he'd changed, could they start over?

"Anything for the baby."

And there was the real reason for his efforts. "What are you doing here, Ty? Do you have a message from Carter? I thought the crew was supposed to be finished shooting at this location yesterday."

"We finished up a little while ago. The crew's disassembling everything in preparation for the next location shoot. Carter gave me tomorrow off. I was wondering if you wanted to go to the ski lodge with me. I've heard they have a wonderful spa. A day of pampering, perhaps? The latest in a truly Ty-dazzling display of charisma." He took a mock bow.

As wonderful as that sounded, she still had to work. "Day job, but thanks for the invite."

His expression flip-flopped once more before he turned his attention to her horse. He came over and greeted Cinnamon with a light nose bump. She whinnied her approval, obviously remembering him from the rodeo. "You never answered my earlier question. Can I ride Cinnamon? Gordon and I went riding yesterday, so I'm acquainted with that trail."

She wavered. Cinnamon could use a long ride, and Ty was an excellent rider. More so, he and Cinnamon were already acquainted. Ty wanted to prove he was trustworthy. There weren't many better ways in her book than taking care of a horse. Not just any horse, either—her beloved Cinnamon.

Still, it was harder than she thought, and this was only a small taste of what it would be like when it was his turn to spend time with their daughter. Cinnamon nickered as if telling Sabrina that the mare didn't have all day when she could be outside in the brisk Colorado sunshine while it lasted.

"Elizabeth will appreciate having extra time with Andromeda this afternoon." Sabrina gave her reluctant approval. "I'll saddle Cinnamon while you change at the guesthouse."

"I'm good to go. One pleasant part about this commercial is I'm already wearing my trademark boots."

He followed her to the tack room and insisted on hefting the saddle while she carried the blanket, bridle and reins. She'd have protested more, except a slight twinge of back pain bothered her enough to let him help.

She led Cinnamon out to the corral and watched Ty ride away with a small wave. The first of many such occasions. Would it ever get easier?

CINNAMON WAS A joy to ride. Patient and intelligent, the mare knew the trail and remembered him from their previous meetings. Even with winter peeking around the corner on this late afternoon, the trail designed by Gordon was a sight to behold and a joy to traverse. Cinnamon kept her footing and forged forward with purpose, almost as if she was on her best behavior for Ty.

Was this a hint of the future? Would their daughter be on her best behavior for her father? Or would she act out, separated from her mother?

Ty pushed that out of mind and spurred the mare onward, allowing her to show him her mettle. The chilly wind embraced horse and rider with the craggy mountains surrounding them, their white sides a reminder of the changeable winter weather. They raced past a brace of aspens, their silver branches bare, waiting for spring to come alive once more. Nearby, green bushes dotting the hillside reminded him this was a working ranch with cattle foraging this late in the year.

Too soon, he and Cinnamon returned to the stable. Ty looked around, expecting Sabrina to be the first to greet him after returning with her beloved mare. Instead, one of the older grooms approached him, explaining Sabrina's work emergency. Ty brushed the mare while the groom put everything away.

His next stop would be finding Gordon and asking him if he could stay in the guesthouse through the holidays. As much as he'd been looking forward to Christmas with his family in Wyoming, his Colorado family needed him just as much. Truthfully, he might need Sabrina and the baby more than they needed him.

Somehow, he had to find a way to tell Sabrina he was using the baby as an excuse. Everything he'd been doing had a benefit of helping the baby, but that wasn't the reason anymore. Seeing Sabrina smile and having her near him tantalized him into wanting more. Last night's revelation about Evalynne only helped explain why she didn't track him down in person. Evalynne's actions weren't just a ripple in Sabrina's life; they'd left as deep a crater as his father's death had in his.

His phone rang, and he steeled himself when his mother's image appeared on the screen. This was the first time they'd had a chance to chat since he found out he was going to be a father.

"Hi, Mom." Now was the perfect opportunity to break it to her he wasn't coming home for her anniversary. But first, he'd find out why she called. "How are you? How are plans for the party going?"

"Merry Christmas. The party's coming together, but Grandma Eugenie fell and sprained her ankle. She's okay, but it'll mean so much for her to see you again."

Disappointing Hal's mother, who'd taken him in as her own? Hopefully, when she found out she was going to be a great-grandmother, all would be forgiven. "Then I'll have to tell her myself that I can't come home."

"Oh, no." Mom's dismay came through. "The commercial production will run over after all?"

Soft whinnies came from the stalls, and Ty headed outside the stable. "No. Carter is doing everything he can to finish on time."

"Hold on a second, dear. Hal just finished checking on the cattle." Ty waited while his mother told Hal about the newest detour. It wasn't long before she came back on the line. "Hal said we can postpone the party for a few days."

"I won't be coming at all." He blew out a deep breath, but he couldn't risk that the baby might be born while he was in Wyoming. "I'll be staying here in Violet Ridge. If you ever visit, you'll love the town, Mom. So will Devon, especially the ski slopes. I have a free ski pass, and then next week there's a holiday pet parade." And he was planning on taking

Sabrina and incorporating that into one of the days of charisma.

"I see." Disappointment laced both words. "You're staying in Violet Ridge to ski."

"There's more to it than that." He ran his hand over his stubble. How did you tell your mother important news, like his impending fatherhood, over a phone call? *Very carefully.* "Do you remember Sabrina MacGrath from the rodeo? The one you and Hal traveled to Casper to see?"

"The rodeo clown?"

"We began dating…"

"That's wonderful, dear. Is it serious between the two of you?" His mother's voice held a note of excitement. Of course, she'd narrow in on this part of the conversation. "Bring her home to the party. We'd be more than happy to have her here for Christmas."

"Actually, we're not dating now." His stomach clenched at having to reveal his part in the breakup, namely that he had been the breakup. "Well, we fell in love, but I broke up with her."

"I don't think she'd appreciate it if you invited her to the party, then. Hold on a minute. Hal's saying something." He spent the next few minutes rehearsing how to tell her about the baby when she returned. "Hal needs me in the stable. Surely the skiing can wait, but then again you wouldn't be the Ty we all know and love if you cut your trip short. We'll be here if you change your mind."

She hung up, and he let out an exasperated sigh. *There it was.* The presumption he'd give up something important for a few hours of fun. Then again, she had just cause for saying that as he'd often postponed trips home because a sponsorship opportunity prevented him from traveling to Juniper Creek. And while that was true, he'd also taken the opportunity to kick up his boots and have a marvelous time.

Maybe he should call her back and explain the real reason. No, he already disappointed her and Hal today. He couldn't pile on everything at once.

He spotted Gordon in the distance and headed his way, deciding to ask about the use of the guesthouse. "Good afternoon, Mr. Irwin. Do you have a moment?"

"How many times do I have to tell you? It's Gordon, not Mr. Irwin." He patted Ty on the back. "Sabrina and Elizabeth were supposed to meet me at the house so I could look over the invoice for the new bits, but I must have missed them. I'm sure Sabrina said she needed to order them today."

Ty frowned. "Sabrina and Elizabeth aren't here."

Gordon's eyes lit up at whatever was in the distance. Ty looked over his shoulder and found Evalynne headed their way.

"Ty, I'm glad to see you. I was looking for Sabrina, and the person who answered the door at the main house said to check the stable." Evalynne greeted him and ran her hand up and down her scarf as if she was nervous. "Oh, hello, Mr. Irwin. Good to see you again."

"Please call me Gordon." He dipped his cowboy hat in her direction. "If you're going to be in Violet Ridge for the holiday season…"

He cleared his throat and stepped back. Was that a blush Ty saw spreading over the older man's cheeks? Gordon Irwin had the reputation of being one of the most savvy ranchers in Colorado, yet he seemed like a lovestruck teenager.

"Yes, I'm staying at the inn." Evalynne resumed toying with her scarf. Her cheeks were rosy, too. "For so long, I've put my career over my daughter. It's too late to change the past, but I'd like to be involved in her life now."

"Sabrina and Elizabeth aren't here," Ty said, feeling somewhat like a third wheel.

"Oh. I see. I'll wait for her at her home then." Evalynne shoved her hands in her coat pocket, her puffs of breath coming out more often. "Have a good evening, gentlemen."

Gordon cleared his throat and shuffled his feet. "I'd be honored if you had dinner with me."

"Excuse me?" Evalynne blushed a deep shade of red, the same shade Ty had often spotted on Sabrina's fair skin.

Gordon kicked at the ground with the tip of his boot. "Never mind. It was a bad idea."

She reached out and touched his arm. "No, it's a lovely idea. I'm just surprised you want to have dinner with me. After all, you're seeing me at my worst." She removed her hand and wrapped her arms around her chest. "I'm not proud of the way I've treated my daughter."

"When my wife died, I worked long hours on the ranch, throwing myself into my work. One of my sons moved away and pursued a career in law. The other is serving in the military," Gordon said. "Even though we lived under the same roof, I was going through the motions and closed myself off to them in my grief. Now, they both live elsewhere."

All of this wasn't encouraging to Ty. If well-meaning folks like Gordon and Evalynne had made a mess of parenting, how could he expect to do any better even with the same intention?

"It's kind of you to try to cheer me up, but I have a question for you. Are you asking out Evalynne?" She bit her lip and leveled a serious look at Gordon. "Or Evie MacGrath?"

Gordon squinted as if giving her question careful consideration. Then he gave a swift nod. "While I'm sure Evalynne is a stimulating dinner companion, Evie MacGrath sounds like she'd have a heckuva lot more in common with an old rancher like me."

Ty's phone rang. He didn't recognize the number on the screen. Gordon glanced down at the phone and frowned. "That's Elizabeth."

Shivers ran down Ty's spine, and he hurried to accept the call before it went to voice mail. He hung up a second later. "Sabrina's at the doctor's office. She might be in labor."

SABRINA WAITED AS the nurse practitioner wrapped a blood pressure cuff around her upper arm. "Can Elizabeth come back here with me? I'd feel better if I had someone by my side."

"Hold that thought and any other words while I do this." The nurse practitioner breathed on the end of her stethoscope before listening to Sabrina's heartbeat. She then noted the numbers on the sleeve.

"How's my blood pressure?" The room wobbled, and Sabrina's anxiety skyrocketed.

"A little elevated, but nothing in the danger zone." The nurse entered Sabrina's stats into her tablet. "Elizabeth's here? Is Kelsea busy this afternoon?"

Kelsea Sullivan had accompanied Sabrina to most of her appointments as Sabrina drew the line at either Will or Lucky attending them with her. Although they'd only known each other a short time, she and Kelsea were already close friends. "I texted her. I don't know if she's coming or not."

"Go ahead to room number three. There's a sonogram machine in there. We'll check to see if everything's okay with the baby or if we need to admit you to the hospital." The nurse wrapped up the blood pressure monitor and placed it in a drawer.

Sabrina's worry mounted as she walked the long trek down the hall. She wasn't at full term yet. And some mother she would be. She hadn't purchased a car seat or enough diapers.

After she changed into the cloth gown, she waited, wishing for a blanket or something to keep her warmer. Elizabeth joined her and held her hand. "I called Ty. He's on his way."

Sabrina released her grip and then played with the edge of the cloth gown. "I didn't want him to cut his ride short."

"He was already finished—"

A knock on the door cut her off, and Sabrina prepared herself for the doctor. Instead, Kelsea entered and hugged Sabrina. The bubbly blonde removed her woolen cap and placed it on Sabrina's head. "You're freezing, aren't you?"

Sabrina nodded and plucked at the thin fabric of the hospital gown. "I must have received the summer model."

Her friends laughed and then sat on either side of her. Without discussion, they grasped each of her hands. *This.* Friendship was why she moved to Violet Ridge. They dropped everything for her when she needed them. They weren't just her friends; they were her family.

Kelsea squeezed her hand. "Will and Uncle Barry send their best."

Sabrina smiled. "Let me guess. Uncle Barry thinks the baby's arrival will be big, really, really big."

Everyone chuckled as Uncle Barry's favorite expression was well-known in Violet Ridge.

"He might have used that exact phrase," Kelsea said. "But Will said to tell you that our niece should stay where she is a little longer. He hopes he doesn't meet her until next year."

Will voiced what Sabrina was feeling inside. "The good news is my back stopped hurting during the car ride." Sabrina rubbed her tailbone.

Another knock, and Sabrina's muscles tensed at the doctor's arrival. To her surprise, Evalynne entered the room with Ty on her heels. In all the rodeos where Ty waited in the chute on a ferocious bronc, she'd never seen this kind of fear on his face before.

"One, two, three, four." Ty counted and stopped before he included Sabrina. "Four concerned friends. That's not what I had in mind for today."

"I don't choose when she's born, Ty." Once again, his predilection for fun was coming between them. "Fun and games are fine in their place, but I have to make sure she's okay. Today might be the day we meet our daughter."

She shivered, not sure if it was in delight or

foreboding. If their daughter was born today, she'd rely on her friends to come through for her with the long list of supplies she'd need before she brought her baby home.

Ty frowned. "I was trying to relieve the tension in the room. You still think so little…"

A knock heralded Dr. Zimmerman's arrival. She stepped inside the room and arched her eyebrow. "There are three too many of you in here."

Elizabeth and Kelsea released Sabrina's hands and stood. "We're outvoted," Elizabeth said. She and Kelsea navigated around the sea of bodies before glancing over her shoulder with a calming smile. "We'll be in the waiting room."

Dr. Zimmerman clutched her tablet to her chest, the dimness of the room hopefully hiding the heated blush rising to Sabrina's cheeks. "And I haven't met either of your other guests before, so they should also wait outside."

Evalynne and Ty headed for the door with Ty's hand reaching for the knob first. "Wait." Sabrina wanted them in here with her. "Ty is the baby's father, and…"

She stopped. Just because Evalynne acknowledged who she was in private didn't mean she wanted Sabrina to tell the world.

"I'm Evie MacGrath, Sabrina's mother." Evalynne extended her hand to the doctor, who squinted.

"Has anyone ever told you that you look like the singer who just came to town? Evalynne?" Dr. Zimmerman placed her tablet on the counter before squirting hand sanitizer on her hands.

"Yes." Evalynne approached Sabrina and laid her warm hand on her shoulder, meeting her gaze. "It's your call, Sabrina. I can wait with Elizabeth and your other friend if you'd like."

While Sabrina had no misconception that Evalynne would once again answer the call of success, she liked that her mom was here now. A little too much. "Your granddaughter needs all the support she can get."

Dr. Zimmerman called for the nurse and bustled around the room, gathering supplies. The nurse handed Sabrina a blanket, and she was thankful for the warmth and privacy. The doctor made her way over and began asking questions about Sabrina's earlier backache and donning blue latex gloves. "Lie back and we'll get started." Then she squirted warm green goo over Sabrina's belly. "Okay, Dad and Grandma, we're going to make sure the baby is healthy and staying put."

Ty reached for Sabrina's hand, and tingles carried over her arm and in the worst of all possible places, a doctor's examination room. It must be the worry manifesting itself. Just to make sure, she glanced at him, his plaid flannel shirt snug while stretching across those broad shoulders. He sent a small wink to her, not a flirting blink, but a reassuring one.

Just as music did with Evalynne, Sabrina knew the lure of the rodeo for Ty would also win out over the sanctuary of her bunkhouse. She'd just have to enjoy the ride while it lasted.

Then she switched her focus to the doctor, who moved the ultrasound wand until the heartbeat rang out strong and reassuring. A gasp drew Sabrina's gaze away from the monitor, and she saw Evalynne wipe the moisture away from her eyes. Then Sabrina's attention returned to the screen, Ty's hand large and warm in hers.

An image of the baby came into view, and he gasped. He squeezed her hand, awe in his expression. "We did that?"

The doctor laughed and moved the wand back to its resting place. "That's one way of putting it. Your daughter is rather feisty and likes her present living quarters." She printed out a series of pictures and handed them to Ty before flicking on the lights. "Sabrina, you had Braxton-Hicks contractions. They're common at this late stage and are often confused for actual labor."

She finished her explanation and delivered instructions before exiting the room. Evalynne followed, giving Sabrina space to change. Ty's mouth was ajar while he stared at the sonogram pictures. She couldn't keep up the pretense that she'd cut him off after the twelve days. "Ty."

He glanced over and saw her clutching her clothes. "Oh, you want to get dressed? I'll join everyone else in the waiting room." His gaze held hers and he smiled. "Although I have to admit, that is quite the fashion statement."

She'd almost forgotten she still wore Kelsea's favorite knit cap. She removed the beanie and traced the snowflake pattern. "And I have to admit that all of you fitting into this room was funnier than my clown car. The vein in Dr. Zimmerman's neck almost popped out when she saw the four of you."

"There are five of us here. Gordon's in the waiting room."

"Mr. Irwin is here, too?"

"He drove Evalynne and me here."

While everyone coming together on her behalf warmed her to her toes, it was also a reminder this was a doctor's office. A deep conversation about their future could wait for her cozy living room later, especially with a crackling fire and maybe some popcorn or a sugar cookie. A little holiday music playing in the background would only add to the ambience. "Let's update everyone and go home. I still have a freezer full of enchiladas if you'd like to come over for dinner."

"What time?"

"How's six?"

"I'll be there."

She blew out a breath when he closed the door behind him, grasping the sonogram pictures.

SABRINA AWAKENED FROM her nap, refreshed after the earlier detour to the doctor's office. She sniffed the air. Something smelled wonderful, and she hurried to her kitchen only to find Kelsea and Will giggling and swatting at each other with oven mitts.

Will caught sight of her and sobered, a guilty look coming over him. Sabrina chuckled and entered the kitchen. "You don't have to be the stern father figure twenty-four seven, Will. Don't stop laughing on my account."

Sabrina had to hand it to Kelsea. No one else ever made Will loosen up and look at the lighter side of life like his new wife. For a while, Ty had offered that same support to her. Maybe Christmas was the time for new beginnings.

Kelsea snatched the mitt from Will and opened the oven door. "We were just talking about the latest Uncle Barry mishap." She glanced over her shoulder and smiled. "Why don't you pull up a chair? This one's a doozy, even for him. Will, tell her about the alpaca who woke us up this morning."

Will shrugged. "When you leave the back door open at our ranch, you need to be prepared for everything." He launched into the story of the alpaca rambling inside while Will poured his first cup of coffee.

Sabrina laughed so hard her sides hurt. "Life with Barry is never boring."

"You could do with a little less excitement yourself." Kelsea removed the reheated enchiladas from the oven. "You've been through a lot over the past few days. Evalynne's your mother?"

Sabrina nodded. "She never signed over full custody to my grandparents."

"Well, I have something that I hope will be soothing and delicious to complement your meal." Kelsea went over to the refrigerator and produced a green concoction, placing it before Sabrina. "It's a mango-ginger smoothie. I asked my neurosurgeon father about prenatal development. He thought I was pregnant before I corrected him. Once I set him straight, he told me to take care of you. You made a good impression on him at my wedding."

Sabrina stared at the smoothie's unusual color before taking a small sip. To her surprise, it was delicious, and she admitted it. "By the way, your father was much more amenable than I thought he'd be, considering everything I'd heard about him."

"He's mellowed since our talk. Clearing the air really helped our relationship."

Kelsea and her father had overcome some major issues between them. What about her and Evalynne? Did they even have a relationship? Evalynne indicated she wanted to start over. So much had happened over the past twenty-three years, from braces to her first rodeo appearance. Her mother had missed it all. She sipped more of the fruity concoction. "How so?"

"Getting him away from work presented us with a more level playing field. We each had misconceptions that blew into mountains taller than Pikes Peak. He's trying to be a father now. That's the important part." Kelsea bustled around the kitchen, wiping down counters.

Before she talked to Evalynne, she'd have to consider what she wanted out of the relationship. Friendship or a mother? Giving her another chance would be risky, but there could be rewards for both of them. Even for the baby. Besides, Evalynne might need her as a friend more than Sabrina needed her as a mother.

As hard as it was to admit, Sabrina wanted someone else's opinion. She longed to hear what Ty had to say.

Her phone pinged with a text, and Sabrina hopped down from the stool. "It's the stable. I have to go."

Sabrina donned her coat, and Will did the same. "I'll go with you."

"I can handle the problem by myself." Her defenses rose at the implication she couldn't do her job.

Looking at her protruding bump, she might not be able to do the physical labor much longer, but there was still paperwork and other duties to perform until the baby came.

"I wanted to see Cinnamon and run an idea by you," Will explained as he buttoned his coat.

"Oh." Sabrina nodded and waited while Will kissed Kelsea.

Kelsea's laugh followed them out the door. In the stable, Sabrina consulted with the groom and checked on Margarita, Gordon's mustang. She entered the stall and patted the horse's flank. "What's going on, girl?" Looking around the stall, Sabrina noticed unchewed grain pellets and then studied the way Margarita was holding her head. "Toothache, huh? I'll call the vet tomorrow."

Sabrina thanked the groom and added that to her to-do list before joining Will, who was talking to her mare. He stopped at her approach. "Any chance I could borrow Cinnamon in January? I'll make it worth your while."

"As if I'd take your money," Sabrina scoffed. "But you have a stable full of horses. Why Cinnamon?"

"Lucky is returning in January, and Cinnamon has rodeo experience. I was hoping he could ride her alongside my horse, Domino."

Sabrina squealed at Will's news. "It's definite then. Lucky will be here in January." She waited for his nod, and then she sighed. "I hate that he's not spending the holidays with us."

But, come to think of it, he never did. He always found some place else to be, someone else who needed him more.

"I called him when Kelsea told me you might be in labor." Will stared at her. "Are you overdoing it?"

Asked like the older brother she'd never had. Even though he only had a few years on her and Lucky, Will was an old soul. "I've barely lifted a finger in the past few days." And that was the truth. "The grooms exercise the horses since I can't ride. And between Ty and Kelsea, I haven't had to make dinner or any other meals."

Sabrina walked over, and Cinnamon turned her attention away from Will. The mare raised her head and nuzzled Sabrina's shoulder. Sabrina reached in her pocket and gave the mare one of her favorite peppermints. She lavished attention on Cinnamon while Will kept a close eye on Sabrina.

"There's physical exertion, and then there's just plain stress," Will said. "Kelsea and I are here for you."

And they would be when Ty returned to the rodeo. "Thank you. I'm not naive. I know music will eventually lure Evalynne back, same as Ty and his fans."

"It still boggles my mind Evalynne is your mother." Will didn't sound too upset at her keeping that from him.

"The world doesn't know about me." That might have been a gift horse in disguise. "I'll take my cues from her. I was just as surprised as anyone when she showed up at the doctor's. While it's a big adjustment, I'm happy she's here for now."

"What about Ty? I know plenty of married rodeo contestants who have a home base, a family, and still compete. Does he make you happy?"

Spoken like a true older brother. Will had always treated her like the sister he never had and Lucky like his younger brother. They'd celebrated birthdays and holidays together, and she knew Will would become her daughter's wise uncle while Lucky would be a steady and calm influence. She rubbed Cinnamon's muzzle, the soft hair reassuring.

"Yes, but he's only here for the baby. Unlike Evalynne, he's made no secret that everything he's doing is for her."

Will arched an eyebrow. "I wouldn't be too sure of that. I've seen the way he looks at you."

A nice thought, but one she wouldn't lose sleep over. "I don't think he'll ever be able to forgive me for not tracking him down in person to tell him about the baby."

Will scrutinized her, and she rested her face on Cinnamon's muzzle. "Talk to him. Clear the air," he said. "What he's doing over these twelve days is too much to be only about the baby. He must be doing this for you, too."

She glanced around although she didn't know why. These ten horses could keep a secret, but she had to be upfront with Will. And whether it was a practice run for telling Ty later or because Will was the brother she never had, she wasn't sure, and it really didn't matter.

"I have to get something off my chest. Then I'm eating a whole plate of enchiladas." As if on cue, her stomach rumbled. "I lied to Ty. When he proposed the twelve days of charisma, I humored him. Anything to get him out of my life forever."

"Come again?" Will's lips thinned to a straight line.

She didn't blame her friend. What she'd done was pretty low. "He said he'll abide by my decision. When he ended our relationship earlier this year, I was devastated. I thought I could guard my heart by going along with his idea since it was only for a little while. My mind was made up. Twelve and out. It seemed easier to get on with my life without him." Her ears pricked up at the sound of a twig snapping. She backed up, intending to investigate when she noticed Andromeda pawing the floor in the next stall. Sabrina chuckled and gave Elizabeth's horse a peppermint. "I didn't forget your nightly treat."

Andromeda whinnied and settled down. The noise disappeared. Will shook his head, as he scrutinized her face. "That doesn't sound like the Sabrina I know."

Sabrina looked at the ground and made a circle in the straw beneath her boots. "You're right, and I've since realized how wrong I was. Ty needs to be in the baby's life." And she wanted him in hers.

"You need to be open with him." Her stomach produced a louder rumble, and her cheeks heated. Will pointed toward her bunkhouse. "After a plate of enchiladas."

"When did you get to be so smart?" Sabrina grinned and hooked her arm through his.

"Probably when I booked that flight to Atlanta to tell Kelsea I love her." They walked back, and she felt lighter after having confided to someone.

She had to be honest with Ty. Once again, her feelings for the handsome cowboy were spiraling out of control. Trust, once lost, was hard to gain back. While difficult to admit her initial misgivings, Ty deserved to know she was approaching tomorrow with an open mind and heart. Slowly, he was earning her trust and Ty-dazzling her.

CHAPTER NINE

MY MIND WAS made up. Twelve and out. Sabrina's words from last night echoed through Ty's mind as he drove toward the cabin. Rather than staying for dinner where he wasn't wanted, he had texted his regrets, claiming he needed to practice his lines. Anything to avoid her. He could no longer stay at the guesthouse and risk running into Sabrina now that she made herself clear; she wanted no part of him in her life. So, at the crack of dawn, he had found Robert and offered to take him and Phineas to the location site a day early. This way, he and the dog could familiarize themselves with the set and their marks. Anything to stay on schedule. If the shoot ended early, that was fine with Ty.

The wind buffeted the sides of the car, and gray clouds gathered in the distance. Ty concentrated on the road to the cabin, situated on the northernmost edge of the Irwins' ten-thousand-acre property. They climbed in elevation, and the air already seemed thinner. Snow fluttered down, but this was a light dusting, as far as Ty was concerned. The four-wheel-drive truck he borrowed from Gordon maintained its traction and would continue to do so even if the conditions worsened. Still, the back roads weren't salted like the principal routes. That could be an issue for the production vehicles with their heavy equipment.

A bump on the road jarred him, and Phineas whined. "Sorry, fella." The distraction almost caused him to miss the turnoff for the cabin. Massive pines hid the narrow avenue that resembled a trail more than a road. He swerved sharply, and his GPS confirmed where he was supposed to be. The road seemed to go on forever before a clearing presented itself. There, front and center, sat a picturesque log cabin. Large flagstones formed the foundation, which wrapped around the length of the cabin. Two piñon trees flanked the front porch, and a forest of pines and aspens surrounded the area, providing seclusion and privacy. They were a long way from the ranch and stable. *Perfect.* Parking the car, Ty searched the area for the cargo trucks or any other traces of life, but found nothing. No curls of smoke coiled out of the stone chimney. Where was the crew?

Robert whipped out his cell. "I'm not getting any service here." He held up his phone and waved it around. "What about you?"

A quick look confirmed the obvious. "Me, neither. I'm sure Carter and the crew are on their way."

Ty emerged from the car. No sooner had he opened Phineas's door but the grateful dog jumped down and bounded away. Robert joined Ty. "If you'd get my bag, I'd appreciate it."

"What bag?" Ty hadn't packed any luggage since they'd return to the ranch tonight. Hopefully very late.

Robert frowned. "I asked you to get the cargo by the door and load it into the truck."

While he was in a bit of a fog from last night, Ty remembered Robert's request clearly. "I thought you meant Phineas." Ty pointed at the dog, who was taking great delight at sniffing the trees despite a light layer of snow covering the ground.

Robert groaned. "I meant Phineas's equipment bag. I need it for the shoot."

Snowflakes floated down from the darkening skies. Maybe it would be for the best if they returned to the ranch. Navigation might be next to impossible once snow accumulated, even in that truck. "Okay, we'll go back for it," Ty said.

Robert clapped for Phineas and then shook his head. "Carter should be here any minute, and I know where I left it. Phineas can stay with you. No need for him to endure another car ride when he has all of this to explore."

"Can you drive a stick shift?" Ty eyed the knee brace around Robert's leg.

"For longer than you've been alive." Robert tapped his gray hair and then patted his brace. "Leg's gotten stronger the past few days. This is mostly just a precaution now, so I don't wrench it again. I'll be back in less than an hour. The forecast says the snow will clear by then."

A glance at the foreboding sky gave him pause. Ty wasn't so sure about that, but he'd feel better once the crew arrived and he had something to do. Helping unload the booms and the poles might exhaust him so much he'd get a good night's sleep tonight. He watched Robert drive away while Phineas came to his side, his head tilted.

Once the truck was out of sight, Ty reached

into his pocket for the bacon he'd stored there. "This can't become a habit. Last time."

Phineas gobbled up the treat and then his velvety brown ears perked up. He sniffed the air and took off running. Ty planted his head in his palms for a brief second. No sooner had Robert entrusted Phineas to his care than the dog ran off. Maybe it was for the best Sabrina had no intention of allowing him into their baby's life. He had a way of letting the best things slip through his fingertips. A stab of regret sliced through him, but he'd deal with that later. Right now, he had a dog to catch.

He whistled and called out the dog's name. Out of breath, Ty stopped running and leaned against a pine tree, dread gnawing at him while snowflakes melted against his face. "Phineas!"

He'd never felt this type of fear. Losing something entrusted to his care had never happened before. Concern for Phineas made him that much more aware of every sound, every square inch of his surroundings. He was sure that type of awareness would be needed with the baby, but he'd never know. He could involve lawyers, but he wouldn't. He'd walk away and go back to being fun-loving Ty. Just what everyone expected of him. No more, no less. Phineas emerged and trotted toward him, looking pleased as all get out at the big stick in his mouth.

Ty's mouth dropped open. The dog was covered in thick, gooey mud that clung to his dark brown fur. "Really? You're out of my sight for a minute, and you get into trouble."

He shouldn't be too surprised by the dog's predilection to find trouble in two seconds flat. If anything, it was better he was learning this hard truth from Phineas rather than the baby. Phineas sat near Ty's boots, the delight emanating off of him for his momentous find. Almost as if grinning, the dog lowered the stick and laid it at Ty's feet. His heart melted at the sight. "Okay, you're forgiven, but that doesn't mean you're getting out of a bath."

Phineas wagged his long tapered tail, and Ty had a change of heart. "Sabrina and I will have to come to some sort of understanding, but without lawyers. I might as well combine fun and responsibility from here on out." Ty threw the stick in the cabin's direction. Phineas darted toward it while Ty stopped halfway and waited for the dog to return. He did so, and Ty repeated the action. They played the game all the way to the steps of the cabin. "Time for your bath."

Once again, Ty searched down the long road and listened for the rumbling sound of the vans full of equipment, but heard nothing. He blinked, unused to the silence. On purpose, Ty packed his schedule with activity. Training, rodeos and publicity. His life had revolved around those activities for the past seven months, really the last twenty-seven years, every minute jam-packed with experiences he longed to live before the family genetics caught up with him. It was easier to live every moment as if it was the last. Recently, though, that had nothing to do with genetics and everything to do with the Sabrina-sized hole carved when he left her.

He stopped and paused. There were no horses or cattle in sight, no fans clamoring for autographs, and nowhere he needed to be. For a second, the walls closed in around him, and he itched from people withdrawal. Who was he without the rodeo and his fans around him?

Had he replaced his father with something fleeting? Adulation that would go away as soon as he left the spotlight and another rodeo star filled his boots.

Maybe he had done just that. Maybe those months with Sabrina had been more than fun.

They'd been a promise for a better future, and he hadn't been able to face that.

He breathed in the crisp mountain air, the snow cold and refreshing on his heated cheeks. For once, he didn't have anywhere to be, nothing pressing on him. Instead, he was alone with himself, really alone, for the first time in forever. He'd use this time to savor what was around him.

Content, being still didn't feel half as bad as he thought it would.

SABRINA PARKED HER Subaru in the clearing and closed the door behind her. Of all the people at the ranch, Carter had asked her to deliver a message to Ty during a light snowfall. With Elizabeth standing beside her, nodding her agreement that she could spare her barn manager for a few hours, Sabrina had no choice but to agree to fetch Ty from Mr. Irwin's hideaway cabin. With Robert nearby and able to drive again, Sabrina wasn't the most obvious choice for this task. If she had to make a guess, though, it seemed Elizabeth was playing matchmaker and had found a way for Sabrina to spend some much needed time with Ty as they'd be alone in the car on the way back. Well, as alone as they could be with Phineas, but he wouldn't interrupt what she needed to say. The perfect opportunity to admit her change of heart had dropped into her lap.

At least the snow had tapered off in the past few minutes, although she wouldn't have guessed that from the heavy gray clouds gathering around the mountain cliffs.

With a yawn, she conceded Ty would have to take the wheel for the return trip so she could nap and rest. Sabrina emerged from the car and slipped her arms through her coat sleeves when ice pellets struck her cheek. Dog tracks led toward the cabin. Ty and Phineas must be waiting inside. She carefully arrived at the icy stoop and opened the front door.

No sooner did she do so than a scruffy brown animal darted past her. A scream escaped from her throat. Rooted to the spot, she stood still, her mouth ajar. That flash of brown, though, raced for the trees, and Sabrina's heart continued racing.

"Phineas! Come back here so I can dry you off!" Ty's voice called out from the rear of the cabin. "You can't escape."

Phineas? Of course. Worse yet, Sabrina had aided his escape. He'd freeze outside with a wet coat.

Ty appeared at the archway separating the living room from the rest of the house, and he'd never looked so good. His flannel shirt sleeves exposed his muscular forearms. A slight layer of stubble graced his jaw, bringing out the ruggedness in him. Her stomach fluttered.

"Um, he escaped." Sabrina found her voice at the same time he acknowledged her presence.

"What are you doing here?"

There it was, the same iciness that had marked his voice the night he broke up with her. She didn't understand what was coming then, and she didn't know why that tone was back now.

Except he had grown close to Phineas, and she might have jeopardized the dog's life. "It's my fault he's out there. I'll bring him back."

Ty rushed to the open door, shock coming over his face. "He'll freeze out there." He cupped his hands to his mouth and yelled, "Phineas!"

The wind picked up, and a frigid chill penetrated her. Sabrina squeezed the knob hard, the thought of the sweet dog being outside in the elements almost more than she could bear. Ty started out on the porch, and she reached for him. "You're not wearing a coat."

"He's out there, wet and alone."

Fear gripped her throat at anything happening to either Phineas or Ty. At that moment, the dog broke through the trees and ran for the stoop. He swept past them, heading straight for the elegant cream sofa and jumped on it. Relief washed over Ty's features. He let out a sigh and gripped the towel in his hands while she closed the door. Ty ran over and blotted the moisture off Phineas's coat while whispering words of affection to the shivering dog. If she harbored any doubts Ty was going to make an excellent father, they were gone now.

Sabrina joined them. Ice chips fell off his thick fur and melted. Phineas looked happy to be back inside, and she couldn't blame him. She reached out and scratched behind his ears. "My apologies, Phineas, but don't run off again like that, okay?" It was almost as if the dog grinned at her, and she turned to Ty. "You're going to make a good father."

She didn't know who that admission shocked more, her or Ty. He gave one last rub and wrapped the towel around his hands. His jaw clenched, and he went over to the square window. "Why are you here?"

He didn't even look at her. She thought yesterday at the doctor's office had marked a new chapter in their relationship. Then she'd received his text he wasn't coming for dinner. At the time, she hadn't given it a second thought, falling asleep relieved that she'd tell him everything the next day. The emotional distance separating them in this cabin confirmed her fear. While the baby would always connect them, they'd live separate lives. He was fun Ty, and she was weighing him down.

He turned around, his arms folded against his chest, the towel now draped over his shoulder. She composed herself, regaining a sense of calm. "Carter sent me. He was concerned about getting the RVs and equipment trucks here, so he scuttled this part of the shoot. Instead, the crew's going to the ski lodge. You left so early he couldn't find you to tell you. Then Robert let us know there's no cell reception here. When he heard that, Carter seemed especially relieved he canceled this part of the shoot."

She smiled and expected him to do likewise, but no such luck. Where was that patented Ty grin? She rubbed Phineas's ears, the damp fur more comforting than she'd have thought.

"You can head back, and I'll wait here for

Robert. By then, Phineas should be dry and ready to go."

"Robert's staying at the ranch. I was elected to bring you back."

"The snow's coming down harder now. We better hurry before the road becomes impassable." Ty's gaze went to her baby bump with a lingering look of regret.

They bustled out the door, and the snow was falling at a fast clip. The wind whirled around the tops of the nearby pines and aspens. Sabrina reached into her pocket and handed Ty the keys. "Being from Wyoming, you're more accustomed to driving in these conditions. My part of Texas doesn't see snow like this often."

She wrapped her gloved hand around Ty's, his jaw resolute. Sadness swept over her at his building such a strong wall between them.

Phineas jumped in her back seat while she buckled into the passenger seat. Ty adjusted the rearview mirror, and they began the trek back to the ranch. The silence created tension as heavy as the snow falling around them. Her car was rather warm from her first trip, and the heater hummed along with the engine. This should be a cozy trip, but the icy chill emanating from Ty made it anything but. She might as well break through now, or it was going to be a long car ride. "We missed you at dinner last night."

Without warning, the car lurched forward in a pothole. Her seat belt stayed firm, but the impact jolted her. He looked over, alarm on his face. "Is the baby okay?"

The baby reacted with a swift kick to Sabrina's ribs. "We're both fine." She turned around, and Phineas wagged his tail. "So's Phineas."

The snow, now coming horizontally, swirled outside the window. Ty adjusted the wipers. "Can you check on cell reception? This storm seems to be gaining in intensity."

She could say the same about him, but she did as he asked. "No bars." She checked, but she couldn't access her apps either. "Or any updated weather info."

With the snow hitting the windshield with more force than earlier, Sabrina stayed silent so Ty could concentrate on driving. A giant thud rocked the ground, reminiscent of the loud sound from a few days ago. "What was that?" Fear shook her voice.

Phineas whined. She turned and found the dog shaking, a wild look in his eyes. She reached out and calmed him by cooing softly. Then she focused on Ty, who also seemed unsure.

"I don't…" His sentence was cut off when he slammed on the brakes.

The seat belt once again stopped her from crashing into the dashboard. Phineas yelped.

"What the…" Her words trailed off when she spotted the huge pine that had just crashed to the road.

CHAPTER TEN

THE BRAKES GROANED, and the car halted not two feet from the massive pine tree trunk. Judging from the lack of snow on the top, this was the crash they'd just heard. Ty jumped out of Sabrina's Subaru, shaking after the close call.

The fresh smell of pine filled the air along with displaced earth. Roots and splinters of wood marked the upturned area where the tree used to stand. Turning, he discovered they were blocked in solidly with the tip of the pine leaning against the grove on the other side. Too tall for them to scale over, and not enough room to go under.

Unless he had a chain saw, he and Sabrina weren't going anywhere, anytime soon. The wind picked up, the swirling chill biting at his cheeks, the whistle through the tops of the trees the only sound for miles around.

He pulled out his phone and traversed the length of the pine until one bar appeared.

Carter and Hal came to mind, but Ty needed to make this call count. He pressed the contact for Gordon, who answered immediately.

"Where are you?" Worry tinged Gordon's voice. "Is Sabrina with you? Evie's here with me, ready to scale the walls."

"We're on the turnoff road to the cabin. A giant pine fell, and we're blocked." Adrenaline pumped through his veins at the close call. A few minutes earlier, and they'd have been on the other side, continuing to the ranch. And yet...?

The pine could have landed on the car. Shivers ran through him at such a close call. Considering his rodeo days, that was saying something.

"Hold on a second." Muffled voices on the other end were too distant for him to make out the words. "Everyone's talking at once. I can't hear Ty. Evie wants to know if Sabrina is safe."

"Yes. So is Phineas." Ty could make out Evie's cry of relief. "Can someone come get us?"

"It's too dangerous. The storm's intensifying rapidly. The forecasters are now calling it an unexpected blizzard. We could get anywhere between fifteen and twenty inches of snow in the next few hours. It'll be heavy at first, and then taper off to light snow. Can you make it back to the cabin?" Gordon asked.

No sooner had he said yes than silence greeted him. He hadn't even had time to ask for someone to contact his family or tell Carter or Robert what happened. He believed the latter two would get the message; his family not so much. The adrenaline dissipated, and the cold bit through his coat. The intensity of the wind nipped at his cheeks, and snow pummeled his face.

He hurried into the car and shut the door, conserving the heat. "I talked to Gordon."

"It's a good thing your phone works out here. Mine doesn't." She comforted Phineas, who was panting heavily. "How long before someone gets us? An hour? Two?"

Only dark gray clouds surrounded them, making it seem like nightfall was about to descend rather than high noon. "We need to return to the cabin."

Sabrina wiped the snow off his sleeve, the coat now damp from the elements. "Shouldn't we stay put? How long until they come for us?"

He hesitated too long, and her eyes grew

wide with concern. "The storm's getting worse. It's a full-fledged blizzard now."

A BLIZZARD? STUNNED, Sabrina pulled herself together while reviewing her Subaru's emergency kit. She hadn't planned on needing it today, and it didn't contain provisions for a dog. Apprehension clenched her stomach while tension froze the interior.

This time last year, she'd have given anything to be snowbound with this rodeo star. Her and Ty and a cabin in the woods? It would have been wonderful.

With a baby on the way and Ty's distant attitude, she wished she were back at the bunkhouse with the horses close by. She let out a gasp at Cinnamon, enduring this without her.

"I know this isn't ideal, but the cabin's big enough for the both of us." Ty's hands were stark white from gripping the steering wheel for dear life. "I'll keep to myself."

"What's wrong with you?" Sabrina snapped, the shock of the circumstances finally giving way to measured annoyance about Ty's attitude. "Yesterday we made progress, and today it's like we're strangers, if not worse."

Ty pulled into the circular driveway in front

of the cabin, the snow piling up quickly. "Progress depends on two people making an honest effort."

What was he talking about? She was doing everything she could, including driving to warn him of an impending storm, only to get caught in the scary blizzard herself. "I missed something."

Phineas whined, and both of them whipped around to find the dog shivering, his large brown eyes soulful and longing for the dry warmth of the cabin. Her heart softened as they were making a fine mess of this. If they couldn't keep a dog happy, how would they keep a baby happy?

Their gazes met, and she knew he was thinking along the same lines. Without another word, they hurried inside with Phineas ahead of them, the swirl of the wind blowing the snow around, creating almost whiteout conditions.

Thankful for shelter, Sabrina assessed the cabin and let out a long, low whistle. As far as shelters in a storm went, this one was at the top of the list. Mr. Irwin did nothing in half measures, and right now, Sabrina was happy he hadn't started here. A massive stone fireplace occupied an entire wall with two dark brown recliners facing a comfortable cream sofa with lots of soft pillows and a plush throw blanket. Phineas jumped on the couch and snuggled in for warmth. Sabrina could spend the next few days happy and content on that spot, except one glance at Ty changed her mind.

"I don't know how long we're going to be here, so we can either get whatever's wrong into the open or make each other miserable for the next couple of days," she said.

The conditions outside the window only confirmed her fear. No longer were the pine trees and mountains visible. Only a whirl of blinding white greeted her.

Ty's gaze was focused in the same direction. "First things first. I need to find out if there's extra firewood and a generator in case we lose power."

Even though she worked on the Double I, this was her first visit to the cabin. "I remember hearing about a shed out back at one of the employee meetings."

"I'll check." Ty headed for the door, and she hurried to him. His face scrunched up at the effort to open it. Once he did so, snow covered the stoop and fell inside. The conditions had worsened a hundredfold. On his way outside, she laid her hand on his arm, his coat not hiding the firm muscles. "Don't make *us* come looking for you. Hurry back."

He gave a curt nod and checked the environs before folding up his collar and heading toward his left.

She closed the door behind him, and Phineas jumped off the couch. The dog trotted over and whined, pawing the wooden surface. He looked at her as if he expected her to keep Ty safe. "Yeah, he gets under your skin faster than you'd think possible, doesn't he?" She arched her eyebrow and then shrugged. "Or fur, as the case may be."

No luggage, no toothbrush, no doctor at a minute's notice. She proceeded to the kitchen, hoping Mr. Irwin kept some emergency rations here. Otherwise, the granola bars in her emergency kit would have to tide them over, and she wasn't sure whether those would agree with Phineas.

TY NUDGED THE door with his elbow, his arms full of cured wood for the working fireplace in the great room. Even with the power still working, this would help make their surroundings toasty and comfortable for the time being. It was the least he could do for

Sabrina. He could barely feel his toes, and he wasn't sure his cheeks would ever be the same. Growing up in Wyoming, he considered himself familiar with the cold, but nothing had prepared him for these types of conditions this high in altitude.

The door flew open, and Sabrina gasped. "Come in! You're frozen solid."

She reached for his elbow and guided him inside. A delicious aroma from the kitchen filled the air, and a crackling fire greeted him. Phineas's head popped over the top of the couch before disappearing once more. Somehow, in the short time he'd been outside, she'd transformed the cabin into a home with dog, hearth and food.

Ty unloaded his haul of three massive logs on the hearth next to the fireplace. Then he took off his coat, placing it close enough to the fire to dry but not too close so it would go up in flames. He'd located the generator in case they lost power. Still, that was the least of his worries. What if the baby came while they were trapped in the cabin? She'd be five weeks early, and there might be complications. It wasn't like he went around delivering babies every day. Sabrina—

"Ty?" Sabrina's gentle voice cut through

the overwhelming questions. "Remember what the doctor said yesterday? The baby hasn't dropped yet, so we should be out of here before she makes her appearance."

How did she do that? Know what he was thinking when he had said nothing? Here she was, glowing in the ambient lighting of the cabin, her brown hair down and lustrous around her shoulders. But that wasn't the only thing said yesterday. Her conversation with Will made it too clear she had no qualms about cutting him out of the baby's life. "I heard you yesterday. I know."

"Then why do you look so worried? If I thought the baby would come today, I wouldn't have driven here." The shadow lifted from her eyes, and she laughed. "Is that what's concerning you? The fact I drove to the cabin to relay a message? I had no idea the weather would go downhill so fast, and it sounds like this blizzard surprised everyone."

"I heard you tell Will your mind is made up. That you went along with the twelve days with no intention of trying to mend fences." He tugged off a glove and muttered something under his breath. "Ouch!"

She reached for his hand and pulled him close to a standing lamp. Switching it on, she examined his finger. "I see a splinter. Wait here. I found a first-aid kit in the kitchen."

He tried squeezing out the offending piece of wood, to no avail. Phineas raised his head and lowered it once more, along with his eyelids, as if deciding his nap was more interesting. Sabrina returned with a medium-sized red first-aid kit and rummaged inside until she extricated a pair of tweezers. Ty squirmed. "I'll pull the splinter out," he said, reaching for the tweezers.

She yanked her hand away and then laid the kit on the end table. "Hold still and listen." Her hand was warm compared to his icy digits. "You only heard part of our conversation. If you'd have stuck around, you'd have discovered I also told Will I was wrong to judge you so harshly and intend to give you a real chance."

Without further ado, she plucked out the splinter.

"Really? You want me in the baby's life?"

The reflection of the flickering flames shone in her deep brown eyes. She'd never looked lovelier. She replaced the tweezers and came over with a tube of antibiotic ointment and a Band-Aid.

"It's a shame you didn't trust me enough

to ask." Sadness caught in her voice as she wrapped the plain beige bandage around his finger. "We're back where we started with nothing to show for it."

They were close enough for him to feel the baby kick. "I wouldn't say nothing. We have an important *someone* to show for it."

Her rueful smile contained a fraction of its normal vibrancy from the past week. "I'm going to ladle out a bowl of soup and take it—"

Lights flickered out, and the hum of the refrigerator ceased. Only the light from the fire broke through the darkness. He brought her close. "Good thing I found the generator."

"Good thing I found candles. They're on the kitchen counter." She raised her chin, the crackling embers the only other sound. "Why are you smiling? You haven't even warmed up yet."

Her presence alone, though, had that effect on him. He held up his finger, her handiwork already taking away the sting. "It's all better."

"It wasn't like I had to sew stitches or anything like that." The fire highlighted the rosy pink of her cheeks.

He drew closer, and her light floral scent filled him with a calm he wouldn't have thought possible under the circumstances. "It would have been easy for you to sit on the couch with Phineas, yet you built a fire and made lunch for us."

They both turned in Phineas's direction, his soft snores bringing forth chuckles. "It was nothing. The soup was already in the freezer. It's stocked solid."

"Don't discount yourself." He reached out and caressed her chin, something he'd wanted to do for as long as he'd been in Violet Ridge. "You were an amazing rodeo clown, and you're an outstanding barn manager."

"Are you using flattery as the basis for creating something stronger between us?"

Whispers were louder than the faint sound of her voice.

"There's already something between us." He raised her gaze to his.

She moved closer, and he wrapped his free arm around her waist. Standing on her tiptoes, she kissed him, her lips warm and sweet. He'd missed her so much in the past seven months. He entwined his fingers in the silky strands of her hair. The kiss deepened, and falling off a bucking bull was less intense than the vortex of emotions colliding within him. His heart pounded almost right out of his chest.

Attraction coursed through him for the one woman he'd fallen for, the one woman he'd been unable to forget. Everything about her was familiar yet different, sweet yet sweeter.

Something punched his gut. *The baby*. He'd almost forgotten about the baby. Kissing her was incredible, but when they separated, he saw something in her eyes he'd never seen before. *Apprehension*. Somehow, amid something wonderful, the chasm between them reared its head once more.

"Ty." *Uh-oh*. That didn't sound good. "We have to talk."

The wind whistled outside, the sound penetrating and constant. "I'm not going anywhere."

Even though he'd found where the generator was located, there was no way he was risking his life in these conditions. One look out the window confirmed that this was a full-fledged blizzard, visibility not extending beyond an inch of the pane. Snow swirled, and from here, he could see it was already piling up in inches. He was staying inside, where they had everything they needed.

She led him to the couch, and they were careful not to disturb Phineas. The dog had other ideas. He jumped off and circled around the hearth before settling into a cozy ball.

This was the picture of domesticity he always feared before now. A dog, a beautiful woman and an isolated cabin cut off from the outside world. This reminded him of a time long ago. A whistling sound awakened him from a deep sleep, enough to seek comfort on the night of his eighth birthday. He sneaked downstairs with his Labrador retriever. The wind buffeted the siding of the small house his family lived in, close to his father's job as a teacher and his mother's job as a vet tech. His mother and father smiled at each other in front of the fire, clinking goblets together, laughing. He went back upstairs and fell right back asleep, secure in their love. Less than a month later, his father died.

Sabrina rubbed his arm. "You're a million miles away. Talk to me."

He blinked, back in the present. "Oh. It's nothing."

She clutched a pillow to her stomach. "Let me in. Can you at least tell me why you broke up with me? I thought we were happy together."

He rose and stoked the fire with the iron poker, the embers crackling and popping, the heat penetrating his icy defenses. "I was happy with you, happier than I'd ever been."

She joined him at the hearth. "Why are you fearful of being happy? After all, you mount bulls that would scare most people."

He kept poking the log, the orange and yellow of the flames captivating and evocative. "My father, Tyrone, died of a heart attack when he turned thirty-five."

"How old were you?" She stilled his hand and removed the poker, placing it back with the other fireplace tools before leading him over to the couch and sitting next to him.

"Eight. He died at the same age as his father, and his grandfather before him." Too many generations to be a coincidence. He turned to Sabrina, lit only by the glow from the fire. "I turned thirty-four this past April."

Even in the dim light, he saw her squint and shake her head. "So, the fear of following in your father's footsteps and dying young caused our breakup?" Her voice grew deep and husky.

When she put it like that, it sounded rather weak. "Three generations of Darlings died at the same age."

"Three generations of MacGraths had perfect pitch. Still doesn't mean I can sing a note.

Well, I can sing, just not the right note." She gave a warbled laugh and reached for his hand. "You and I have had extensive physical screenings for our job. If you had a hidden heart defect, the doctors would never have cleared you to ride in the rodeo."

"At his funeral, I promised myself I wouldn't leave anyone behind." Ty stopped once more as the holes in his boyhood promise became canyons.

"Maybe it's time to think about how proud he'd be of the man you've become. He must have been very special, considering what a big promise you made to yourself." She squeezed his hand.

"He was my father, my mentor, my everything." Would their daughter look at him in that same adoring way?

"Childhood promises run the gamut of emotions. When Evalynne didn't show up at my birthday party, I promised myself it didn't matter." She tried to rise from the couch but didn't succeed. The second time was the charm, and she crossed to the fire. "I realized this week her decision to value fame over family came at a high price for us both."

He hadn't updated her on that part of his conversation with Gordon. She joined him at the fireplace. "She was frantic with worry on the phone."

"Evalynne promised she'd come for me and she left me behind. Your father didn't leave you on purpose, and you promised you wouldn't leave anyone behind, but you did. You left me." Sabrina breathed in and out. "Maybe the takeaway is considering whether we can keep our promises before we make them."

"What are you going to do about your mother?"

"Take it one day at a time. See if she's serious about wanting a relationship."

Sabrina could just as easily have been talking about him. He might not have kept the promise he'd made to himself when he was eight, but he could keep the twelve days of charisma alive. Sometimes the parts of life that were the most fun could carry a weight of truth and heft not clear on the surface. Look at Sabrina, the best rodeo clown he'd ever shared the ring with. Her rapport with the crowd had them laughing loudly at her antics while gasping at her mastery in distracting the bull and saving the rider from harm. Laser-focused about her purpose, she still had fun with the crowd.

"I promised you an unforgettable twelve days. How am I doing?"

She bumped his arm. "So, you orchestrated an entire blizzard to get me alone and snowbound for the next day of charisma?"

Sabrina's giggle turned into a snort, and then a sheepish expression came over her face. She went completely still.

"Hey, that snort is one of the cutest things about you. I hope our daughter has that same laugh." She arched an eyebrow, but he nodded. "As hard as it is for me to admit it, I don't have that much pull with Mother Nature."

She clasped her hands over her chest. "Ty Darling, my illusions are shattered. I'll never be able to look at you the same way again."

With any luck, she'd still feel like that when the twelve days of charisma ended.

CHAPTER ELEVEN

THE PILLOWS ON the couch looked inviting, but they hurt Sabrina's back. She shifted her weight and reached behind her, adjusting the pillows until she found a tolerable position. Phineas whined and came over, nudging her hand. "I'm fine. I just can't get comfortable."

The pain in her back knifed through her once more, and she groaned. At that moment, the lamp flooded the room with light. *Thank you, Ty, for finding the generator.* As if by some miracle, the sliver of pain faded into oblivion. She rubbed Phineas behind his ears. "It's only stress. I'm fine now."

The front door opened and in strode Ty. He shivered and shrugged out of his parka. "Glad Gordon is tall and rangy. His coat kept me warm, and I think the worst of the storm is over."

Ty headed for the kitchen, and she couldn't help but worry he was holding something back. She followed him. He rolled up his shirtsleeves, allowing her a good look at his arm muscles, well-developed from years of training for the rodeo. After a long whiff of the chicken tortilla soup resting on the front burner, he closed his eyes, his face appreciative of the aroma filling the small space.

She stood resolute. "What aren't you telling me?"

He ladled some soup into a bowl and held it close to his chest. "I'm going to turn off the generator tonight to conserve the natural gas."

Phineas came over and stopped at Ty's feet. Ty reached for the box of crackers and threw one to the dog. He snapped it up in one gulp and sat patiently for more. Sabrina clucked her tongue. "Don't be fooled. I found the dog food and fed him."

"Lucky for us that Irwin keeps the place well-stocked." Ty added tortilla strips to his soup.

"Most likely it's on account of Elizabeth. She's thoughtful that way." She frowned. "I hope she'll take care of Cinnamon for me."

"I'm sure she's treating Cinnamon the same as Andromeda." Ty was generous with the sour cream and sprinkled some green onions on top.

How would Ty's future girlfriends treat

their daughter? They weren't a couple, so it was inevitable he'd settle down with someone else. A spurt of jealousy cascaded down her spine at the thought of Ty becoming involved with any other woman. She fixed her bowl and led him to the living room. Sitting only brought the pain back with a vengeance. Wincing, she rearranged the pillows behind her. That didn't help.

"Sabrina?" Ty placed the bowl on the end table and moved it when Phineas gave the contents a polite sniff. "What's wrong?"

She waved him off. "Nothing. Barometric pressure can affect pregnancy, that's all."

Ty leaned forward, panic welling in his eyes. "How long has this *nothing* been going on?"

She finally found a comfortable position and relaxed. "Since you powered up the generator. It's nothing."

He glanced at his watch and fiddled with it. "If you say so."

"I say so." She clutched one of the pillows to her chest. "Eat before it gets cold. I'll just close my eyes for a minute now that I know you're inside, safe and warm."

No sooner did she fall asleep than the pain returned. She sat up with a start. "Ouch!"

Ty turned pale. "You were asleep for seven minutes."

Her heart began racing, and her breath came in spurts. This cabin was not an ideal place for the baby to be born. And she and Ty were only now taking the first steps in re-kindling their friendship. They needed more time to sort out their relationship. Not that they had one. That kiss had been pure magic, and she'd give anything for that to be the start of something new and deep between them. However, she couldn't forget his expression when she said she wanted to give him a real chance. All he'd talked about was being part of the baby's life.

Not hers.

"It could have been a bad dream." Denial was good. She wasn't ready to be a mother. She didn't exactly have a great role model, although she credited Evalynne for taking the first step of mending fences. And what kind of mother drove to an isolated cabin while seven-and-a-half months pregnant? "We're stuck here, aren't we?"

"I have an idea." He went to the parka and pulled out a transistor radio. Turning it on, he fiddled with the dial. Static greeted them until he found a station with Christmas music.

He tapped his foot and then continued tuning the dial.

"…six inches more over the course of tonight. A winter warning is in effect for the following counties…"

He switched off the dial. "Yes, but we can make the most of it. How about exploring the cabin with me?"

"Good call. My legs are cramping from not getting enough exercise."

Ty nodded as if he liked that idea. They spent a little time in the covered porch. While the windows probably provided a spectacular view of the mountains on a normal day, this day was anything but that, the snow swirling and accumulating in mounds. They proceeded to the bedrooms, the master bedroom even more luxurious than the first. He insisted she take the master while he and Phineas claimed the smaller room.

"How are you feeling?" he asked when they arrived at the master bathroom.

She eyed the Jacuzzi with longing. Forgoing a soak in that tub and refraining from ice-skating would be worth it once the baby was born, safe and healthy. "I'm fine. See, nothing…"

A hard pain split her abdomen, and she

clasped the edge of the door frame. Ty blanched, his face nearly matching the white color of the subway tile. "Six and a half minutes."

"The baby. Can't. Be. Born. Here." She paused between each word, taking deep breaths like she'd learned in the classes she and Kelsea attended together.

He ushered her to the living room. "We'll drive to the tree and climb over. Then it should be a breeze."

"First babies are notorious for taking their time." Sabrina's laugh didn't have any confidence behind it. Fear welled inside her, and she pushed it aside. Her baby needed her to stay strong.

They bundled up and clipped a leash to Phineas's collar. After a tight hand squeeze, Ty opened the door. A wall of snow, over two feet high, greeted them and fell inside the cabin. Her jaw dropped.

"This is nothing in Wyoming. Just a trace." Ty stepped back and tapped his chin.

"Why are you looking at me like that?" Sabrina frowned.

He moved toward her, his arms held out wide. "I'll carry you to your SUV."

She held up her hands. "I'll walk." She pointed to her boots. "They're water-resistant."

They carefully stepped out into the pristine surroundings until they reached the car, and Phineas jumped in the back seat. Sabrina fastened her seat belt while Ty cleared the windshield. Returning, he turned the key in the ignition. *Nothing.* Her mouth went dry. "Why isn't the car starting?"

Ty examined the dashboard and then groaned. "You know how we were in a hurry to get inside the cabin? I didn't turn off the lights."

"The battery's drained, isn't it?" Another pain gripped her, and she held on to the console that divided the driver from the passenger seat. Her breathing technique helped her until the contraction ended.

He checked his watch. "Seven minutes since the last one."

She scrunched up her face. "Are you sure? I thought they were six and a half minutes apart." He showed her the timer on his watch, and she shrugged. "The more time we have until she comes, the better."

How was she going to handle motherhood? She was in the middle of nowhere with no diapers, no cell phone coverage and no name picked out for her daughter. Her breaths came out faster.

Ty reached over and squeezed her hand. "Do you want door A or door B?"

He'd lost control, that had to be it. "How can you be flippant at a time like this?"

Her heart rate soared, and she clutched the console.

"We can either panic, or we can stay calm. Door A is the safest route. We go back inside, deliver the baby and get her to the hospital once the storm blows over." He made that suggestion sound so feasible, and yet she saw the fear in his eyes if something went wrong.

"What's door B?"

"You trust me to get you and Phineas to the log."

"You can't carry me the entire way." Although that thought would be appealing in different circumstances.

"Trust me." He grinned and left the car, her mouth open.

She turned to Phineas in the back seat, his tail thumping. "He's something else, isn't he?"

Minutes later, Ty returned, wearing snowshoes and pulling a big sled. She emerged from the car, the snow up to the tops of her thigh-high boots, Phineas's leash in hand. He grinned and bowed. "Your chariot awaits. I saw this in the generator room. It's perfect."

Sabrina glanced at the cabin, and then at Ty. "You're having the time of your life, aren't you?"

His grin grew wider. "It's not every day your daughter's born. I can either approach this with fear and trepidation or rise to the occasion."

With a glance at Phineas and a pinch to her forearm, she climbed onto the sled. "It's a good thing you're a rodeo star with arms of steel."

"Aw, Brina." For the first time since the breakup, he used his pet name for her. "You noticed."

HALFWAY DOWN THE long isolated road to the fallen pine tree, Ty paused. The skies shifted to a misty shade of gray rather than the near slate color of earlier, the brightness with the snow almost blinding. A blanket of white created a beautiful panorama with the pines and aspens reaching their lacy arms toward the sky. For all of its splendor, it fell short of Sabrina's natural beauty. He looked over his shoulder and noted her on the sled with Phineas beside her, the snow up to his chest.

She leaned over and whispered something in Phineas's ear. Then she looked up and saw him watching her.

"You stopped." She wrapped her scarf around her neck. Her pink cheeks, rosy from the wind and excitement, reminded him of the first time they met after she rescued him from a charging bull. "Are your arms tired?"

Not with so much on the line. Fear, simple yet intense, took hold of his heart. They were in the middle of nowhere with a baby about to come into the world. Adrenaline pounded in his ears. If he failed either her or the baby? He wouldn't have Sabrina jumping out of a barrel, rushing toward him, handling the bull in such a way so he could escape. They were alone out here, and it scared him.

It was time to face his fear. "The constant training for the end of the season is coming in handy." He flexed his arm muscle invisible under the thick parka, her chuckle making all those hours in the gym time well spent.

He stopped and approached the sled. She handed him a bottle of water and hesitated, as if she was debating whether to say something. He gave her space until she was ready to talk. "I watched the finals," she admitted, while transferring her gaze to Phineas. "Your comeback was quite the feat."

That wasn't the comeback of the year he cared the most about winning, however. Not that this tenuous relationship with Sabrina was a game. He wanted another chance with her, her vivaciousness and caring spirit so integral to his life that he knew his future wouldn't be the same without her.

"I wouldn't have guessed that. After all, I was the grade A jerk who didn't return your calls or emails." The fact she watched presented him with new hope they could start a new chapter after the twelve days were over.

"Well, I might have said a few choice phrases while I was watching." She pretended to put her hands over her belly as if placing a pair of noise-canceling headphones over the baby's ears.

"I have another reason to succeed this year. I want her to be proud of her father." Speaking of which, he tapped his left wrist. "When was the last contraction?"

She blinked, and then a look of pure joy came over her. "I haven't had one since we left the SUV." She checked her watch. "It's been over an hour."

She launched out of the sled and ran over to him, clutching him tight as Phineas ran circles around them, barking to get in on the joyful moment. A sense of relief washed over him. "More of those Braxton-Hicks contractions, then?" he asked.

Her nod was his answer. She looked at the sky. "How about we head back to the cabin? Unless you can get a signal here and someone might come for us?"

He checked his phone. No bars, but he had a series of texts waiting for him. "Hold that thought." Scanning them, he latched on to one. "Gordon says there's a satellite phone in the living room. We can call him with that."

"What are we waiting for?" She walked alongside the sled, Phineas wagging his tail as he settled onto the wooden platform. "Luxury cabin, here we come."

Suddenly, being stuck with her seemed all the more wonderful.

AFTER SABRINA GREW tired of walking, Ty insisted she climb back into the sled. The cabin came into Sabrina's view once more, a most welcome sight. Her home for the night was proving quite a haven while providing an atmosphere of trust. Not only had she kissed Ty, but she also admitted she'd watched him compete in the rodeo championships.

But every time they seemed like they were at a place where she could bring up a second chance, he always returned the subject to their baby. Was it wrong for her to have him want her in his life as Sabrina, who happened to be the mother of his child?

No, it wasn't. In the past, she'd been rejected, and she had to stand up for herself. She was worthy of love, and she wouldn't settle for anything less than being loved for the special person she was.

The sled slid to a stop, and Ty turned around. "All ashore!"

She laughed and stepped out of the sled, her boots sinking into the snow. "That's the best you've got?"

He shrugged and rubbed his arms. "Once feeling is restored to all major limbs, I'll be more ready with the quips."

Phineas huffed from his sitting position, and she couldn't blame him. "You miss Robert and your home, don't you?" He rose to all fours, the fur on his back rising. "Ty? Is something wrong with Phineas?"

He paused from coiling the rope. "Good boy, Phineas. Release." He finished his task. "He's used to certain commands. Guess he was guarding you, but he needs a break."

She cricked her neck. Standing felt all the

better after sitting in that position. "I'll help you put the sled away."

"No need to do that." Ty raised the circle of rope and placed it on his shoulder. Then he lifted the sled as if it weighed nothing. "I'll let you in on a secret. It's fiberglass and is quite light."

So much like their former relationship. She shrugged and carried on. "Please show me the generator. You can teach me how to use it." That was a skill she needed.

"Okay. Come on. You too, Phineas," Ty said. The dog sniffed the ground, a low growl coming forth, and he refused to go with them to the shed. Instead, he neared the cabin. "He must be ready for that couch again. We'll hurry."

With some reluctance, Ty led the way to the storage area. She listened while he explained the different mechanisms. He stepped back and watched her check the fuel valve, moving the choke rod from right to left. She crossed her fingers for luck and then flipped on the engine switch. The generator hummed, and he gave her a thumbs-up. That behind her, she could no longer hold back the yawn she'd been suppressing.

"You sure do know how to show someone

a good time." She teased him, grateful for the chance after the earlier tension.

He grinned and hung up the snowshoes. "Wait until you see what I have up my sleeve for tomorrow."

They walked to the front of the cabin, their hands entwined. Their boots made giant circles in the pristine layer of snow that blanketed the earth. They approached the cabin, but something seemed off. Phineas still sat there, the fur on his back raised.

"Did you close the door when we left?" Sabrina's voice quavered at the end of the sentence.

"I thought you did." All traces of levity left Ty as a crash came from the living room, most likely the lamp falling to the floor. "Stay back."

What was inside the cabin? Another look at Phineas confirmed it wasn't him. And it couldn't be a bear. They started hibernating in the area around mid-November. That left quite a selection of wildlife in the area that might have smelled the food and welcomed a chance to escape the blizzard. Mountain lions, bobcats and moose were all winter predators on the minds of the Double I ranch hands.

Ty might have grown up in Wyoming, and he definitely knew how to proceed with caution around a two-ton bucking bull. That didn't mean he was prepared for whatever was waiting for him in the cabin.

With a gulp, Sabrina searched the area covered by mounds of snow as far as the eye could see. The multiuse tool in her pocket could be effective, but it was rather small. She made her way over to the copse of aspens and kicked around the base until her boot came in contact with something. Reaching down, she picked up a large branch. Phineas barked as if she was going to play with him. "Not now."

She smiled for Ty's benefit, working up the courage to face whatever was in the cabin.

Please let it be raccoons.

A deep breath in and out, and then she hurried to Ty's side as he cautiously approached the door. He looked over his shoulder and frowned. "I thought you were staying back." He glared at her midsection. "The baby."

She held out the branch. "Then you take this."

"Let's see what's in there first."

He pushed the door until it opened all the way. Sabrina gripped the branch so tightly her knuckles hurt. A female elk stood in the living room, and it glanced up as if frozen. Then she ran past them, out the door, into the woods.

Admiration lingered in his eyes. "You're brave." He motioned toward the branch.

"Extra firewood." She entered the cabin and placed in on the hearth before shaking her head. "Never mind. Aspens are too soft for burning."

He whistled for Phineas and then shut the door. "But not too soft to protect our family."

CHAPTER TWELVE

ONCE THE ELK was long gone, he and Sabrina stood back and stared at the shambles left behind. Shards from the ceramic bowls were scattered on the kitchen floor. Hoofprint tracks in sour cream and guacamole led to the living room. Something told him this wouldn't be the most unusual situation he'd find in the next few years. Considering Sabrina always kept him on his toes, it wasn't too hard to imagine their daughter doing the same.

"Gordon gave clear directions on where to find the lockbox in the living room. It has the satellite phone in it. I'll find it before we clean up." Phineas darted over and sniffed the food dotting the kitchen floor. "Correction. First, I'll put Phineas in one of the bedrooms and then find the phone."

Ty situated Phineas in the master bedroom. Returning to the living room, he found Sabrina with a trash bag, picking up large broken shards. He located the metal lockbox and groaned at the distinct hoofprint, the size of an elk's, in the center. Ty opened the box only to find the satellite phone in smithereens. So much for using it to call Gordon now or anyone if Sabrina went into labor.

He walked into the kitchen and found Sabrina sweeping the floor. She looked his way, and he held up the shattered lockbox. "The elk destroyed the satellite phone."

Sabrina rested her chin on the tip of the broom. "Well, at least Gordon knows where we are. As soon as it's safe, I'm sure he'll send someone for us."

Ty threw the lockbox into the trash bag. "Evalynne sounded quite emphatic that he do so at the earliest opportunity." He pointed at the broom. "Why don't you let me finish cleaning while you take a nap?"

"You know the perfect thing to say to a woman." She held out the broom and moved toward the bedroom.

Phineas ran out of the room and wagged his tail as if waiting for the next piece of bacon. "Sorry, Phin. No extra treats. As it stands, you're lucky Elizabeth stocked up on dog food."

After he swept away all the remnants of the

ceramic bowls, taking extra care so no left-over fragments would harm Phineas's paws or Sabrina's feet, Ty found ground coffee in the refrigerator and brewed a pot of coffee. The rich aroma sent a second wind through him. Cozy comfort solidified his inner strength to face whatever was ahead. He waited for the coffee and appreciated the elegant surroundings. The interior designer did a top-notch job, and Ty made a mental note to ask Gordon for a referral. He could see himself coming home from a rodeo to something like this.

Where was his home now anyway? He glanced at the closed bedroom door before searching the cabinets until he found the mugs. Wherever Sabrina was. It was time to face the truth. The way she held that branch fiercely on the porch? When he was the first Darling male in generations to blow out thirty-six candles on his birthday cake, he wanted to see her there.

How could he convince her he wasn't a flight risk again? He added some cream into the dark liquid and stirred.

Something else nibbled at his mind, and he hummed a Christmas carol. "What's missing, Phineas? What does this room need?"

Contact with the outside world, while nice,

wasn't quite what he had in mind. His earlier pledge to savor what was around him was one he could still get behind. Unlike the promise he made when he was eight, this one bene-fited him, infusing him with calm and peace. He went over to the front door and cracked it open, cold air rushing in to greet him along with a good three feet of snow. The trill of a Colorado junco reached him, the only sound for miles around.

He hummed a bar of "White Christmas," the irony not escaping him. The treetops were loaded with snow, and he let the quiet of the day seep into his soul. Cupping the mug, he closed the door and went over to the window. He didn't turn on the transistor radio or reach for his phone. He was alone with himself, and that was enough. For once, he wasn't worried about the next activity that would catapult him into a whirlwind of fun.

The coffee tasted wonderful, and Phineas pawed at the door. He let him outside and watched him romp in the snow. Perhaps this time away from the hustle and bustle of the holiday season was what he'd needed most of all. This was like that second in the chute when the noise of the crowd dimmed to noth-ing, and it was the two of them alone: him and the bull. Nothing else mattered except being in sync with the bull and making sure that for the next eight seconds, he held on and enjoyed the ride.

Gordon would send someone as soon as it was safe, but maybe he needed to grasp this moment for the opportunity it presented, the same as he always savored that last second in the chute, hoping for the ride of a lifetime.

Humming the last bars of the Christmas carol, he finished his cup of coffee and then headed for the shed. He knew just what the cabin needed.

SABRINA RUBBED THE sleep away from her eyes. Was it only this morning when she arrived at the cabin? Part of her was surprised she woke up this late in the evening, while another part demanded to use the facilities. Thank goodness the cabin possessed indoor plumbing.

In no time, she paused at the archway leading to the living room. It was as if she walked into a Norman Rockwell painting. Phineas sat in front of a roaring fire while Ty was assembling a Christmas tree?

"What on earth?" She laughed as Ty pointed

to the artificial tree. He made a goofy face. "Where did you find that?"

"In the shed with the generator and the sled. I went out there to look for another satellite phone. No luck on that front, but I did find this." Ty finished assembling the branches and hummed the last bars of "O Christmas Tree."

"Since we're running the generator for power, I'm leaving off the lights."

Sabrina touched the storage container marked ornaments. "That's fine, but you went to so much trouble bringing this in from the shed when we won't be celebrating Christmas in the cabin." She shuddered and listened to the radio. The latest forecast confirmed another storm was heading their way. "It sounds like we'll be here a couple more days, but I hope the weather clears up before Christmas. I have a feeling that if Gordon doesn't mount a search and rescue team soon, Zelda and Nelda will."

"I wouldn't put it past Evalynne either." Ty stepped back and sized up his efforts. "About Christmas."

She opened the lid, pulled out a box of red, green and gold balls and inserted hooks through the small openings. "You don't have to worry about me. While you're celebrating your mom and Hal's anniversary, I'll be with Will and Kelsea and Will's family, which includes his cowhands and uncle and new aunt. They've invited me for Christmas Day, and Will's uncle claims this is going to be the best and biggest Christmas ever."

Ty inspected the ornament selection and chose a box of long finials. He started hanging them on the tree. The layer of dark stubble on his chin added an air of maturity with a hint of mystery. Her stomach tightened at how good he looked in the fire's glow.

"I can see why you love Violet Ridge so much. Do you think Will would consider adding one more plate to the table?"

"For you? I thought you were going to Wyoming." Sabrina started decorating the other side of the tree while Phineas came over to see what they were doing.

He sniffed the balls and then went back to his spot in front of the fire and curled up.

"There's no way I'm leaving Violet Ridge until the baby's born."

"I'll talk to Will—" His laughter stopped her from finishing her sentence. "What's so funny?"

"Five golden balls—" he pointed at the tree "—for the fifth day of charisma."

She joined in the laughter, and the joy of Christmas came alive for her. This time in the cabin was unique, even more special because of this man. While she'd been sleeping, he'd cleaned the kitchen, found a Christmas tree and stoked the fire. Even with a blizzard in the rearview mirror, he brought the fun with him.

"All that's missing is music," she said. He adjusted the radio dial and gave up when only static met them. "Come on. You're brave so you can listen to my warbling."

She reached for the radio and set it down. Her mood light, she smiled and hummed a few bars. He joined in, his husky baritone more than compensating for her off-key pitch. They went through a catalog of favorites while they finished decorating the tree.

He rifled through the box and chuckled. "You'll never believe what I found."

That glint in his eye proved he had something up his sleeve. "Mistletoe?" Sabrina asked.

"That would have been perfect, but I found this instead." Ty stood on his tiptoes and perched a stuffed bird atop the tree.

"A partridge on a pine tree." She laughed until she snorted. "How fitting."

Stepping back, he sniffed the air. "There's still one more thing." He shrugged on the parka and disappeared outside with Phineas before returning with the dog and his arms loaded with greenery. "That fresh pine smell. A tree isn't a tree if it smells like the attic."

She had to hand it to him. He'd turned a critical situation into an evening to remember. His larger-than-life personality dominated the cabin and filled it with a gaiety she hadn't felt, well, since he broke up with her. Tonight was full of surprises, not the least of which was his intention to stay in Violet Ridge until the baby was born. And yet a bigger surprise, one that wasn't a shock to her system, came over her as she watched him play with Phineas. She was falling for the rodeo star.

He'd proven in the past few weeks she could trust him with their daughter, but could she trust him with her heart?

CHAPTER THIRTEEN

THE NEXT DAY, Ty closed the door behind Phineas. Following the dog to the living room, he dried him off with a fluffy burgundy towel and then wiped his paws. Hal used petroleum jelly on the ranch dogs' paws in winter to protect them from salt and other chemicals, so Ty used the small packets from the first-aid kit even though the road to the cabin wasn't salted as it was impassable. Sabrina's SUV was half-covered with snow after another six inches fell in the middle of the night.

"They won't be able to come today, will they?" Sabrina plunked a tea bag in the cup with a rueful grin.

He shook his head and held up the radio. "Not with the fresh powder that fell overnight, and there's more expected today." Gray clouds gathering on the horizon had him concerned. "I'm even doubtful about tomorrow."

She blew out a deep breath and sank onto

the couch. "Will there be enough gas for the generator?"

He'd turned it off last night before they went to sleep and awakened to Phineas curled next to him in the bundle of blankets in the second bedroom within hearing distance of the master. This morning, they found embers among the ashes smoldering in the fireplace, and he'd replenished the fire. Then Ty dug a pathway to the shed and turned the generator back on. "I found one more tank, so we should be good for a few more days if I continue turning it off at night. Were you warm enough? The baby didn't complain about the cold, did she?"

A shadow fell over Sabrina's face. "No complaints."

She rose and went to the kitchen. He couldn't blame her, only himself, for her being here. Her concern for the baby's safety had been obvious from the beginning. If it wasn't for him heading to the cabin a day early, she'd be safe and cozy in her own home. Sabrina was so close and yet so far from her friends and her doctor. He understood how she must be going stir-crazy with worry that something might go wrong.

He had to distract her, but how? His mother's

special holiday cookies! Those always cheered him up. "Cookie time!"

"Did Elizabeth leave cookie dough in the freezer?" Sabrina opened the door and peered inside. "I don't see any."

"I know my mom's recipe for ginger cookies by heart. I always make them with her. What about you? Didn't you make cookies with your grandparents?"

"No. Grandma and Grandpa worked full time until I left for the rodeo circuit. In their off hours, we were always outside, hiking or going on long horse rides. Neither of them loved to cook. Their idea of Christmas cookies is the big blue tin that's at every checkout counter."

"You've never baked holiday cookies?" He scoffed at the very idea. "Fear not. I'll be gentle."

"I'm in!" She closed the refrigerator door and licked her luscious lips. "They'll taste warm and gooey, right out of the oven, and the cabin will smell wonderful."

He gathered the dry ingredients and found enough flour and sugar on hand. "See if the elk left us any cinnamon and cloves. She decimated our supply of fresh vegetables."

"Good thing our baby isn't craving kale. Peanut butter, though? Yum." Sabrina located the spice rack. "Yes to cinnamon. No to cloves."

"I can make that work." He whistled and bustled about before stopping in his tracks, taking care not to collide with Sabrina. "You always call her the baby. What's her name?"

She blinked and stood at the counter next to him, her smaller shoulders brushing the side of his arm, her softness affecting him in such close proximity. "I haven't decided yet. Winter and Stormi are now off the table, and I promised myself I wouldn't name her Noelle if she arrived on Christmas Eve."

He found some mixing bowls and baking sheets. "Good call."

She followed his instructions and creamed the butter and sugar while he sifted the flour and other dry ingredients. "I'd like to use MacGrath as a middle name. A tribute to my grandparents."

"I remember your concern about their health. Are you going to visit them once the baby's born?"

"I've had some good news about my grandmother. She's doing well, but Grandpa Bob isn't well enough to travel, so I plan to take her to Texas next summer."

He should go to Texas with Sabrina and

the baby and meet the pair that had raised Sabrina, but he'd most likely be in the thick of the rodeo season. He blended the ingredients together. "If I can arrange a weekend off, I'd like to go with you and meet our daughter's great-grandparents."

"They'd like that."

Her soft sigh endeared her to him all the more, her affection for her family sincere and loving. He showed her how to form a ball of dough and then set the timer. After the first batch was in the oven, he wiped his hands on a towel.

"Do you want me to take her to Wyoming to meet your family?" she asked.

He hadn't thought about it. He pondered what Hal and his mom would probably do. "Mom will come to Violet Ridge right away. Nothing will keep Jenny Middleton away from meeting her first grandchild."

Sabrina formed more dough balls out of the remaining batter. "What about you? Do you have any names you're particularly fond of? What about your middle name?"

He started running water in the sink. "I've seen the nursery. You have everything so perfectly prepared that I'm surprised you haven't chosen a name."

She scraped the rest of the dough out of the bowl. "You changed the subject too quickly. Don't you want me to know your middle name?"

"I don't know yours."

"Eden. Sabrina Eden MacGrath. There's a tradition in my family where the oldest daughter's name starts with *E*. My great-grandmother was Edith. My grandmother's name is Eloise, and my mother, as you know, is Evalynne." She found a towel and started drying. "She wanted to break tradition but didn't stray too far."

"I like that." No sooner were his arms up to their elbows in bubbly hot water than the oven timer dinged. "Eden Darling? Eloise Darling? Do you like either of those?"

Sabrina found an oven mitt and swapped out the baked cookies with the other sheet. "I'm not letting you off the hook. What's your full name?"

"You don't want to know." He finished rinsing off the last bowl and placed it in the drying rack. Then he looked inside the refrigerator and pulled out a bottle of lemon juice. "Do you want lemon or vanilla icing?"

She waved a warm cookie under his nose. "Come on. Tell me."

"That's not a good implied threat. After all, you can't eat all those cookies by yourself." He mixed powdered sugar with the lemon juice for the icing.

"Try me." She grinned and bit into the cookie. Her face melted into pure happiness. "Oh, this is so good."

"They'll be even better with icing."

Her chest deflated. "If you say so."

He rolled his eyes. "Tyrone Eustace Darling V."

A quiver of laughter broke out before she stilled her lips. "I'm glad she's a girl. You wouldn't have been able to talk me into Tyrone VI."

He fluttered his eyelashes and put on his best puppy face. "Aw, you wouldn't have humored me for the sixth day of charisma?"

She let loose the laughter with that snort on the end, the one he was so crazy about. "I thought the eggs in the cookie recipe were your tribute to the six geese a-laying."

He crossed his chest with his arms and staggered backward. "I trust you with one of my innermost secrets, and this is how you repay me. With laughter." He squinted and looked at the bowl of icing. "I'll have to retaliate."

She hurried over to the other side of the couch in good time. "You wouldn't and definitely not in here. Mr. Irwin paid an interior designer a pretty penny for this beautiful cabin." She glanced at the spot where the lamp once stood before the elk damaged it. "And we already owe him for what the elk destroyed."

He swiped his finger in the icing and pointed in her direction. "Yes, I would."

A minute later, he smeared the icing on her plump lips, their softness yielding under his fingertip. She licked off the icing. "I won't laugh at your name again."

Suddenly, he wanted a family with her, including a possible sibling to the one coming soon. Perhaps a brother and they could revisit him being the sixth or, more likely, agree on another name. Or a sister who'd shadow her older sibling. "You didn't hurt my feelings."

Her gaze intensified, and the bond between them was back, stronger than ever. The oven timer broke the spell and woke up Phineas, who howled. Ty went to the door to see if someone was outside. There was only ice and snow as far as the eye could see. Four feet and counting. "No one's out there, Phin, old boy."

The last sheet of cookies came out of the

oven, and they fell into a rhythm icing the first batch. Sabrina placed the knife in the sudsy sink. "So, we have Christmas cookies, but no name," she said.

He tasted one. "It's better this way. A little mystery in our lives."

A crack of thunder filled the air and shook the cabin. "What was that?" Sabrina asked.

They both went over to the living room window and looked outside, with Phineas popping up between them.

"Thundersnow." Ty swallowed the cookie and groaned. "It usually happens near the Great Lakes, but it also occurs in Colorado. We're in for more snow and high winds."

"And snowbound for even longer."

SABRINA THUMBED THROUGH the set of books on the library shelf. Without the internet or working phones, she was at her wit's end for something to do after lunch. Last night, a search of the cabin had yielded checkers, Candy Land and Monopoly. Somehow, Ty had managed to win every game before she retreated to the master bedroom with a few cookies to tide her over till morning.

The bookshelf offered few choices, and she fingered the bindings, looking down at the baby bump. "Okay, baby girl. You have your pick of a book about range management, a guide to raising cattle or an illustrated history of Colorado."

Riveting options. These might be Mr. Irwin's reading preferences, but Sabrina would give anything for a good romance or mystery to pass the afternoon away.

Ty came over, whipping the dish towel onto his shoulder. "Uh-oh. You look like you're ready to climb the walls. Ah, books. What looks interesting?" He glanced at the options and winced. "Or maybe we'll think of some other form of entertainment."

She raised her eyebrows. "That's quite a line, Ty."

"Think of the baby, Sabrina." He acted as if he was shocked and put his hands over the baby bump. "I had something quite innocent in mind. I'll teach you how to clog."

She blinked and rubbed her ear. "Did you say clog? As in plumbing?"

"As in dancing." He pointed to his feet and tapped his boots against the hardwood. "My grandmother is one of the best cloggers in Wyoming. She runs a dance studio and taught Devon and Peyton. Devon's won quite a few dancing competitions."

"How did I not know this before? While I don't think I'd make the most graceful dancer right now, I'd love a demonstration." Sabrina settled on the couch and leaned her elbows on her knees.

"I walked right into that one, didn't I?"

She nodded and pointed to the area in front of the fireplace. "Is that enough room?"

"I'm not as good as my sisters. You can wait and they'll show you."

"Keep trying." She hugged a pillow to her chest and Phineas jumped up beside her.

"I don't have the right shoes."

"Does that matter?"

He shrugged. "Actually, boots are rather close to the wooden heels of clogs."

"This show will be perfect for the next day of charisma."

He sought any excuse and latched on to the obvious. "No music."

She went to the kitchen and came back with the transistor radio, fiddling with the dial until the twangs of country music filled the air. "Look at it this way. I've never been to a clogging recital, so you'll be the best that I've ever seen."

He began some limbering exercises and then dipped into a deep bow. She sat spellbound while he danced an entire routine. The song ended, and he wiped away the sweat dotting his brow. She awkwardly got to her feet and delivered a standing ovation. "You did your grandmother proud."

"Grandma Eugenie is Hal's mother. She's the best."

Out of breath, he came over and sat next to her, the closeness of him making her aware of his thigh muscles, strong and supple. Surprised at every turn by Ty, she searched her mind for something safe, something that wouldn't make her so aware of his attributes. The perfect thing came to her. She rolled his grandmother's name on her tongue. "Eugenie." It had an old-world charm about it. "I like that name. It's traditional and modern at the same time. Do you think this little one would like it?"

He faced her, a bead of sweat from the performance falling down the side of his face. She stopped short of wiping it away. His cheeks softened with a lopsided smile. "Eugenie MacGrath Darling. Maybe Genie for short?"

"I think we just decided on her name." *Together.* She liked that most of all. When they worked with, instead of against, each other, they were pretty impressive.

They sat there, and he linked her fingers with his. The crackling of the fire was the only noise in the room, the silence sweet and not oppressive. Minutes went by as they watched the hypnotizing flames of the fire, beautiful yet dangerous.

Finally, she tore herself away from the sight and stretched her back. "I'm getting cabin fever."

"Are you up for another round of Candy Land?" He grinned and flexed his fingers.

"It's still early afternoon. Maybe we should head to the log and see if we can get a signal?" She glanced out the window, wondering how long until someone would come and take them home.

"Tired of me already?" His voice cracked at the end. "Or is that your way of telling me we need to get to the hospital?"

"It's more like I don't want to lose four games in a row." That was only part of it. She hated feeling useless and much preferred some sort of action to waiting. That was why she loved being a rodeo clown. This type of helplessness was what she'd fought against for years. Now it resurfaced, and she clenched her hands by her side.

He fiddled around with the radio dial until a meteorologist's voice came through. Snow and ice with a side of ice and snow. No heading out today.

He tapped her shoulder until she faced him. "I feel like I should be doing something," she said. "I know Elizabeth is taking care of Cinnamon, but my horse is my responsibility. I'm AWOL as far as my barn duties are concerned."

"There was a blizzard and then thundersnow." Ty squinted and tilted his head. "Sometimes doing nothing is the best way to let others do something. It's like in the ring when you save us rodeo contestants from the bull. We have to let you do your job so everyone gets out alive."

"I'm not used to being the one who's trapped." Sabrina admitted.

"It's the perspective that matters. I prefer to think of us as destinationally challenged." Ty's eyes widened, and he stepped backward, diving onto the couch on his back. Phineas must have thought Ty was playing around as he jumped on Ty's chest and wagged his tail. "Oomph."

Sabrina joined them. "So, you're saying I should relax since I have nowhere else to be?"

"You have a Christmas tree, cookies and me." Ty propped himself on his elbows and grinned. Phineas licked his cheek.

Her heart did a somersault. If only that were true. She wandered over to the bookcase. "We might as well look at the illustrated history of Colorado together."

She moved the three books around and found a book that had fallen behind the illustrious trio of ranching tomes. She pulled out a slim volume and showed it to him. "*A Christmas Carol.* Have you ever read it?"

"I've seen movies based on it, but I've never read it. How about you?"

She shook her head. "My grandparents loved to be outside. I don't think I ever saw them read a book."

"I bought Hal a hardback copy from his favorite thriller author for Christmas. He's always reading."

"Do you think your parents will enjoy reading to Genie? Will they want to be involved in her life?" Sabrina fretted, wanting Genie to have as much love in her life as possible.

He made room for her on the couch, and she shifted her weight until she found a comfortable position, something that was getting harder with each passing day.

"Come closer." He wound his arm around her shoulders and pulled her close. The fire and Ty. Life didn't get any better. "My mom and Hal will love Genie. They'll do anything for her, same as your grandparents did when they raised you."

A reminder that both of them found security and love after life-changing events. She snuggled next to him, reveling in his warmth and solidity. "This is cozy with the fire and the blankets."

"There's something about snow and a good book in the winter." He drew her closer. The woodsy scent of pine and vanilla and Ty captivated her.

All her assumptions about Ty went out the window. He enjoyed his fun, but there was a hidden depth to him. Like others, she'd been quick to assume the worst about him and hadn't taken the time to dig beneath the surface. When they'd dated, he'd shown a glimpse of those layers, but nothing like the man she'd gotten to know better since he landed in Violet Ridge.

He protected Phineas, and he went out of his way to arrange for the éclairs and enchiladas for her. While they'd been snowbound, he'd risen to the occasion, surprising her with his baking and clogging skills.

This was a man she could fall in love with, if only he wanted her in his life.

He waggled his eyebrows. "Anything can be fun…"

"It just depends on your perspective." She finished his sentence for him and opened the book.

"Nelda and Zelda would be very proud of you." A reminder of the friends she'd made in Violet Ridge. Soon enough, she'd be back in town and see them again. Maybe she should relax and enjoy this time with Ty, just the two of them. He elbowed her and looked over her shoulder. "Are we reading it together? If so, let's put it between us, and I'll tell you when I'm ready for you to turn the page."

"How about we read aloud and alternate chapters?" She turned the page. "Or, as the book says, alternate staves."

"I wouldn't miss it for a third National Rodeo Championship buckle."

THE NEXT EVENING, Ty donned the parka and grabbed the snow shovel. Another morning of snow had given way to a calm afternoon.

Ty breathed a sigh of relief. Then again, if he had to wait out a blizzard, this cabin was the place to do it. "Come on, Phineas." He motioned to the dog while keeping his voice down to a low whisper. Anything so Sabrina could enjoy a needed nap before dinner. "I'll dig the tunnel for you."

Ty opened the front door and marveled at the stillness of the late afternoon. Dusk would descend on them soon with the sky's brilliant shade of robin's-egg blue ceding to a pearlescent gray, soft and ethereal. The blinding white of the snow, forming a layer of lace on the nearby aspens and pines, was evident as far as his eye could see. A high chirp echoed in the mountains, and a junco alighted on a nearby aspen. With no fresh snowfall since eleven, more birds had started to make their presence known. All of this pointed to a good chance that tomorrow someone might arrive to take them back to the Double I.

He wouldn't wait around, though. With every minute, his worry increased that Sabrina might go into labor. The radio meteorologist called for sunny skies tomorrow. Over dinner, he'd broach the subject of pulling Sabrina and Phineas to the fallen pine tree in the morning, barring any signs of another sudden storm. Then he'd help them climb over the log and lift the sled as well. From there, Sabrina could monitor her phone until bars appeared.

Phineas frolicked in the snow, and Ty hoped Robert wasn't too concerned about his dog. The commercial had been on his mind all day, along with his family. With the two costars sidelined at the cabin, Ty wasn't sure Carter could remain on schedule. That was, if he hadn't shut down the production altogether. Without the satellite phone or cell reception, Ty had no way of knowing how the blizzard impacted the shoot. Any chance of alerting his family to his whereabouts was also impossible. He could only cross his fingers that Gordon had let them know he was okay. Then again, Hal and Mom were accustomed to going a couple of days without hearing from him when he was in the thick of a rodeo competition. They probably figured he was having fun and forgot to call.

Ty trekked to the shed. The remaining gas in the generator was running low, and they could go without electricity for a few hours. Conservation was key in case the forecasters were wrong and more snow came tomorrow. Turning it off, he headed back to the cabin. Whistling for Phineas, they rushed inside the cabin, where he flicked on the flashlight, taken from Sabrina's emergency kit, from his coat pocket. After taking off the parka and hanging it on the coatrack, Ty removed his boots, dried Phineas's paws, then applied a thin coat of petroleum jelly.

As Ty went about his remaining tasks, he noticed the small covered porch nook featured a spectacular view now that there wasn't a whiteout. He straightened one of the seven origami cloth napkin swans he'd assembled. Then he opened the drawer with candlesticks and tapers. Within minutes, the cabin glowed from the flickering flames.

"Ty?" Sabrina's low husky voice sounded from the other side of the cabin. "How long did I sleep?"

"A couple of hours." He brought her into the nook. "I hope the baby had a good nap."

"Oh, Ty." Her mouth dropped open. "This is beautiful."

Not as beautiful as she was, fresh from slumber. The candlelight emphasized the pregnancy glow. Her chestnut hair, thick and shiny, surrounded her face as if in a halo. Her inner light captivated him, her kindness and spunk charming audiences on the rodeo circuit and him alike.

What was he going to do about it?

Her soft chuckle broke the spell, and he followed her gaze to the origami swans. "Seven swans a-swimming?"

"Seven swans a-skiing is more like it, considering this is Colorado." He pulled out a chair for her and then pushed her in to the makeshift table.

"How did you know how to shape these into swans?" she asked, reaching out for one and then stopping short. "We don't have internet access. Or was there a book in the kitchen I didn't see? The Complete Guide to Origami Napkins and Other Tricks for Bored Rodeo Stars Stuck in a Snowbound Cabin?"

"How did you know?" He chuckled and sat across from her. "Actually, I owe this to Devon. Along with tea parties, she went through an origami phase, a knitting phase, playing the bassoon phase and painting pet rocks phase. Peyton is steadfast, more like Hal in that respect, while Devon likes something for a week and then moves on."

"Origami, clogging and a gourmet baker?" She reached for the rubber band around her wrist and tied back her hair. "I'm impressed."

"Not guilty as charged. I can only bake the ginger cookies because those are my mom's favorites, and I spent all afternoon on the fanciest of dinners." He paused and moved his hand to the handle of the lid on the silver platter. "What did you tell me earlier the baby was craving?"

"Peanut butter sandwiches." She scrunched her nose. "Not the most romantic of dinners."

"Ah, but we're not the most usual of couples, are we?" He waited a long beat and then removed the lid with a flourish. There on the silver platter sat a mound of peanut butter and jelly sandwiches, all without crusts, cut diagonally. "For your dining pleasure."

She burst out laughing and reached for one on the top. "This is perfect." She leaned over and kissed his cheek, her soft skin burning its imprint on his stubble. He'd have a beard started by the time they returned. While he liked it, he had no doubt he'd have to shave it off for the commercial, for continuity reasons.

After a bite, Sabrina moaned with delight. "I will have to thank Elizabeth for stocking peanut butter. I think I could have just had peanut butter this entire time and been fine."

Ty wiped a smudge from the side of her mouth. If he had to be snowbound again with anyone in the entire world, he'd take Sabrina every time. He couldn't have asked for a better companion for these few days. *Companion?* He made her sound like Phineas, who was sitting nearby with an expectant air of falling scraps, when she was so much more to him.

And if it was just the two of them, without a baby's welfare at stake, he could spend the whole winter here with her.

But this time with her had to end, if for no other reason than the baby's safety. They had to consider Genie in all of this.

"Speaking of time, what do you say to waking up early and heading out to the log? The radio forecast calls for clear skies. Once we get closer to the ranch, you can call Gordon or Elizabeth." He presented the rest of his plan, ruing they couldn't stay longer.

"While it would be nice to see what other hidden talents you have up your sleeve, I agree we need to get back to town."

"So, you're game to travel on the sled again?" Ty popped a bit of sandwich into his mouth.

She grinned and finished a bite. "Of course."

"What do you want to do first once we're back on the ranch?"

"Look in on Cinnamon." She smiled, and they started comparing their favorite saddle makers. Their hands bumped as they reached for the last half at the same time, but he let her have it. Who'd have guessed that the best dinner he'd had in years, if not ever, could be something as simple as a peanut butter and jelly sandwich? It wasn't the sandwich as much as the company.

She rose and ventured to the window, the view picturesque. The deep scarlet glow of the sunset was captivating, and he joined her. The pink sky over the snowcapped mountains took his breath away, almost as much as the woman next to him. She crossed her arms against her chest and shivered. Ty wound his arms around her, wanting to share his warmth with her. "This time with you has been special," he said.

She froze under his touch. "Those were the words you said to me on your birthday, the same night you broke up with me this past April."

He groaned. How had he managed to make a mess out of his last birthday, a celebration which should have marked the beginning of something unique and lasting? Just because he wanted them to start their future now, that couldn't be. Not here. This was a break from reality, not a stepping stone to more.

"I'll always treasure this time." He tapped

his fingers on his forehead and rubbed the spot that was starting to throb. "I said that on that fateful night, too, didn't I?"

Out of the blue her face relaxed, and she laid her cheek on his shoulder. "Sometimes, the same words can have different meanings depending on the context." Then she lifted herself on her toes and kissed his cheek. "I wouldn't trade being here with you for all the horses in Mr. Irwin's stable."

Considering how much Sabrina loved Cinnamon and the Double I Ranch, that was saying something. "Or for all the belt buckles from the next five National Rodeo Championships."

"Or for the entire monetary value of the actual twelve days of Christmas." She chuckled and stepped back, the candlelight playing with the expressive curve of her cheeks. "Besides, it would be a pain to have all those birds everywhere. Swans, geese, turtle doves. They'd be even messier than a baby."

"I was scared." He blurted out the word, finally confirming what she'd wanted to confront the other day, but he wasn't upset about baring his soul to her. He'd never been able to be this honest with anyone else. Opening up to people risked everything. Not opening up?

That was even riskier as it led to a life without commitment, without fun, without love. "I was scared I'd leave you behind. I won't do that to you again."

A smile lifted the corners of her mouth. To put her mind at rest, he added, "Or Genie."

And like that, her shoulders deflated, and she yawned. "Thank you for a lovely dinner, Ty. *The baby* appreciates it."

She turned on her toes and left. Phineas looked at him as though Ty had eaten an entire Porterhouse steak and left him nothing before the dog followed Sabrina down the hall, his nails clacking against the hardwood. The door click reverberated in the silent cabin.

SABRINA FINGERED THE copy of *A Christmas Carol* and then placed the book back on the shelf. Together they'd read three of the five staves, ending when the bell struck twelve and the Ghost of Christmas Yet to Come was about to visit. Their stopping point seemed appropriate, given the circumstances. This time at the cabin had been part of a wonderful Christmas Present, the kiss and experiences the start of what she'd hoped would be the beginning of many more Christmases yet to come.

However, she'd been deluding herself. Naive, to say the least, she'd poured herself into that kiss on the first day, believing someone had come back for her. Not just anyone. Ty.

That, along with the other unforgettable moments in the cabin, had given her the false hope they could have a second chance at a relationship, this time for keeps.

And yet for all their talk last night about words, the truth in everything he'd said since he showed up in Violet Ridge couldn't be denied any longer.

Then the baby will get enchiladas.

The baby needs a lullaby.

For Genie.

From the start of the agreement centering around the twelve days of charisma, Ty had been upfront with her. He wanted to prove to her he would be trustworthy for the baby's sake. She'd been so wrapped up in his charming self that she believed they were on the verge of something lasting that would lead to a lifetime of Christmases yet to come. But he'd meant what he said. He was doing this for the baby, not for a second chance at love.

Until last night, her heart hadn't received

the message. Now, everything fell into place. She could trust him with Genie; she just couldn't trust him with her heart.

With a pang of regret, she pushed the book into place. It was for the best they hadn't finished reading it together.

The front door creaked open, and Ty ducked his head into the cabin. "Are you ready? There's nary a trace of a snow cloud in sight, but we both know that could change at a minute's notice."

She nodded and grabbed two pillows from the couch. She cleared her throat and turned toward him with a smile she didn't feel inside. "Thought this might help cushion the ride."

A wide grin broke over his features, even more devastating with a couple days of stubble gracing those cheeks, highlighting his rugged appearance. He tapped the side of her head. "Smart and beautiful."

Her heart leaped with that Ty charm and magnetism on full display. She crossed to the door, and he kissed the top of her head. "Those should keep you still enough so the jolts don't send you into early labor. We don't want anything to hurt Genie."

And just like that, her heart thudded in her chest. So much for second chances for her and Ty. Giving him the pillows, she zipped up her puffy turquoise coat and threw the thick scarf around her neck. With a yank of her gloves, she didn't even look back at the interior one last time.

Instead, she got moving and carefully lowered herself into the sled, accepted the pillows from Ty and settled them around her. She caught sight of Phineas playing in the snow. Despite the growing ache inside her chest, she laughed at his antics. Maybe she should think about getting a pet for her and Genie, a cat or dog to keep her company while Genie stayed with her father. One more thing to consider when they arrived home, along with sending someone else to retrieve her SUV.

Ty donned the snowshoes and then flexed his muscles before reaching for the rope. Between him and Phineas, her laugh was genuine. She'd have to find some way to tamp down her attraction for him. Her heart was just too fragile.

Instead of looking at Ty, she drank in nature's beauty. Signs of the blizzard's aftermath greeted them on the long trail. Branches lay scattered on the high tufts of snow; others hung low under the heavy weight. She listened for a moment. No cars, no tractors, no whinnying of horses. The chirping birds and the sled crunching through the snow and ice were the only sounds for miles around. Her cheeks stung from the cold, and yet she disregarded any discomfort. The open landscape dotted with trees gave rise to the white-capped mountains, majestic on the range.

A few minutes later, Ty stopped the sled. Phineas danced in the snow and bounded over to him. Ty rubbed the dog's ears, his laughter echoing in the morning air. The bond between the two was obvious, and she hoped he wouldn't be too sad when they had to part. Ty came over to her and reached for the backpack lodged under her knees.

"It might be easier for you if I get off the sled. I need to stretch my legs anyway." She extended her arm, and he helped her to a standing position.

Phineas jumped in and wagged his tail as if expecting it was his turn next.

They both laughed, and then Ty found his reusable water bottle. "Have you been drinking enough water? It's important to stay hydrated. Dr. Zimmerman said so."

"I'm good, Ty." She huffed and managed to get to a nearby tree, beginning a series of stretches she often used prior to her rodeo routines.

He followed her, and that was the only bad part of being alone in the vast wilderness. There was nowhere to run.

"Missing the cabin already? This might help." He grinned and pulled out a chocolate and peanut butter candy bar, a close second to her beloved éclairs.

"Darn you, Ty Darling, for being so charming." She accepted the gift and was about to take a bite when the sweet smell wafted to her.

This wasn't something she should bite off in anger. This gift was one to be savored and appreciated. The sentiment overwhelmed her, and she said, "Thank you. And before you ask, yes, the baby also thanks you."

He was so close she could see the sapphire flecks in his eyes. They darkened, and he shifted his weight. "What's wrong, Sabrina?"

She bit into the chocolaty peanut butter goodness, the smooth taste melting in her mouth. She let the flavor seep into her before answering. "How are we going to do this, Ty? Are you going to take time out of your schedule and visit her in Violet Ridge for the first couple of years? Will you wait until she's older before she accompanies you on the road?"

"This is where you want to get into those details?" He waved his hand at the landscape.

"Not really." She polished off the treat. "I was hoping…"

The pause lengthened, and she rested her back against the tree trunk. Dislodged snow fell and landed on her head. Ty started laughing, and then he grew serious, wiping the bits of ice and snow off her nose. The softness of his insulated gloves brushed against her cheek. "What were you hoping?"

His whisper surprised her, considering they were the only people for miles around. "I was hoping you'd forgive me for not telling you in person."

"I did a long time ago." He moved toward her, propping his arm on the trunk, his face inches from hers. "Do you want to know what I'm hoping for?"

She nodded, the crackling crispness of the air twisting her stomach into knots, a testament to the tenderness and attraction that had always flowed between them. "I'd love to know."

"There's nowhere for miles around to train for the rodeo, yet the Violet Ridge Rodeo

Roundup brings a strong lineup of contestants." He kept rubbing her cheek with the back of his glove. She leaned into his touch. "I'd fill a void, but I need a partner. Someone who loves horses and the sport as much as I do."

"So, you want to start a training center?" She lifted her gaze to his. Dare she believe that scorching look was for her and her alone?

"Someone's given me a reason to think about the future. Acting's not for me. I love the rodeo." He neared, the puffs of breath misting the air between them.

Every fiber of her sparked to life with his being so close. "I need to know, Ty. That someone..."

A noise cut through the air, and he took a step back, cupping his ear. "Do you hear that?"

In the distance, the hum of an engine became clearer, and Phineas barked. Ty separated from her side and hurried toward the dog. From the vantage point of the tree, Sabrina saw a most beautiful sight near the horizon. A tractor with a snowplow attached to the front chugged along the path. Following a safe distance behind came a utility terrain vehicle. Phineas jumped out of the sled and came over to Sabrina as if guarding her.

A few minutes later, the tractor approached and cut its engine. Sabrina's pulse raced as she spotted Will in the cab. While she had a few issues with his timing, her good friend was still a welcome sight. "Will!"

"Why am I not surprised you two aren't waiting in the cabin for your ride home?" Will stepped out of the tractor and opened his arms wide for a hug. Sabrina went directly into them.

A minute later, the UTV caught up to the group, and Sabrina released Will when Elizabeth emerged from the vehicle. She came over and embraced Sabrina. "Cinnamon and the horses are doing well. We'd have been here sooner, but we went into emergency mode at the Double I after the blizzard. So far, so good as far as the cows and the other ranch animals are concerned. Even the stable cat and kittens are snug and accounted for."

Relief flowed through Sabrina about her horse and the other animals. "Thank you for looking after Cinnamon for me."

"As soon as we cut the log into three sections, the tractor did the rest, but what about you and the baby?" Will acknowledged Ty with a nod before pointing to her bump. "Are you okay?"

Sabrina reassured everyone, and Ty threaded his arm around Sabrina's shoulders. "Can we finish this discussion back at the ranch? We had to cut the generator's power last night. I don't want Sabrina to freeze."

With that, Will rushed over to the sled and loaded it in the rear storage area of the UTV. In minutes, Sabrina sat in the front next to Elizabeth while Ty and Phineas rode in the back. As much as she was thrilled to return home and see Cinnamon, the timing of Will and Elizabeth's arrival couldn't have been worse as she'd been on the verge of asking if he could care for her as Sabrina and not as Genie's mother.

But then again, that was the story of her and Ty's tempestuous relationship.

CHAPTER FOURTEEN

"CUT!" CARTER COMMANDED at the end of Friday's scene. "That's a wrap for Phineas. The rest of us report Monday for the closing shoot at Irwin Arena. We'll finish on the twenty-third come snow, sleet, rain, or shine."

Everyone joined in applause for Phineas. The camera operator dismantled the equipment for transportation while Robert hovered over Phineas, adding his accolades, the dog never leaving the trainer's side. Ty couldn't help but feel a little sad the dog would move on to his next role so easily, but he enjoyed every minute with the affable creature.

Ty headed for the wardrobe RV, but Robert called out his name. Curious, Ty held back.

"If there's ever anything I can do for you, just say the word. I can't thank you enough for taking such good care of him." Robert bent down and ruffled Phineas's fur. "Phineas is more than an actor. He's a splendid companion."

"He is the best." The dog's ears perked up, and he preened as if he knew Ty was praising him. "He guarded Sabrina and kept us company."

"If you're interested, Phineas has sired a litter that's about to be born. Taffy is also a bullmasador. I have claim to the pick of the litter, and I'd like you to have him or her. A gift from Phineas and me." Robert moved his hand, and Phineas barked like he was giving his seal of approval. "For you and Sabrina."

Ty didn't correct Robert's misunderstanding of his and Sabrina's relationship status. He started to turn down the offer, but stopped. The reason he'd never accepted responsibility for a dog was his firm belief he'd follow in the footsteps of his father and so forth. Now, he had a new lease on life. While not knowing what the future would bring was half the fun and beauty of the experience, he was now prepared to meet whatever it held with joy.

Even with the demands of the rodeo, he'd find time to train and take care of a puppy. Watching a pup grow up alongside Genie was too much of an offer to resist. "Thanks, I'll take you up on that."

Another advantage would be keeping in touch with Robert. He'd get updates on Phineas and share reports about the puppy's progress. A win all around.

The two exchanged information, and Ty couldn't wait to see Sabrina's face when he told her he was set to become a responsible pet owner. He neared the corral and watched Sabrina approach Cinnamon and feed her horse a carrot. Cinnamon's muzzle grazed Sabrina, and she leaned into the mare. The shared moment of affection hit Ty hard.

After finding out about the puppy, Sabrina was the first one he wanted to tell. When she believed he might be in danger, she prepared to defend him from the elk with her presence and an aspen branch. She turned a dinner of peanut butter sandwiches into the best meal of his life. His head spun, and the world flipped on its axis.

He was in love with Sabrina.

He might have started the twelve days as a way of winning back Sabrina's trust and ingratiating himself into the baby's life, but sometimes the future had a way of bucking up and taking you by surprise. Fun wasn't the same without her. He wasn't the same man without her.

While she was now willing to share Genie with him, that was no longer enough. He wanted to walk alongside her, reminding her of the fun in the minutiae of life while her grit grounded him in the important matters.

With a determined step, he'd see these twelve days through. Only by finishing what he started could he win back the trust of the woman he loved.

DESPITE HER BEST efforts to find some excuse to get out of escorting Ty to the Violet Ridge Holiday Pet Parade, here she was on her free Saturday afternoon, along with most of the town. Main Street was closed for the length of two blocks while tourists and residents alike scoped out the prime spots for watching.

Sabrina searched the crowd for Ty, intent on getting through to him that this experiment was at its end. The twelve days of charisma were fine when she needed to learn to trust him again, but she conceded that Genie needed her father in her life. In fact, he'd succeeded in his task too well. She now trusted him as a fixture in their daughter's life, but she could no longer trust herself around him. What could she do at this point? Ty loved Genie and would be a phenomenal father.

The problem was he cared for their daughter, but not her.

Somehow, she had to separate their lives once more.

Something honked at her from behind. Without warning, she stepped aside, and a scooter with a toy poodle in the basket passed her. Stumbling into someone, she murmured an apology and turned around.

"I'll catch you anytime." Ty's voice registered before he did.

The head rush she experienced almost made her go back on her stance to keep her distance. Since arriving home after being snowbound in the cabin, she'd tried convincing herself that their time together and that unforgettable kiss loomed larger in her memory, a result of the circumstances and not Ty himself. The kiss resulted from forced proximity and nothing else. He was a blizzard of activity when she wanted sunshine and stillness. They weren't meant to be. She righted herself and thanked him. "I can take care of myself."

"Yes, you can, but it's nice to have someone help once in a while."

His handsome face issued a distinct challenge. Was she up to sharing her life with him, meeting whatever came at them with this force that was always close to blowing her away?

In this moment, there was nothing she wanted more. She narrowed the gap between them, thankful for the extra inches her boots afforded her. Standing on her toes, she reached up, her lips finding his. No mere kiss, the contact with him warmed her despite the distinct chill of the winter air. This close, she breathed in the woodsy scent of him, and he deepened the kiss. Her head swirled with the giddy feeling of being on the precipice of something that could shield both of them from whatever life threw their way. They were both survivors, and they could face the future together.

With reluctance, she pulled away. "I guess looking out for each other can have its benefits."

He smiled and grasped her elbow while taking care not to bump her with either of the two portable chairs slung over his shoulder. "Come on, I used my sources to find out the best vantage point for the parade."

He led her to a spot where a pair of familiar Violet Ridge residents waved with all their might.

"Merry Christmas, Ty," Nelda said. Her coat was unzipped, allowing him a glimpse of her geometric red and fuchsia Christmas sweater.

"And Happy New Year, Sabrina," added Zelda. Her bright green hair matched her vivid jumpsuit. "My granddaughter's in the parade with her pet hamster…"

"They're the cutest little pair of elves you'll see today." Nelda finished her twin's sentence. "And Jaxon and his parents turned his wagon into a makeshift sleigh for his pet pug. Jaxon's rat had to stay at home, though. His father put his foot down."

Sabrina sent a silent thank you to Jaxon's father while Ty set up their chairs. Then he raised a picnic basket and winked at the sisters. "I have enough éclairs to go around." He motioned to Sabrina. "Take your pick."

With a murmured thank you, Sabrina settled in the navy chair. "Just let me sit here until the baby's born."

The festive sounds of bells alerted them to the start of the parade. Two elementary school students held a long banner announcing the tenth annual Violet Ridge Holiday Pet Parade. Ty leaned over and whispered, "Perfect for the tenth day of charisma."

Before she could tell him it was also the last day, he handed her an éclair and a grin.

For once, she let herself enjoy the moment. "Yes, it is."

The parade began in earnest, and Ty reached over and grabbed her hand. Together, they chuckled and compared notes while the procession passed them. Leading off the festivities were Robert and Phineas, riding along as passengers in a convertible. Robert threw out candy and smiled at their group. Behind them, elementary school students held their heads high while leading their Shetland ponies in fake antlers and red noses clipped to their halters. Following on their heels, owners held birdcages high while one family in matching candy-cane-striped pajamas accompanied their dog in a similar outfit.

Jaxon passed, pulling his pug in a sporty wagon decorated as Santa's sleigh. Nelda jumped out of her seat and yelled an effusive greeting. Jaxon waved back, his face lighting up as he spotted Ty, who clapped and raised both thumbs in approval. Sabrina marveled at the creativity. In no particular order or reason, dogs and goats strutted along Main Street with their owners. It was just good fun, and she got into the spirit.

Ty scooted his chair over to hers and leaned

closer. "Is that a rabbit in the crate decorated like a Christmas tree?"

She squinted and shook her head. "The side says it's a ferret."

"I love it!" Ty's breath caressed her cheek like fine cashmere.

He clapped while more goats swaggered past in their holiday finery. They were followed by a family with coordinated costumes, each dressed like a character from the Grinch, down to the toddler dressed like Cindy Lou Who. "The beagle looks just like Max."

"I can't wait to bring Genie to her first pet parade next year." He squeezed her hand. "We'll have so much fun."

The last group of dogs passed, their owners waving to the crowd, who began dispersing. Zelda rubbed her hands together. "Nelda, do you have any cider left in your thermos?"

"Not one drop."

Ty stood with a jaunty step. "I saw a booth that was selling warm beverages. I'll be back in no time." He looked at Sabrina. "Do you want cider or hot chocolate?"

"Surprise me."

He reached into his backpack and pulled out a thermal blanket. "This should keep you warm while I'm gone. I don't want the mother of my daughter catching hypothermia." With a wave, he was off in one direction before he doubled back, rolling his eyes with a chuckle. "You have me all mixed up."

Nelda sighed, and Zelda patted her chest. "Be still…"

"My beating heart," both sisters said in unison. Then their eyes grew wide at the same time.

"Did he just say…" Nelda began.

"What I think he said?" Zelda finished her twin's sentence. They faced each other and performed a high five.

Nelda did a little two-step in front of Sabrina. "Our favorite rodeo star will have another reason to visit Violet Ridge more often."

A light snow began to fall. Zelda reached into her purse and pulled out her woolen cap, tugging it on her bright green hair. "And the way he looks at you?" She winked at Sabrina, who shifted in the chair and realized this talk was bordering on the uncomfortable. "That's love, right there."

Sabrina used the opportunity and lifted herself out of the folding chair, only to fall back again. "He doesn't love me."

Nelda chuckled and patted Sabrina's arm.

"Of course he does. That boy has stars in his eyes."

"He acts like he just fell off the feistiest bull in the rodeo whenever he sees you." Zelda sighed, thumping her hand over her heart. "My Wayne was a keeper like Ty."

"Yep. Wayne looked at Zelda the same way Ty looks at you," Nelda confirmed while waving hello to a passersby, who greeted her and her twin. "I'm happy for the two of you. Ty's special, and we'd do anything for him."

Could the pair have a point? Did they see something in Ty's demeanor that proved he saw Sabrina as more than just the mother of his child? Their earlier kiss proved their relationship was taking on an extra dimension. She was no longer the little girl sitting at the window waiting for her mother to arrive at her birthday party. If she wanted the answer to whether Ty wanted a second chance, it was time to jump out of the barrel and make her presence known.

Ty HEADED BACK to the parade site, taking care and protecting from passersby a cardboard drink carrier filled with hot apple cider. A bevy of footsteps and a mass of giggles behind him alerted him that a group was in a hurry to pass him. He moved over, and a flash of bright yellow whizzed by him before coming to a halt in front of him.

"Eek! There you are!"

Somehow, he kept a grip on the drinks. A yellow parka with a hood lined with fake fur covered the face of the woman speaking, but Ty would recognize that voice anywhere. "Devon?"

His sister lowered the hood, her grin blinding. She reached out her arms and laughed when she noticed his hands were full. "Looks like I'll have to wait a little longer for a Ty hug."

"What are you doing here?" The joy at seeing her was replaced with a wiggle of worry. "Did Mom and Hal send you?"

"Nope." His mother's voice came from behind. "We came too. Merry Christmas, Ty!"

Mom and Hal appeared out of nowhere, and Ty grinned while keeping a tight grip on the drink holder. "Where's Peyton?"

Ty glanced around for the older of his two younger sisters. "Someone had to stay behind and keep the ranch running. Peyton insisted she wouldn't run the place into the ground. She did such a good job while we attended the rodeo finals, I agreed to her terms." Hal patted Ty's back. "Good to see you, son."

Shocked to his core, Ty had never expected his family here in Violet Ridge, especially considering the plethora of chores at the Juniper Creek Ranch. Speaking of family, there was something important he had to get out of the way before Nelda or Zelda announced his impending fatherhood on the Grandmas for Ty Fan Club social media sites. Sweat formed on his brow, and he inhaled a deep breath of that chilly mountain air.

"There's someone I want you to meet."

Mom chuckled and nudged Hal. "You were right. That was the reason he wanted to talk to us tonight." She came over and squeezed Ty's shoulders. "I was convinced you might quit the rodeo, but Hal guessed there's a special someone."

Two special someones actually, but words escaped him. Ty stood there petrified as if a two-ton bull was headed his way. Just like in the actual rodeo arena, Sabrina appeared out of nowhere and came to his rescue.

"I see more of your fans found you." Sabrina propped the folding chairs against the building and reached for the drink holder, accepting it from his grip. "Let me hold that for you in case they want your autograph."

It was Devon's turn to laugh. "Whoever this is, I like her. She came up with the solution about how to free Ty's hands, but I don't want an autograph. I'm claiming my Ty hug now."

His sister threw her arms around Ty's middle with the same enthusiasm she greeted everything in life. Sabrina's mouth dropped open, and her face asked a thousand questions. He hurried with the answers. "This is my sister Devon and my parents, Jenny and Hal Middleton."

Mom reached for the cups and sent a regretful glance Sabrina's way. "Thank you for holding those for Ty. I hope you don't mind if his family takes him away from his friends for the rest of the day. He has a big announcement for us."

A flicker of hurt crossed Sabrina's face while she handed Mom the drinks. "I wouldn't dream of taking Ty away from his family."

The double meaning was clear to him, and Ty stepped into the fray. "Mom, Hal, Devon, this is Sabrina MacGrath."

Hal extended his hand Sabrina's way. "Any

friend of Ty's is a friend of ours. Pleased to meet you."

"Likewise." Sabrina accepted the handshake and picked up the chairs. "Sorry you missed the pet parade. It was a lot of fun."

His mother composed herself and smiled, her hands now full with the cardboard drink holder. "That's our Ty. He lives for fun."

Exasperation rose in Ty. After winning two professional rodeo championships and celebrating his thirty-fourth birthday, his mother still viewed him as a fun-seeking thrill hunter. No matter that was how he'd seen himself for a long time.

Sabrina pulled herself up to her full height, her puffy turquoise coat hiding the baby bump. "Ty deserves more credit, especially considering how he defended us from an elk and dragged us over a mile so we could get to safety."

Everyone switched their gazes from Ty to Sabrina, and his heart swelled with love. Not only was she defending him, she was going on the offensive and spouting his merits. Could she have forgiven him for the way he broke up with her earlier this year and then going through the first seven months of her pregnancy, including being hospitalized with a bout of dehydration, alone?

Mom glanced at him. It was now or never. "By *us*, Sabrina means her and our daughter. We're having a baby."

CHAPTER FIFTEEN

THE STUNNED LOOK on Jenny's and Hal's faces only confirmed they were as shocked at Ty's announcement as she was. Sabrina reeled for the exact opposite reason. Ty hadn't informed them about the baby.

"I'm not leaving Violet Ridge until the baby's born." Ty reached out for the cup holder. "I was going to tell you tonight on the videoconference call."

Hadn't she learned not to judge him so quickly yet? If she was wrong about this, what else was she wrong about?

Devon clenched her fist and pulled it toward her chest like victory was hers. "I finally get the inside scoop about something before Peyton." She faced Sabrina. "I'm going to be an epic aunt. I want to know everything about you. Do you have any brothers or sisters? That doesn't matter. They'll still love me because I'm awesome. How did you meet Ty? Was it romantic? He has a romantic side, you know, but he doesn't show it to everyone. But duh, you obviously know him very well. I can tell you and I are going to be great friends."

Jenny placed her hands on Devon's shoulders. "Please excuse Devon. She said her first words early, and she's been our chatterbox ever since."

"I don't mind. I'm an only child." Sabrina reassured Jenny, while trying to regain her bearings and remember all the questions. "Ty and I met at the rodeo. I don't think you'd call it romantic, although Ty was flat on his back at the time." Her cheeks heated, and she rushed forward with her explanation. "I used to work as a rodeo clown, and we met when I rescued him."

Hal chuckled. "I'd have like to have seen that. When's the baby due? June? July?"

Snowflakes dotted her nose and melted on her warm skin. "She's due in January," she said.

Jenny coughed in a weak attempt to hide her obvious surprise, and then a blissful look descended on her face. "My first grandchild!" She reached over and hugged Hal. "Our first grandchild. A little girl."

Sabrina felt as though she was intruding on a family moment. "I'm sure you and Ty have a lot to talk about." She began backing away. "And I only took this morning off. I have to get back to work."

Jenny broke away from Hal and reached for Sabrina. "You're not getting away from me without a hug. If Devon's a chatterbox, I'm the family hugger." Jenny enveloped Sabrina in a firm embrace, the smell of ginger and cookies surrounding her, rather fitting for Genie's grandmother. "Can your boss spare you this afternoon? Wait, I thought you said you're a rodeo clown."

Another reminder of how she couldn't escape her past despite her feet planted firmly in the present. "I used to work as a rodeo clown. Now I'm the barn manager at the Double I Ranch, northwest of town."

Hal's eyes lit up like Christmas had arrived early. "Then we need to talk. I'd love to hear your ideas on training protocols for two-year-old colts and fillies. Peyton and I..." Despite her interest, Sabrina started shivering.

"Honey, Sabrina's getting cold." Jenny interrupted Hal with a smile.

Ty thrust the cup holder in Sabrina's direction. "The hot apple cider's probably cold by now, but it might still be warm."

She accepted one of the drinks. "Zelda and

Nelda were whisked away by their grandchildren."

Ty offered the other three to his family, and Devon pounced on one while people continued to file past them. "Thanks," the bubbly teenager said.

Jenny and Hal accepted the other two, and Ty threw the holder into a nearby compost receptacle. Sabrina tried once more to make a graceful exit. "It was a pleasure to meet you."

"Do you have family in the area?" Jenny pulled her back into the conversation.

Sabrina hedged her answer. "My best friend owns the ranch adjoining the Double I…"

She stopped talking when she heard her name. Whirling around, she found Evalynne and Mr. Irwin heading her way, and they were holding hands.

What had happened while she and Ty were snowbound in the cabin?

"I'm so glad we found you." Evalynne approached and stopped short. "Do you mind if I give you a hug?"

Still unsure of how this relationship would work, Sabrina accepted Evalynne's offer. One hug didn't change the past, but it might signal a new beginning. She nodded and let Evalynne envelope her in a hug, her gardenia scent different from Jenny's, but they'd both be part of Genie's future and that counted for something.

Evalynne broke away and motioned for Gordon to join her. "While you and Ty were at the cabin—" she hugged Gordon's arm "—we talked nonstop, and then he invited me to the pet parade today. Wasn't that a great show?"

"Excuse me," Devon interrupted Evalynne. "Has anyone told you how much you look like Evalynne? Except older and without as much eyeliner."

To her credit, Evalynne chuckled and grinned. "I've never met her face-to-face, but I'll take that as a compliment."

Jenny let out a sigh of exasperation. "Please don't mind my daughter Devon." She glanced at Sabrina and then at Evalynne. "I see the family resemblance. Are you Sabrina's mother?"

"Yes, I'm Evie MacGrath, and this is my friend, Gordon Irwin." Introductions commenced while Sabrina drank the still-warm cider.

The cinnamon tang helped her gather her senses around her while everyone exclaimed their surprise about the news. She met Ty's gaze, and he rolled his eyes. Then he held his hands together like a cradle and swayed them. *Are you okay?* he mouthed over everyone else's voices.

She nodded, and he reached for her. He pulled her under the canopy of the nearest storefront. "You look like you need a minute away from everyone."

"You're right." She watched the group as they laughed and exclaimed over the baby.

"That's settled." Gordon turned around and located Ty and Sabrina. He signaled them, and they returned to the fold. "Elizabeth and the grooms can cover you this afternoon so you can spend some time with Ty and his family."

Sabrina opened her mouth to protest, but Evalynne started talking first. "And Jenny and I are going to spend the afternoon planning an impromptu couples' baby shower." Evalynne's eyes sparkled, and Sabrina didn't doubt that she wanted a second chance.

"A shower? Thanks, but I have everything I need," Sabrina protested, not wanting to draw extra attention to herself.

Jenny and Evalynne looked at each other and giggled. "Oh, darling, it's not about what you need, and you always need more than you think you do. It's a party to celebrate!" Evalynne hooked her arm through Sabrina's.

"This is late notice," Jenny said. The snow was starting to come down with more force, and her knit hat was getting covered with white flakes. "Maybe we should settle for a family dinner party instead. If tonight works for everyone, that is."

"When are you going back to your ranch?" Evalynne asked. "Wyoming, isn't it?"

Jenny glanced at her husband. "Well, we were planning on heading back tomorrow morning."

"I know my wife too well." Hal placed his arm around Jenny's shoulders. "You want to stay with Ty and Sabrina, don't you?"

"If you don't mind being separated on our anniversary." Adoration reflected in Jenny's gaze as Hal reassured her he'd be fine doing just that. "With everything going on, I think we should reschedule the party, or cancel it altogether."

"Of course. That goes without saying. We'll plan a celebration next year for our first grandchild. After all, I plan on spending many more anniversaries with you." Hal squeezed her shoulder and kissed her.

"We can book a return flight for you, depending on availability with the holidays so close. Peyton or one of the ranch hands can pick you up at the airport, and Devon can stay with me." Jenny's eyes shone bright with excitement. "We'll take turns driving back in the SUV."

"Sounds like a plan." Hal nodded to Jenny and their daughter while Gordon looked at the skies, gray clouds accumulating by the second.

"How about we finish planning this event at my ranch?" Gordon offered. "From what I already know about Evie, she'll make it happen, even with the holidays fast approaching."

His face was filled with admiration, and his tone caused the group to disperse with a promise to meet at the main ranch house.

Was there something happening between her boss and Evalynne? Sabrina shivered about her job prospects once Evalynne decided it was time to move on for the sake of her career as she had once before.

Ty came over and wrapped his scarf around Sabrina, taking care to stay close. "I don't want you getting cold." Sabrina reveled in his gaze, and the rest of the group blurred as she focused solely on him, that smile of his for her and her alone.

Maybe the more important question was whether Ty would move on as he had earlier this year.

THE REST OF the weekend and Monday passed by in a whirlwind of activity. Starting work earlier than usual on Tuesday morning, Sabrina relished the silent time in the stable. This moment of the day when the dawn peeked around the snowcapped mountains and everything was still and calm, and starting anew. She used the ax and chipped away the light coating of ice on the trough outside. Then she put away the ax and made sure there was drinking water in each stall. When she fetched the bucket for carrying grain, she only filled it halfway. With this being the last week until she shifted to exclusively desk work, she took her time with her morning duties, avoiding anything too heavy to lift.

Spending time with the horses actually grounded her. They didn't want to know her opinion on whether she preferred pink and silver or pink and gold balloons for this evening's impromptu baby shower. They also didn't care if she had her gifts wrapped and under the tree, as tomorrow was Christmas Eve. For the record, she didn't.

She reached into her pocket and pulled out a handful of oats for Cinnamon, her mare relishing the treat, nuzzling her palm and giving a soft whinny. "I can't wait to go on a long ride, either." Cinnamon nudged her hand until Sabrina stroked her muzzle. "Okay, that's not all I want, but I can't have everything."

Last night, she'd dreamed of Irwin Arena, driving around the perimeter of the inside corral in her clown car before hunkering down in the barrel while Ty shot out of the chute on a ferocious bull. Then he fell off, and the bull pounded him before she could reach him. The bull set its sights on her when she catapulted awake. Her recurring dream was becoming more and more vivid, most likely on account of the last days of her pregnancy. Genie's security came first. She'd given up her former career for good.

Mews came from the rafters, and she climbed the first couple of steps and peeked into the loft where the stable cat tended her kittens. Happy and content, the cat laid on her side while the kittens clamored for milk and warmth. Life in the barn was enough for the cat, and it would be enough for Sabrina.

It would have to be. Someone had to keep both feet on the ground for their daughter's sake.

"Sabrina?" Ty's voice came from the doorway, and she stopped herself from falling off the ladder.

Her heart still racing, she climbed down the few steps and wiped the dust off her jeans. "Come see this." She gestured him over before placing her finger near her lips so he wouldn't make any noise.

From her vantage point, she watched his face light up upon seeing the mother cat and kittens. For a full minute, he stared at them before reaching for her hand. "New life is all around us," he said.

Sabrina let the warmth glide over her, and then she motioned for them to give the cat her privacy. She jerked her thumb toward her office. "Come with me."

They entered her office, and she checked her to-do list. Rising early after her nightmare and subsequent discomfort from not finding a comfortable position, she was ahead on her tasks.

"We're up to eleven pipers piping. Does eleven guests a-gifting count?" He leaned against the door frame and looked too good for someone who probably just got out of bed. The low lights of the stable caught the charcoal of his hair, setting off his deep tan from years of ranching and training outdoors. "I'd have asked you sooner, but we haven't had a moment to ourselves for the past two days."

"With good reason." She loved getting to know his parents and sister, and rightly so. They were delightful. "Your family drove all the way to Violet Ridge so they could hear your news in person."

That kind of unconditional love was priceless in her book.

"Hal couldn't get a flight out until today, so he'll miss the shower, but Mom and Devon are over the moon about the baby and the party." Relief settled on his shoulders. Until now, she hadn't realized how nervous he'd been about telling his family about Genie.

"They've worked hard to get everything ready." Kelsea and Will were coming tonight, along with everyone from Will's ranch, the Silver Horseshoe. "Gordon offered the main house, and the mountain backdrop at night will be spectacular."

"I've been talking to Gordon about local properties. He's agreed to put me in touch with some backers about the possibility of the training facility." Ty stepped into the room. "Zelda's also on board and offered her connections as former mayor."

What began as an off-the-cuff comment might be coming together. If he lived nearby, would that give them an opportunity for a second chance? Or would she have to endure seeing him settle down with someone else? "I'm glad Nelda and Zelda can come tonight."

"Hmm, there may be more than eleven guests a-gifting."

She settled into her seat and fought the urge to take off her boots and rub her ankles. "Ty, it's time to give up the ghost."

"Which one? The Ghost of Christmas Past, Present, or Yet to Come. We never finished reading that together. What about you and me and Dickens on Christmas night?" Ty's eyes sent a silent appeal.

"The ghost of the twelve days of charisma. We decided a long time ago you're going to have a role in Genie's life. There's no reason to go through with this any longer." Her soft sigh filled the air.

He walked over to where she sat and reached for her hands. His presence filled her small office. "Yes, there is." His warm fingers caressed the side of her jaw, and shivers skittered down her spine. "A very important reason to finish what we've started."

She gulped, the trust she once thought elusive now firm in her grasp. She was done running. "And what's that?"

"There's new life all around us, Brina. Those

kittens. Even Phineas is going to be a doggy daddy, and I'm adopting one of his puppies." His fingers continued their exploration of her skin, touching the delicate area around her earlobe, his heat searing into her. "I'm planning for the future. For you and Genie."

There it was. If only he'd stopped two words earlier, she'd be on cloud nine. She broke the contact between them. Instead, she bit the inside of her cheek to keep from groaning in frustration. "I'm happy for you, Ty."

"There's a *but* in there." He frowned, and a cloud came over those blue eyes.

"I want to believe in the possibility of us again."

"That's the beauty of this season. The possibility of more." He brought her close and waited until she nodded. Then his lips brushed hers, the kiss sweet and full of promise. It held hope and light and more.

"You don't play fair." She licked her lips, the taste of him lingering there.

That frown melted into a grin. "In the rodeo ring, always. Everything else in life is up for grabs." He steadied himself and gazed right at her. "Except for us. I don't want to let you go again. My spunky Sabrina."

His Sabrina.

"Then we need to look forward. To the future."

"I need to finish these twelve days first. For me, as much as for us. I'll up my game for these last two days." He dipped his head with a chuckle. "Until tonight, my lady."

With that, Ty left her office. The minutes ticked by, and she collected herself so she could get back to the horses. Her cell rang, and she glanced at the screen. Why was Luis Rodriguez calling so early the day before Christmas Eve?

"I'd have thought you'd be off for the holidays, especially since the start of the circuit isn't for another four months. Why the urgency since tomorrow's Christmas Eve?" she asked.

"We hired another rodeo clown, but he called last night. He can only work for the first part of the season. No one else has applied for the job, and I need someone reliable and experienced." Luis's desperation came through over the line.

"Thank you, but I have a job. Besides, I won't be able to train and get in shape until six weeks after the baby's born."

"That's why I'm calling now, so you can make arrangements." He laid out his terms, and she whistled at the generous offer. It was almost as stunning as Ty's exquisite kisses.

She was tempted to accept. She missed the rodeo so much. Hanging up her costume was like denying part of herself. If Ty was serious about the training center, she could teach other rodeo clowns, and Luis could have his pick of candidates. And yet she'd promised Gordon and Elizabeth she'd work for them. A promise was a promise. But tonight, at the shower, she could approach them. See if they could find someone else in a four-month time frame. Excitement at the thought of returning pumped her with joy. "I'll think about it."

They ended the call, and she hurried to get on with her day. While pouring Andromeda's feed, her wrist throbbed, the one she sprained two years ago. The baby kicked, and she knew the answer. There was no way she'd take that kind of risk in the rodeo ring with Genie so young. Her daughter's security meant too much.

She'd text Luis after Christmas with her decision not to return and let him know that it was final.

TY DELIVERED THE final line and pulled at the jacket lapels. Feeling more comfortable in the middle of Irwin Arena, which was practically his backyard, he delivered what he hoped was a winning smile to the camera. Only a limited area was set up like a rodeo with a yellow fence backdrop and red dirt. Extras from the town occupied seats in the stands, a touch organized by Carter with the help of Nelda and Zelda. Earlier this morning, Ty had gladly spent two hours posing with each person and signing autographs.

"That's a wrap on this Tuesday evening with six hours to spare before it's officially Christmas Eve. Thanks, everyone!" Carter stepped away from the camera. Everyone on the set applauded, including Ty.

After a brief speech to his fans thanking them for their time, he hurried to the costume trailer. The shoot had run longer than expected, and he only had an hour to get to the Double I Ranch where Elizabeth was officially hosting the couples' baby shower in her living room, although his mother and Evie had coordinated everything. It wasn't the typical baby shower, but Sabrina wouldn't be the typical mother, either. Few women would have ventured forth in the snow after a blizzard or wielded an aspen branch to defend him, not just herself, yet she endured the conditions for a chance at returning home. A special woman, indeed.

With not much time to spare, he needed to run downtown, pick up his chocolate éclair order from Emma, and Sabrina's Christmas present from Setting Sun Jewelers, a necklace with a turquoise heart and matching beads. On Christmas morning, he intended to bare his soul to her. That she had his heart and would have it always. Forget the Ghost of Christmas Yet to Come. The future wasn't about ghosts but grasping life by the horns with the people you loved.

The baby was a bonus, though. Loving Sabrina was the real prize, bigger and more important than any belt buckle. Sharing experiences with her was better than all the solo fun he'd had over the past thirty-four years.

His step became lighter, and he couldn't wait for the baby shower and the twelve days of charisma to be behind them. His genuine gift to Sabrina would be his love, if she wanted it.

"Ty!" At the sound of his name, Ty stopped and turned. Carter was heading his way, but why wasn't he breaking down the set and storing the equipment?

"I thought you'd be in a hurry to get back to

Denver." Ty waited until Carter reached him at the steps of the wardrobe trailer. "And your son's first Christmas."

"Yeah. Erin found him the cutest rocking horse. He's going to love it." Carter fished his phone out of his jacket pocket and brought up a picture.

"Could you ask Erin where she bought it? Genie might be ready for one of those next Christmas." Listen to him. What a difference a couple of weeks could make. Was he that surprised? After all, Scrooge had changed overnight. Or, at least, he thought that was how the story went. He and Sabrina still had a couple of staves left.

Carter nodded and entered the trailer with Ty. Maureen handed Ty a box of makeup remover wipes, and he plucked out two, thankful he'd be using these towelettes for the last time. Acting was now in the rearview mirror. Ty finished removing the layers of makeup, only to find Carter watching him, an expectant look on his face. "I have an offer for you. How about a few minutes at the Bighorn Blaze before I hit the road?"

Ty removed the jacket and handed it to Maureen, who hung it with the others. "I'm already late. I'm going straight to the Double I from here."

"I'll make this quick then. My production company has a full slate of projects next year, and we just signed a few more that would benefit from your dynamic presence."

Carter had trouble taking no for an answer. Ty just didn't love acting, and wouldn't miss it one bit. A knock on the trailer door halted Carter from expanding on his offer, but Ty didn't need to hear any more. While Maureen rushed over to the door, Ty faced Carter. "Thanks, but Gordon and I are touring a couple of properties for sale after Christmas. One more year on the rodeo circuit…"

Ty stopped talking as the shock from the arrival of his agent, Belinda, left him speechless.

"Merry Christmas, Ty. Let's talk about your acting career and the bottom line, shall we?"

CHAPTER SIXTEEN

JENNY AND EVALYNNE seemed pleased with themselves, and they should be. Sabrina couldn't believe how festive the Irwin ranch house living room looked, blending traditional holiday and baby shower decorations. Even the massive Christmas tree in the corner had been outfitted with pink lights. Walking over, Sabrina gasped as pacifiers and rattles and other gifts hung from the branches.

Evalynne separated herself from Jenny's side and joined Sabrina, handing her a cup. "A hot drink to warm you up."

"Thank you." Sabrina accepted it as couples began arriving. Will helped Kelsea with her coat while his uncle Barry did likewise with his new wife, Regina. Everyone waved, and Sabrina watched the door, waiting for Ty to show and sipping the wassail, the proportions of apple cider, orange juice and lemon juice blended to perfection. "This is delicious."

Evalynne raised her cup and clinked Sabrina's. "Gordon's chef is a wonder." Evalynne's cheeks grew red while her gaze crossed the room to where the rancher was speaking to his daughter. "I met the staff and the ranch hands during the blizzard. Gordon and I talked for hours."

As if on cue, Gordon came over and patted Sabrina on the shoulder. "Do you mind if I steal your mother away? I have some people I'd like Evie to meet."

Sabrina watched them walk away, Evalynne's whispered words bringing a boom of laughter she'd never heard out of Gordon before. Elizabeth sidled over to Sabrina's side. "My father is quite taken with your mother."

Concern for what would happen once Evalynne grew tired of the domesticity came over Sabrina. "I promise this won't impact my work."

Elizabeth waved Sabrina's concern away. "I just meant I haven't seen my father this happy since my mother died." She raised her cup and drank some wassail. "Then again, my father hadn't been happy for some time before that. They were separated when she was diagnosed with cancer."

"Oh." Sabrina softened and watched Gordon and Evalynne chuckling with Regina and Barry

Sullivan. "You don't talk about your mother often."

"I guess we need to become better acquainted since we're already friends." Elizabeth's ability to get to the heart of the matter was one quality Sabrina liked about her boss. "Is she staying here for Christmas or going to Texas to visit your grandparents?"

"Staying. My grandparents want me to visit with the baby after she's born. Evalynne offered to arrange a private flight." That type of generosity was beyond anything Sabrina had ever encountered, and she'd accepted for Genie's benefit.

Elizabeth sipped more of her wassail. "Will Ty be going with you?"

Speaking of Ty, where was he? All the guests had arrived, except for him. "I don't know. Excuse me." Sabrina made her way to the window and searched for any sign of Ty.

Since her maternity leggings didn't have pockets, she went into the office where a rack was located for guests' coats. She found hers and retrieved her phone from the pocket. No messages from Ty.

If the shoot had been held up at the arena with retakes, he might not have had the time to text her. She texted him and asked if he was on his way. *Nothing.* Not even three little dots. The baby kicked, almost as if begging her to give Ty the benefit of the doubt. Perhaps they were in the middle of a take, or he could be driving here.

Ty wouldn't let her down on purpose. Not this time. Not considering how he went out of his way to approach Emma to bake her favorite dessert. Or pulled a sled across a mile of snow so they could return to the ranch where she'd have a fighting chance to get to the hospital in case she went into labor. This new Ty was the one who laughed as they read *A Christmas Carol* while Phineas rested his head on her legs.

This Ty still made sure even the most strenuous activity was fun while caring for others and keeping them safe.

This Ty, who'd kissed her back.

Goose bumps dotted her arms, and she whispered the words for Genie's benefit. "I love your daddy. I love Ty Darling."

Holding on to her phone and grabbing her coat, Sabrina made her way back to the living room where Jenny and Evalynne passed around sheets of paper, asking guests to write a wish for the baby. A gracious gesture, and

Sabrina smiled while guests expressed their congratulations.

Ty should be here. She gazed out the window where drips from the icicles fell onto the snow-covered ledge.

Her phone pinged with an incoming text from Ty: Carter waylaid me. At Bighorn Blaze. Wish you were here.

No longer was she the same seven-year-old who waited by the window at her party for her mother.

Nor was she the same woman who stood by while Ty broke up with her. If he wanted her by his side, she would rise to the challenge. She turned and caught Evalynne's attention. Sabrina crooked her finger at her, and Evalynne murmured something to Gordon before heading her way.

"Do you remember a long time ago when you promised to sing at my birthday party?" Sabrina asked.

A shadow crossed Evalynne's face. "I'm so sorry for not coming that—"

"Yes, we need to clear the air later, but that's not what I'm getting at. I need you to stall everyone while I bring Ty to the party." Sabrina shrugged on her coat, the zipper getting tighter around her midsection. "Turn this into an Evalynne holiday party."

"You're asking me to sing?"

"From what I hear, you're pretty good at it." Sabrina reached into her pocket for her gloves. "Ty needs my help."

Evalynne looked at her midsection. "Is it car trouble? Should we send Gordon or your friend Will?"

"Not that kind of help." She reached for her mother's arm and squeezed. "But thank you."

AT THE BIGHORN BLAZE, Ty tapped his boots on the sticky tile floor under the scarred wooden table. Carter and Belinda ordered dinners and soft drinks, indicating they thought they'd all be here for a while. Ty knew otherwise and stuck with water. He'd extract himself from the discussion as soon as he could do so politely. As it was, he'd arrive late at the baby shower. He might have missed it when Sabrina found out about the baby and the gender reveal, but he would not miss out on this night. Ty fiddled with the paper from the straw wrapper, only half-listening to Belinda.

"In lieu of participating in the rodeo, acting in two more commercials for the clothing line along with ads for three of your sponsors is guaranteed. So is a screen test for the hit show on that streaming service. I also have a nibble from the producer of a movie about the early days of the rodeo." Belinda produced a tablet from her voluminous tote, entered the passcode and swiped the screen open. "She saw the daily rushes from the commercial and thinks you'll be the next big thing."

Ty already was a big thing in the rodeo, if he did say so himself. That was, if he didn't sound like he was too large for his cowboy hat. There was nothing like the second of calm in the chute before it opened. When the arena's bright lights and the smell of the dirt rose up and greeted him and the beast before they performed their dance. He loved the rodeo and his fans almost as much as he loved Sabrina.

He'd had enough. "Thanks for driving here on the day before Christmas Eve, but there's somewhere else I need to be."

"Want a ride, cowboy?" The husky voice behind the table belonged to the woman he loved, the spunky rodeo clown whom he wanted to spend the rest of his life with.

"Aren't you Sabrina MacGrath? I never forget a face from the rodeo." Belinda rushed to her feet and extended her hand. "I'm Belinda Wasilewski, Ty's agent."

"Perhaps all of this can wait until after Christmas. You see, Ty has a previous commitment, and I'm here to take him home." Ty faced Sabrina, her slow but sure smile a confident sign she knew she was in control of the situation. Rather than leaving the Bighorn Blaze like she had when she saw him with the blonde, she came over and trusted him.

He'd never loved her more.

Belinda went over to the next table and asked if she could have the chair. She came back and patted the seat. "Ty's screen test is scheduled for the first week of January, so it can't wait. The directors wanted a signed agreement yesterday."

Ty was done. He and Sabrina had a shower to attend. Sabrina, though, unzipped her coat and accepted the chair. "I figured out pretty quickly acting is fun, but it's not where my heart is. It's here in Violet Ridge," Ty said.

"Then let's discuss the magazines that want to interview you before the start of the season." Belinda glanced at Ty, then Sabrina, and then her gaze went to the baby bump. Her mouth dropped.

"Yes, our baby is due next month." With

all his success with the rodeo, the title of father was the one he cherished the most. That was, until he could change his and Sabrina's relationship status and he became her boyfriend, and eventually maybe even her husband someday. Sooner rather than later, if they were both willing.

"Then you must be a part of the magazine interviews." Belinda looked at Sabrina. "I can see the spread now. Please stay and talk some sense into Ty. There's financial security on the line."

While he loved Belinda's enthusiasm, he accepted himself and his love for the rodeo. For the first time, he was open to what the future presented and couldn't wait to get back to the circuit until he opened that training center.

Sabrina rose from the chair. "We have somewhere we need to be. Anyway, I'm retired from the rodeo."

"I have connections, and I'm sure we can get you back after the baby is born." Belinda swept aside the drinks and pulled out her phone. "What's your event?"

"I'm not a contestant. I used to be a rodeo clown. Thank you for the kind offer, but Luis Rodriguez contacted me yesterday. Wait a second. I thought—" A shadow crossed Sabrina's face, and she stared at Ty. "We should be on our way. They're expecting us."

Her voice became icy. He couldn't blame her, as this baby shower was important to her. She was probably thinking of another spoiled party. This time, though, he was the root of the problem.

"I enjoyed working with you, Ty." Carter stood and threw some bills on the table. "But I need to be on my way so I can kiss my son good night and spend some time with Erin."

"We'll videoconference after the holidays." Belinda placed her phone in her purse and followed Carter out the door.

Ty reached into his wallet for his portion of the bill when he felt Sabrina's gaze boring into him. He added his money to Carter's and waved at the server with a grin. Then he reached for his coat on the hook next to the table. "I can't wait for next year. I can already feel it. It'll be the best yet. I have an extra reason to prove my mettle."

"I know. Genie." The exasperation came out in her voice. "She's the reason I'm telling Luis that I'm rejecting his offer."

They went outside where the bitter cold stung his cheeks. He walked with her to her

Subaru. She hurried into the driver's seat, her hand on the door. He stopped her from shutting it. "Why do you keep rejecting Luis? You're my favorite rodeo clown."

"And I don't understand why you're returning instead of going out on top." Sabrina emerged from the car, misty puffs of her breath evaporating in the air. "You could break a leg, sustain a concussion, or worse."

"I trust myself and my training. That's why I want to open that center down the road. Two years sounds about right."

"And what about then? Will you still need one more year on the circuit so you won't disappoint your fans?"

Ty reached into his pockets and pulled on his gloves. He connected the puzzle pieces in his mind. "You don't trust yourself. And you don't trust your training to keep you safe in the arena."

She blinked and fiddled with the ends of her turquoise scarf before barking out a harsh laugh without snorting. "Of course I do."

The energy sapped away from him, and he realized he didn't know this Sabrina, the one who played it too safe. "I remember meeting a woman who jumped out of barrels with the confidence and grace of a gazelle, putting herself in danger while trusting her instincts and training. I fell in love with the woman who lowered herself into a sled in a blizzard, trusting that we would do the best we could for our daughter together. There's an element of risk in everything we do, but we depend on our experience and our training. You're a rodeo clown at heart, and you love the sport."

"I love our daughter and want to give her a good home." Fire entered her tone. "Fun and games are all well and good for twelve days, but what happens when the crowds are gone?"

"Then I leave with grace, knowing I gave it my all, happier for the experience. There's something wrong with turning your back on who you are because you're afraid. I know that better than anyone, because for years I was afraid of leaving people behind who might miss me, but that's no way to live." His shoulders slumped, and his heart shattered into a million pieces. The word *goodbye* hung in the air. This time, though, it came with a sense of permanence.

This time, though, it was so much worse as he'd tasted the sweetness of forever at the cabin.

Sabrina sat in the driver's seat once more, her coat almost touching the steering wheel.

"I'm going to the shower now. After the holidays, we'll work out the best agreement *for Genie*."

He watched as her Subaru left the parking lot. He'd told her he'd fallen in love with her, and yet she thought the twelve days were only about fun and games to him when they meant so much more.

CHAPTER SEVENTEEN

CHRISTMAS EVE DAWNED BRIGHTLY, but the day didn't hold any luster for Sabrina. She headed to the Double I stable, yet her favorite place wasn't a refuge like it normally was. Dreary skies and falling snow were convenient excuses that she could fall back on. Blaming the weather for the surrounding dreariness would be a lie, though. She'd fallen for Ty, who was just like her mother, choosing fun over security, and her.

She checked on the horse feed and paused. She wasn't giving Ty the credit he deserved. Ty didn't choose fun over her, even though it felt like he did. The rodeo, with its crowds and excitement, was a world in itself with constant motion. She loved it, too, but someone had to be the adult and look out for Genie. Her grandparents had stepped into the fray when Evalynne pursued her career. She'd be Genie's anchor, the same as the growing kittens relying on their mother for protection and safety.

"Would you like some help? I know my way around the stable." Evalynne broke the silence.

Sabrina caught her breath, her heart racing at the surprise of another person being in the stable. "I didn't hear you."

"No wonder, considering how your mind seems elsewhere." Evalynne's bright pink coat matched her high boots etched with pink curlicues, both coinciding with the rosy tones in her cheeks. "Gordon and I finished an early morning walk, and I excused myself when I saw you enter the stable."

Sabrina closed the bin and made a note for the next order. "You and Mr. Irwin seem to be getting very close."

"We have a lot in common. He's a good man. Kind and understanding. I'm excited to see where the new year will take us." Evalynne stood by her side. "Can I do anything for you? Carry something?"

"I'm good." Sabrina moved out of the storage room and headed toward the horses. Her mother followed her to Cinnamon's stall. "Can this wait until later?"

Evalynne searched Sabrina's face. "Last

night you were rather upset and went to sleep before we had a chance to talk."

Sabrina grabbed the shovel, her nostrils flaring. "Isn't it a little late for this concern?"

"Yes, and no." Evalynne pulled down on the brown-and-pink knitted hat until it covered her ears. Then she took the shovel from Sabrina and started cleaning the stall. "This brings back memories. You can't take a ranch away from a country girl, though."

"But it wasn't enough, and you chose fame over…" Sabrina stopped short of saying *me*.

"You." Evalynne completed the thought for her. "Yes, I did, and I regret that. I emphasized success over everything. Once my first album was out, I visited Mom and Dad, intending on moving you to Nashville with me. You were about ten, and I saw you riding your horse with the wind in your hair and a smile lighting up your face. Mom said you were secure with them. I couldn't offer you that kind of stability, so I faded into the background."

This was the first she'd ever heard about that. And yet there had been so much Evalynne could have offered Sabrina. Security was only part of what a child needed.

Oh, no. Sabrina had valued security so much she turned her back on what she loved.

That part of her that loved being a rodeo clown was as intrinsic to her nature as anything else. That was what Ty had meant last night. Her eyes misted over, and she faced her mother, who was wiping her tears with her coat sleeve.

"Music is your passion. It gives you purpose," Sabrina said.

Her mother placed the shovel next to the wall.

"So do you. I thought I was doing the right thing, allowing your grandparents to raise you." Her mother's clear voice grew husky with emotion, and Sabrina couldn't hold back any longer.

She flew into her mother's arms, the baby the only barrier between them, and yet it was only fitting that the three generations came together like this. "I've missed you."

Her sniffles filled the stable, and Cinnamon neighed as if checking to make sure everything was okay. Evalynne reached into her pocket and pulled out a pack of tissues, handing one to Sabrina. After blowing her nose, Sabrina reassured Cinnamon.

"You'll make a wonderful mom. Trust your instincts." Evalynne plucked out a tissue and daubed at the corners of her eyes.

"Ty said the same thing last night." Sabrina's throat tightened so that it hurt to speak.

Evalynne led Sabrina into her office and pulled the spare wooden chair alongside the desk chair. She stroked her daughter's hair while Sabrina poured out her regret about what might have been, her eyes closed with the weight of Ty's goodbye pressing on her. Sabrina sniffled, and Evalynne held on tight. "Ty's emergency must have been massive for him to stay away last night. I haven't seen anyone look that much in love in a long time."

Sabrina opened her eyes and shook her head. "Everything he's done, he's done for Genie. He's told me so quite often."

"Oh, honey." Evalynne patted Sabrina's hand. "If he was in Violet Ridge for Genie, he'd have been at the shower last night. What happened between the two of you?"

Sabrina recounted the events at the Bighorn Blaze. "Then he talked about falling for a woman who jumped out of barrels, but it can't be all fun and games, can it?"

Evalynne let go of Sabrina's hand and squinted. "Isn't it best when what you're good at is what you love doing? Don't deny yourself for anyone, especially yourself. Isn't being true to yourself worth the risk?"

Sabrina reached into her desk drawer for more tissues. "It's too late."

"Is it? If I thought it was too late for us to become friends, I wouldn't be in this office with you, and you wouldn't be offering me a second chance. You're opening your heart to me, and that makes me very happy even though I hate seeing you so sad." Tears clouded her eyes, and she accepted a tissue from Sabrina. "I hope you can call me Mom again someday but, for now, how about Evie instead of Evalynne?"

Sabrina wanted to believe Evie had changed. After all, Scrooge had changed. She knew the gist of the ending, even if she and Ty would never finish reading the book together. Those days at the cabin tugged at her heartstrings as much as missing out on the twelfth day of charisma.

Was it too late for her and Ty? He changed for the positive, but looking back, her insecurity had barreled down on her like a bull.

An idea took shape. There might be hope yet. "Evie, I'm going to need your help." And Nelda and Zelda. On Christmas Eve, no less. There was a slim chance for her and Ty, and the baby kicked as if telling her she had to try.

But she wasn't trying for Genie.

She was trying for herself.

Ty LOADED THE last suitcase in the cargo area of Mom's four-wheel-drive SUV. He'd return to Violet Ridge closer to the baby's due date. For now, he'd head to Wyoming and spend the holidays with his family. Why did he have such an empty hole since this was what he'd wanted? Spending Christmas Eve at Juniper Creek Ranch had been his intention the whole time. With a regretful glance at the bunkhouse, he slammed the liftgate.

The problem was his family was here in Violet Ridge.

"Christmas Eve on the road might not be the way you wanted to spend your anniversary, but barring any disasters, I should get you home to Dad by the stroke of midnight." Ty headed toward the driver's door.

Mom reached out and stopped him. "Ty, what's wrong? You didn't get home to the guesthouse until after midnight, and you didn't make an appearance at the holiday party."

"You mean baby shower." Ty clenched his jaw and wondered what was keeping Devon. They had a long day of driving ahead.

"Evie turned it into a Christmas Evalynne party instead of a baby shower." Mom grinned and then the smile faded. "My grandchild's other grandmother is Evalynne. How can I compete with that?"

"It's not a competition, Mom. Just be yourself, and the baby will love you." *Being yourself.* That was what the past two weeks had been about, but while he'd been busy finding his future, Sabrina had been busy holding on to the past.

"You've come a long way since you were eight, Ty. I'm proud of you." Mom hugged him and patted him on his back.

"A long way how?" He separated from her, confusion gripping his insides.

"After your father died, you had the weight of the world on your shoulders. You tried to do everything for me, make everything fun, but you never said you were doing it on my behalf. It was always 'well, Dad would have wanted you to smile more' or 'Dad always rode quarter horses. We should go ride for fun.' I'm glad you're not hiding anymore."

"Back up. I don't remember doing that."

Mom nodded. "You hid behind someone else, thinking you'd seem the stronger for it."

Then the baby will get enchiladas.

There's no way I'm leaving Violet Ridge until the baby's born.

I'm planning for the future. For you and Genie.

Snippets of his words to Sabrina echoed in his mind. Although he'd done everything to get back into Sabrina's good graces, he'd masked his feelings for her and projected Genie onto everything he'd done. No wonder she craved security on her own two feet. Her mother had abandoned her, and then he'd never given her a reason to believe in them. "How did I not see this sooner?"

"Honey, you were eight. I had to work through my grief and help you with yours, although there are days I don't think I did a good job. You held back from love for so long, claiming you were too busy having fun." Mom bit her lip, her anguish for him written all over her face, her caring maternal side, front and center. He hoped he could be a good dad in that same way someday.

His legs wobbled, and he leaned against the car, the cold metal penetrating through the layers of his clothing. He planted his face in his palms. "I kept telling Sabrina I was committed to the twelve days of charisma for Genie, but I did it for her."

"Have you told her that?"

"No. I always brought up the baby whenever

we were together. I never told her I love her, *Sabrina MacGrath*, simply because she's Sabrina." His stomach clenched as, once again, he might have let the best thing in his life slip through his fingers. "And it gets worse."

"This sounds serious. Maybe we should finish this discussion inside where it's warmer." She shivered, and he bustled her inside the guesthouse.

They hung their coats and scarves on the tree by the front door. The enormity of last night weighed on him. Instead of being honest with Sabrina about his feelings, he pushed aside her stated desire to remain on the ranch as barn manager. He must have seemed like he was forcing her into a choice where it was the rodeo or nothing while couching everything in terms of the baby.

"I lost her again." Ty sank onto the plush leather couch, and numbness pierced every inch of him. "She wants Genie to have a secure home, and I told her she was denying herself, same as I was telling you to have fun when you needed to grieve."

"Oh, honey." She sat next to him and patted his shoulder. "She needs your support, but she needs to know you support her as Sabrina and not just as Genie's mother."

He sat straight and wiped his chin with his hands, the thick stubble coming in strong. What should he do? Should he give Sabrina room and leave until the holidays were over? She needed his unconditional support, but how could he prove he loved her for her?

The twelfth day of charisma. He had one more chance, and he stopped. Those days were over. Their purpose revolved around Genie, whom he loved and couldn't wait to meet, but this was about him and Sabrina.

He racked his brain about how to show his support for her and her needs. Perhaps he should go to Wyoming and talk to Hal. It was time to put fun and games in the rear-view mirror. An adult would use this time to regroup. Maybe he should do just that.

His mom's phone rang out a chime. "Devon." She excused herself and went into the other room for the call.

She returned, concern written on her brow. Ty stiffened, his worry for his impetuous and loving sister at full alert. "Is something wrong with Devon? Is she okay?"

"She ran an errand this morning, but she's ready to go home for Christmas now and told me where to pick her up. We'll say our good-byes to you and be on our way." Mom searched his face, long and hard. "Because I have a feeling you're not coming home to Juniper Creek with us."

"I have to stay and tell Sabrina how much I love her." He bit his lip, an idea coming to mind. It was risky, but Sabrina was worth it. "Text Devon. I have to make a quick stop first."

He had to try to merge their past and their future. Somehow, he'd convey his heart to Sabrina without relying on his usual standard of fun and games. His Christmas and their future depended on it.

CHAPTER EIGHTEEN

ON THIS CHRISTMAS EVE AFTERNOON, Ty intended on finding Sabrina after he said his goodbyes to Devon. That shouldn't be too hard as, no doubt, Sabrina would be at the stable, feeding Cinnamon her special holiday horse cookie, a blend of pumpkin, apple cider and oats. Ty tapped the two gift boxes on his lap. Maybe, just maybe, she'd gift him the chance of telling her exactly how he felt. No pretense, no artifice, no fans. Just the truth about how he felt about her.

That she was the special woman who'd rescued him in the arena and then rescued him from a promise that kept him frozen like the elk in the cabin.

If she'd listen to him. No fun, no games. Just straight talk out of the chute.

He frowned when his mother drove in the direction of the guesthouse rather than taking the main road toward town. "Where did Devon say to pick her up?"

Mom continued on the wrong path. "Your sister had a conference call with Hal and me while you were in town." She adjusted the stick shift of the four-wheel-drive. "She's decided to take a gap year away from college."

"What? Why didn't you tell me? Why didn't she tell me?"

"It seems as though everyone was waiting for Christmas Eve for their announcements. It's just as well that we postponed our anniversary celebration. Peyton wants to introduce Angus cattle to our ranch, Devon is taking a year off and you're going to be a father." Mom huffed out a breath. "Really, this is too much excitement."

"What's she going to do? Work on the ranch?" That didn't sound like something Devon would love, but he'd support whatever she chose to do.

"She's been presented with an opportunity of a lifetime. She didn't need our approval, but she wanted it and has it." Mom kept her eyes on the road. This was not the way to Violet Ridge.

"You're going the wrong way."

"Am I?" She inserted a little too much sweetness into those two words. Something was happening, but what?

"Mommm." Ty drawled out the word, but

then something on the side of the road caught his attention.

He rubbed his eyes. What looked like a group of high school band students in full uniform came into sight. Each was playing a small instrument. A triangle? Like the ones on a dude ranch that announced mealtimes? One, two. Ty continued silently counting in his head until he arrived at twelve.

He blinked and shook his head. "Did you see twelve kids playing triangles on the side of the road?" He didn't get much sleep last night, and it showed.

"Hmm. Isn't a triangle a percussion instrument? In a way, I guess that makes them twelve drummers drumming." Mom laughed at her joke but kept driving.

Whatever was happening, his mother was in on it. A group of older men in cowboy hats, coats and boots stood in a row with ropes a flying. Ty counted to eleven. "I'm not hallucinating, am I? You saw eleven men with ropes, right?"

"Eleven lads a-lassoing. Pretty cute." Mom grinned.

She continued driving along the road that seemed familiar. It should, since it led to the cabin where he'd been snowbound with Sabrina, the same one where he pulled her on a sled with Phineas.

They passed a group of kids performing jumping jacks, and Ty didn't even bother to count. He didn't need to since Jaxon held up a sign. Ten Lads a-Leaping: The Twelve Days of Cowboy Christmas.

"That's Jaxon. He's Nelda's grandson," Ty said. "The Grandmas for Ty Fan Club must be behind this. This must be their way of saying Merry Christmas." Nelda and Zelda went through a lot of trouble for him.

"Hmm." Jenny waved at Jaxon while keeping one hand on the steering wheel. "If you say so."

From there, they passed nine cloggers clogging, followed by a sizable group holding up stuffed cows and glasses of milk. Ty laughed. "Eight maids a-milking. I have to give Nelda and Zelda credit for originality." Down the road, he spotted Will Sullivan in what looked like a heated discussion with someone. "Slow down, Mom."

She stopped the SUV, and Ty cracked the window, only to hear Will in a heated discussion with his wife, Kelsea. "Is everything okay?" Ty asked.

Kelsea waved her cell phone around, and

Ty could make out sounds of birds chirping. "Hold those up, Will."

"If I didn't love you so much, I'd be at the ranch in front of the fire," Will grumbled as he held up five of his rodeo championship buckles. "Ho ho ho. Five golden buckles. Bah humbug."

"You have to sing it. Five. Golden. Buckles." Kelsea laughed and wrapped her bright yellow scarf around Will. "You love being part of this and you know it."

"Anything for you and S—"

"A certain someone," Kelsea interrupted her husband with a kiss. Then she stepped back and bent down to the package at her feet. She handed a box to Ty. "Merry Christmas!"

Inside the box were four kazoos, which must represent the calling birds. Kelsea brought one out of her pocket and blew the final notes of "The Twelve Days of Christmas."

Will winced but then gave Kelsea a look of love that sent Ty reeling. What would Sabrina think of all of this? She'd love every minute. More than anything, he wanted to share this time with her.

Mom pressed on the gas once more, and her Subaru made its way past three kids in giant coats, all pretending to cluck like hens.

Around the bend stood Nelda and Zelda, each with one dove knitted in yarn attached to their knit hats. They pointed toward their heads and mouthed something. Finally, Ty understood. Two turtledoves.

Then his heart went pitter-patter as he made out a lone figure on the cabin's porch. As Mom parked the SUV, he could see more clearly. A person in a baggy flannel shirt and patched denim jeans sat on a rocking chair, in front of it, a miniature Christmas tree decked out with colorful lights. The red clown nose didn't disguise the glow on her face. What was Sabrina doing here?

"Only one way to find out, isn't there?" Whether his mother read his mind or he'd said that question aloud, he wasn't sure. Mom leaned over and kissed his cheek. "Someone obviously loves you very much to organize this type of event on Christmas Eve. Merry Christmas, Ty."

Of course. "Thanks, Mom."

He gathered the two gift bags from the floor and paused with his hand on the door, soaking in Sabrina's presence. The white of the snow reflected off her face, and he etched the glow into his memory. Just the sight of her filled him with a sense of calm, ironic since they'd met when she rescued him from a charging bull.

She was everything he ever wanted, and everything he never thought he'd have. Just her. He loved her for her, and he'd support whatever she wanted to do.

Now it was time to let her know just that.

SABRINA CALMED THE fluttering nerves in her stomach. From her vantage point on the porch, she saw Nelda and Zelda send a positive signal her way before everyone started dispersing to enjoy the rest of their Christmas Eve. What was taking Ty so long?

Soon he headed toward her, two gift bags in hand. She popped off the chair as gracefully as she could manage.

"On the last day of Christmas, my true love gave to me, a rodeo clown on a pine tree." She finished singing and honked her red nose.

Donning her old oversized work shirt had been a revelation. Instead of dread, a sense of relief bordering on freedom flowed through her. This was part of her, the same as her mother's musical talent was part of her. Denying this was denying who she was. Ty had denied love for so long, fearful of others grieving for him, that he'd turned her away.

She accepted herself and gave herself the freedom to reach for the stars.

It was time for her to take charge and grab her future.

When she was inches from him, he whispered her name. Was that a whisper of futility or the whisper of hope?

"I need to know, Ty." Courage she'd forsaken for the safety net of security once again flooded her. Or maybe it had always been there, and she only needed to be reminded of who she was. "Why did you commit to the twelve days of charisma? Was Genie the only reason?"

"Experiences aren't the same without you. For so long, I lived for today, for fun and excitement, but that only goes so far without something tangible and real behind it. I found myself when I found you." He kissed her, his touch flooding her with something tangible, something whimsical yet real. He stopped, his lips near her ear. "I love you, and I'll support whatever you decide. If you don't want to go back to the rodeo, I understand."

She stepped back, and her nose fell into his hands. They both laughed. "You were right, Ty. You stopped living when you were eight, out of fear someone might grieve for you, and I stopped living eight months ago out of that same fear. We both had to find our true selves and leave the chute." She grinned. "Even though I will hide under a clown outfit gladly when I return to the rodeo."

Without a word, she plopped the round red clown nose back on her face.

"You, Sabrina MacGrath, have my heart for always." He presented the two bags to her.

"What's this?"

"Your Christmas presents a day early." He looked behind him but, from her vantage point, she could see everyone had already left. "You just gave me mine. You're the true love in the song, aren't you?"

"Yes." She peeked into the bags. "You didn't have to get me anything."

"But what if I claim this?" He reached into the bag and pulled out an éclair. "Are you sure you don't want this?"

"We could share it." She licked her lips. "It's better when you share something you love with someone you love."

Snowflakes started gathering in intensity, and he pulled out the other gifts. "Open them."

"It's a day early." Her protests sounded full of awe and wonder.

"That makes it even more daring and fun."

His grin reached his eyes, twinkling even brighter than the star atop the Violet Ridge Christmas tree. "The big one first."

She ripped off the paper and found a copy of *A Christmas Carol*. Her squeal echoed on the porch. "We never finished reading it."

"I want to start a new tradition with you. Every year, we can reread it together." Earnestness was written on every inch of his face. "Just the two of us. You and me."

"And what's this?" She rattled the long oblong box and unwrapped it in a second flat. The smooth velvet box hinted of jewelry within.

Opening it, she found a necklace of beautiful turquoise beads and a massive turquoise heart, and he placed it around her neck. "Whenever you wear it, you'll carry my heart with you."

He set the gift bags on the chair and pulled her toward him. Snowflakes dotted the surrounding air, and he kissed her, the promise of a future making the kiss the sweetest ever.

She touched the charm against her chest. "I didn't get you anything."

"Of course you did. The Twelve Days of Cowboy Christmas. How did you do it?"

"Zelda and Nelda helped with everything. The Grandmas for Ty Violet Ridge Chapter loves you, and so do I." She kissed him again, giving her entire self. Love involved an element of risk, and she was up for the experience of a lifetime.

She broke away from Ty first. Her back had that funny ache in it, the same ache as it had five minutes ago and six minutes before that. She'd attributed it to sitting on the front porch waiting for Ty, but could it be...? This time, it wasn't Braxton-Hicks. "I have a feeling we're getting one more present today."

Recognition dawned on his face. "Now?"

She felt her water break, and she nodded. "Let's go meet our daughter."

EPILOGUE

THE FOLLOWING MAY, a crowd filed into the Irwin Arena for the last night of the Violet Ridge Rodeo Roundup. From his vantage point behind the chute, Ty looked out at the seats and located his sister Devon, with Genie on her lap. Devon bent over and cooed something into her niece's ear before placing a pair of baby noise-canceling earmuffs on Genie. During her gap year, she agreed to become the auntie nanny to her now five-month-old niece, receiving a salary that would help fund her tuition for the early education degree she intended to pursue.

Thankfully, Genie had arrived safely on Christmas Eve, and he'd been by Sabrina's side for the birth. In the hospital room, he watched the two, amazed at his daughter, who was as beautiful and spunky as her mother. Already, Genie was pulling herself up to stand, and soon she'd be crawling all over their trailer on weekends, their temporary home away from, well, their temporary home. Soon enough, though, construction would begin on his, Sabrina and Genie's permanent dwelling in Violet Ridge on fifty of the prettiest acres waiting for the rodeo training facility. He'd teach competitors, and Sabrina would guide those who wanted to become rodeo clowns.

Footsteps sounded from behind, and then Sabrina made her way to his side, resplendent in her baggy jeans and oversize flannel shirt. "Howdy, cowboy. Haven't I seen you somewhere before?"

She pointed to the giant screen over the rafters where his one-and-only commercial ran on a continuous loop, and then they laughed together. "Yeah, I recognize you, MacGrath. You came with me to pick up our new puppy yesterday."

"Ah, that's where I've seen you before. In the hallway cleaning up after him while I changed our daughter's diaper. I knew you looked familiar, Darling." She grinned before her face assumed a serene look of contentment. "I missed this."

His wife waved around at the lights and the fans, the smell of the dirt and animals rising and filling the air with a tangible excitement, an experience like no other.

"I know." He faced her and encircled her with his arms. "We both love the thrill of the moment, followed by going home to the ones we love."

"Will you be content teaching others?" She looked up at him with those big brown eyes, larger versions of their daughter's.

"You, Belinda and I worked out a schedule that combines the best of both worlds." They'd keep their hand in enough rodeos as long as they wanted to compete while running the training facility for the rest of the year, a permanent home base for Genie and themselves, as well as any siblings that might join Genie in the future.

The lights dimmed before the spotlight shone on the master of ceremonies in the middle of the arena.

"Ladies and gentlemen, we have a special guest to start the night off right." The emcee spoke into the mic and the crowd responded with cheers. "Here to sing 'Misty Mountain' for us is the world-famous country music sensation, Evalynne."

Fans stomped as his mother-in-law entered from the other side of the arena, waving to one and all. She picked up her Gibson guitar and settled the instrument against her body.

"Good evening, Violet Ridge." The sound system amplified her soft voice, and she waved in Genie's direction. "You've opened up your arms to my family and me, and I love you for that."

The applause grew to a thundering pitch, and Sabrina moved in front of him, her back now pressed against his chest. "Is Genie okay?"

"She's wearing her earmuffs," Ty reassured Sabrina.

They turned their attention back to the ring where Evalynne situated herself on the stool in the center of the arena. "I'm dedicating this song tonight to four very special people who've brought joy into my life in the past few months. First, to my daughter, Sabrina, and new son-in-law, Ty, thank you for letting me join your family circle. Next to my granddaughter, Genie, who's now my biggest critic. She always falls asleep to my singing." Her smile went along with the laughter from the crowd. "And finally to Gordon Irwin, who asked me to marry him last night, and I accepted."

She waved her hand in the air, a diamond sparkling in the lone spotlight. A roar came from the crowd. Sabrina turned around, and

Ty leaned toward her. "It was gentlemanly of Gordon to come to us for our blessing."

Her former boss had sweat profusely while asking for their blessing, which they happily gave, not that the pair needed it. It was enough, though, that they wanted it.

The final strains of the famous song, written for his wife, echoed in the arena, and he hugged her tight. She laid her head on his shoulder, her curly chestnut hair tied back for the evening. She'd melted the ice around his heart, and he was the better for it. Spring had come to Violet Ridge, and he counted his blessings, a different man than the one who left Sabrina a year ago. Thankfully, she'd given him a second chance, and he'd taken full advantage of those twelve days, happy she rescued him from his childhood promise that had left him cold and alone. Loving her was a thrill beyond compare, with adventure waiting out of the chute and delivering the ride of a lifetime.

* * * * *

For more romances from acclaimed author Tanya Agler and Harlequin Heartwarming, visit www.Harlequin.com today!